T0198652

THE COMMUTER TRAIN

A Hijacking for Justice

a courtroom crime thriller by
Karl Milde

iUniverse, Inc.
New York Bloomington

iUniverse books may be ordered through booksellers or by contacting:

iUniverse
1663 Liberty Drive
Bloomington, IN 47403
www.iuniverse.com
1-800-Authors (1-800-288-4677)

Because of the dynamic nature of the Internet, any Web addresses or links contained in this book may have changed since publication and may no longer be valid. The views expressed in this work are solely those of the author and do not necessarily reflect the views of the publisher, and the publisher hereby disclaims any responsibility for them.

ISBN: 978-1-4401-8012-5 (sc)
ISBN: 978-1-4401-8014-9 (dj)
ISBN: 978-1-4401-8013-2 (ebook)

Library of Congress Control Number: 2009909977

Printed in the United States of America

iUniverse rev. date: 10/14/09

Of the things we think, say or do:

1. Is it the TRUTH?
2. Is it FAIR to all concerned?
3. Will it build GOOD WILL and BETTER FRIENDSHIPS?
4. Will it be BENEFICIAL to all concerned?

The ROTARY 4-Way Test for Business Ethics

———◆◇◆———

Chapter 1

"*ALL ABOOAARD!*" SHOUTED the conductor. The few latecomers hurried up the steps to the platform to get to the train before the car doors closed. It was 6:31 Monday morning at the station in Wassaic, New York, the northernmost end of the Metro-North commuter railroad.

The doors slid shut and the train started up with a jerk.

Carl Collingwood sat in a car in the middle of the train with a duffel bag on his lap.

Carl's son, Bruce, a young man in his early twenties, took a seat in the front of the first car, just behind the growling Diesel locomotive. There were only a couple of other passengers in this car.

"Ticket?" Bruce Collingwood handed the conductor his ticket. The conductor punched it and gave it back. "You're gonna have to put that up on the rack." He pointed to Bruce's duffel bag, on the seat next to him. "This car fills up pretty fast."

Bruce nodded, and the conductor went on his way, walking down the aisle, stopping to punch the tickets of the few other passengers, and then left through the door at the rear of the car.

The train stopped briefly at Tenmile River to pick up a few more passengers. None got into the front car.

Bruce unpinned a cell phone from his belt and pressed the bleep button. His father, Carl, keyed his phone, "Okay?"

"Yeah. I'm ready."

The train slowed to a stop at Dover Plains. The station platform was filled with early morning commuters who crowded the car doors before they opened. The passengers rushed in when the doors parted, as if at the starting gun of a race, and took their seats.

One of the passengers, dressed smartly in a gray suit, was on a cell phone as he entered the car. Without taking the phone off his ear, he surveyed the available seats and chose one by a window. Mike Snead, President and CEO of Transport International, Inc., was on his way to corporate headquarters from his country estate in the nearby town of Millbrook.

Carl, in he same car as Sneed, bleeped Bruce with his cell phone and said quietly, "He's here."

Bruce pressed an acknowledging bleep, and snapped his phone shut, hitching it quickly to his belt. He opened his duffel bag, took out a wrench, and zipped the bag closed again. Turning around with one swift movement, he used the wrench to unlock the front door on the passenger car, pulled the door partly open and slipped out. One of the other passengers looked up absently from reading the paper, but the unusual occurrence failed to register in his mind.

Outside, the roar of the Diesel engine was deafening. Bruce held on to a bracket with one hand and, with the other, deftly used the wrench to unlock the back door of the locomotive. He pushed this door open and stepped inside.

Bruce bleeped Carl: "I'm in."

Carl got up from his seat, carrying his duffel bag, and sat down next to the man in the gray suit. He placed the duffel on his lap and looked squarely ahead. Snead was oblivious, barking orders on his cell phone to some underling far away. Then Snead pulled a small computer from his briefcase and opened it on his lap.

The train pulled into the Harlem Valley Wingdale station and picked up a few more passengers. Bruce opened his duffel and replaced the wrench. When the train started up again, Bruce reached into the duffel, took out a handgun and zipped the duffel closed again. He then moved forward along a narrow corridor in the locomotive, past the roaring engine, and approached the back of the engineer.

Bruce watched as the engineer stopped the train at the next station, Pawling. He took a deep breath, stepped up to the engineer and, holding the gun to the engineer's head, said sharply but politely, "Hello. Don't move. Don't make a sound." The engineer instantly froze with fear. "I don't want to hurt you or anyone else. Just do as I say."

The train signal changed from red to green. "Go ahead. Take us to Patterson," Bruce commanded. The very frightened engineer did as he was told. Bruce unhitched his cell phone again and bleeped Carl. "We have control."

The train traveled on to the Patterson station, stopped and picked up still more passengers. When everyone was seated and the car doors were closed, the train started up again.

Bruce spoke to the engineer, more calmly now: "Call the dispatcher and tell him the engine isn't running properly Tell him you can make Southeast, but then all the passengers have to get off."

"Y-yes, sir."

The engineer's call came in to the Metro-North Railroad control room, located in Manhattan, above the tracks in Grand Central Station. The dispatcher, Phil Davis, wearing a telephone headset, sat facing an enormous illuminated track board, monitoring and directing the trains. Whenever anyone asked how he liked his work, he'd tell them "It's like a huge real-time video game."

"This is the Chief on Metro two-niner out of Wassaic."

"Come in, Jack. Is that you?"

"Yeah, Phil, it's me," came the somewhat nervous voice over the speakerphone. "We - uh - have a little problem here. Engine's smokin'. It's overheating but fluid levels are okay. I can make it to Southeast, but then I gotta dump all the passengers. They can take the local."

"Shit. Can't you keep that old Diesel running? What did you do? Feed it cow piss up there in the country?"

"You gonna let me stop, or what?"

"Yeah. 'Course. After you unload, back it onto a holding track and shut it down. We'll have someone come up there and check it out right away."

"I'll be there."

"Roger that."

Phil looked at his computer screen to see what trains were scheduled to leave Southeast station after the 6:31 out of Wassaic passed through.

There were plenty of trains to pick up the slack. Next he pressed a button on the console to call maintenance.

"Metro-Central. C'mon back."

"Maintenance."

"We've got a problem with one of our Diesels. He's going to park at Southeast station. Can you get up there?"

"Uh, let's see…Yeah, we've got a guy who can hop the next train out of North White Plains. Is it serious?"

"Serious enough to dump all the passengers."

"Oh. Well maybe he'd better take the truck with the equipment."

"Your call."

"No problem. He's on his way."

"Roger that."

Next Phil pressed another button on his console for the public address system.

"I need an announcement, *now*."

"Okay. Go ahead."

"The 6:31 out of Wassaic is disabled. When it stops at Southeast all the passengers will have to change to the 7:20 on the electric line. We're taking that train out of service."

"Passengers on the 6:31 Wassaic to change in Southeast to the 7:20?"

"Roger that."

Having taken care of this small emergency, Phil went back to watching the trains inch along on the Big Board.

Chapter 2

In the middle car of the train, the passengers listened intently to the announcement.

"The last stop of this train will be Southeast. All passengers are asked to get off and change to the 7:20, which will be waiting just across the platform. This train will not – repeat *not* – be going on to Manhattan. It will be taken out of service."

A huge collective groan could be heard throughout the car as people stopped what they were doing and began to collect their belongings, preparing to get off at the next stop. The man in the gray suit looked disapprovingly straight at Carl, as if Carl were the cause of the problem, and muttered under his breath, "Shit." He shut down the open application on his laptop and closed the screen. "Damn bastards don't know how to run a railroad."

As the train slowed to a stop, the passengers grumbled but began to get up and move down the aisle toward the doors at either end. The man in the gray suit looked at Carl, motioning for him to get out of the way. Carl remained seated and slowly unzipped his duffel bag. When the last passenger in the aisle had passed by, he took out a handgun and pressed it against the waist of the man in the gray suit. "Don't move. You're staying on the train," he announced sternly.

"Whoa. *What the fuck!*"

"I know who you are, Mr. Snead. You're staying right here on this train."

When the train doors opened, the conductors stepped out first and waved their hands at the shiny new electric-powered train across the platform. A number of people on the platform, waiting to board the Diesel express to New York, seemed confused.

"Don't board this train. It won't be going on. Take that one. It's a local to Chappaqua, but then it's an express to New York," explained the conductors, over and over again.

The passengers on the Diesel train spilled out onto the platform, and then scurried to find seats on the local.

When the last stragglers finally emerged, the conductors re-boarded the cars to check for any remaining persons who might not have heard the announcement or who might be sleeping. Finding no one, they too exited the train and joined the passengers on the local. Before he boarded, the head conductor inserted a key in a lock on the side of a door and all the doors closed. He then waved to the engineer, who had his head out the window of the locomotive. What the conductor couldn't see was Bruce standing behind the engineer with his gun drawn.

After receiving the "all clear," the engineer turned to face Bruce. He was still wary, but no longer in fear of his life.

"Okay, what now?"

"Call the dispatcher. Tell him this train has been hijacked. Tell him there's a man in the locomotive with a gun to your head. Tell him we're going to take this train to Washington, D.C."

"But we can't go to Washington. The tracks go to Grand Central, and that's the end of the line."

"Do as you're told."

The engineer keyed the mike and reported in.

"This is Metro two-nine."

"Come in."

"We're at Southeast. Passengers off. Request permission to proceed."

"Permission granted. You can back up now into the rail yard."

"This is a code 99. I repeat, a code 99. This train has been hijacked. There is a man here with a gun. He says we are going to take this train to Washington."

"Just a minute, Jack. This is a joke, right?"

"Phil, you've gotta believe me. There's a guy standing here with a gun aimed at my head."

"Jack, give me a break. This is the morning rush. Quit farting around."

Jack, not knowing what else to do, keyed the mike which stood up out of the dash, and pushed it in Bruce's direction for him to talk.

Almost as flustered as Jack at this unrehearsed turn of events, Bruce leaned down toward the mike and spoke awkwardly into the open channel. "Uh, hello. This is - um - Bruce Collingwood. You'd better do as he says."

"*Who?* Who is this?"

"I – I'm Bruce Collingwood. My father and I are hijacking this train."

"That's *baloney.* You can't hijack a train! It's on a goddamn *track.* And I know exactly where you are at every minute. I see your train right here on the Board."

"Don't you think I know that? You're the guy that throws the switches. What's your name, anyway?"

"I –uh – I'm Phil Davis, the dispatcher. And who the hell are *you?*"

"I already told you. Bruce Collingwood…. It doesn't *matter* who I am. The point is, my father and I are hijacking this train and we have guns. And we're going to take this train to *Washington.*"

"You can't get there from where you are."

"Yes, we can, and you're going to help us."

"Okay, Bruce. Tell me how."

"We're going to stop at Mt. Vernon, just beyond the cut-off to Connecticut and then back up the Connecticut Line to New Rochelle. From there, we can go forward down the main line through Penn Station and continue on to Washington."

"The hell you are! You can expect the police to be crawling all over that train in five minutes, like bears on a honey pot. You're looking at some major jail time, Bruce, whoever you are."

"We're prepared to take the consequences, once we get to

Washington. In the meantime, if anyone tries to stop us, the engineer, Jack here, gets a bullet in the head."

Bruce handed the mike back to Jack, who was decidedly more nervous now.

"Jesus, Phil, don't piss him off. Do as he says!" Jacks voice was shaky, and it caught Phil up short.

"Okay. Okay. You go ahead, Jack. Just take it easy. You read me?"

"You just throw the switches. I'll do the rest."

"Roger that."

Chapter 3

THE CONDUCTORS AT the Southeast station fully expected the Diesel train to reverse its direction and back onto an idle track to wait for maintenance. Instead, the Diesel briefly emitted a loud growl and eased slowly forward, pulling the train back onto the main line. It roared and picked up speed as it headed south, out of the station

"Where the heck is he going?" wondered the chief conductor aloud as he pulled out his phone and quickly called the dispatcher.

"Metro two-nine, calling in. This disabled train is headed south!"

"Roger that. It's authorized."

"What gives, Phil? Where's it going?"

"Can't say."

"Can't or *won't*?"

"Not at liberty to say, dude. Just get your passengers on the next train out and come on down."

Inside the train, Carl stood in the large handicap restroom, with his pistol leveled at the head of Mike Snead. Mike sat fully clothed on the open toilet seat and snarled at his captor.

"You'll pay for this, you shit!" he hissed.

There was a small jerk as the train started up. "Looks like we're moving again. We're going to take you on a little ride, Mr. Snead," said Carl, ignoring the last remark.

"Now, Mr. Snead," continued Carl coolly. "You are going to call your office with your cell phone and tell them that this train has been hijacked, that you are being held hostage, and that you are being taken to Washington, D.C."

"This train doesn't go to Washington, you idiot."

"It will."

"Okay, I'll play your little game. *Then* what?"

"Then I'll let you go."

Mike snapped his phone open and pressed a button. "I want to speak to Shelley, right now!"

"Be sure to tell him to contact the media about your little ride."

"You bet I will. And the F.B.I. too. This is a federal offense, you bastard. You won't get two miles down this track without ending up dead."

"While you're at it, you can tell them that if anyone tries to board this train, you are going to get a bullet in your brain. I mean it."

"Shelley, listen to me carefully. I'm on the usual train – yeah from my weekend place in Millbrook. And there's this crazy guy holding a gun on me. Says he's hijacking this train and taking it to Washington for god's sake…. *Yes*, yes, I know. He's *nuts*! That's just the *point*, I don't know *what* he'll do. They've got to be goddamn careful or he'll blow my brains out…. No, I have no idea what this is about. I'm sitting here in the restroom in one of the cars in the middle of the train. The usual one I get on at Dover Plains on Mondays. Get help. And inform the media. They'll be all over this train, with helicopters and news vans, the works. The F.B.I is good at this shit. They'll board the train and take him out. But I don't want to end up dead. Got it? Go!"

"It's not going to be so easy," commented Carl with a wry smile.

"Oh yeah? Why is that, Mr. . . whoever you are?"

"Collingwood. Carl Collingwood. First of all, we're on a speeding train, in case you haven't noticed. How do you expect someone to board? Fly?"

"They'll drop someone down from a helicopter – whatever!"

"Can't do that. There are electric wires nearby. And bridges too. You can't get in that way."

"So? They'll go alongside and jump on."

"Nope. That won't work, either. There are no roads along the train line."

"Okay, they'll come in the *back,* for god's sake. Who the fuck cares! It's *their* job to get their butts in here!"

"Sorry. They can't come in the back. They don't have the equipment for that. At least not now."

"Just shut up. This train has got to stop sometime."

"Now, *that's* true. We'll just have to wait and see, won't we?"

Carl revealed a worried smile that was not lost on Mike Snead as the train jounced along southward toward Manhattan.

Chapter 4

———◆·▸◂·◆———

JULIANNE GABLES, CALLED Juli, made her way up the steps to the main door of the Channel 8 Building on Tenth Avenue, a three-story structure that blended in well with the nondescript architecture of the area. Channel 8, an independent, also-ran television station, somehow scraped by, notwithstanding a continual lack of funds. Its specialty was reruns of classic oldies, but it kept a skeleton news crew because it could make good money reporting strictly local events and tragedies in the New York metro area. Now and then it even scooped the big alphabet-soup guys: CBS, NBC, ABC, UPN and FOX.

Juli swiped her employee pass through the entrance gate and waved at George, the security guard. Juli was African-American, like George, which gave them a bond that transcended their respective positions in the company. George made just a few dollars more than minimum wage, without health benefits, making it extremely difficult for him pay his monthly rent, food, phone and subway expenses. Juli earned a salary of $36,000 with benefits that, while far below TV journalist standards, enabled her to meet her obligations and even have something left over for an occasional movie. Nevertheless, you could count on George to greet everyone with a smile and a cheerful remark.

"Nice weekend?" he offered as Juli breezed past.

"Same old, same old. How about you?"

"Now that subject's censored," replied George with a grin. "Can't tell it to a nice girl like you."

"Oops. Sorry I asked."

"There's always an opening in my schedule for a new pretty lady."

"I thought the girls ran you ragged."

"You're kidding, right? *Moi*? Run ragged? I don't *think* so!"

"Gotta go. See'ya."

The elevator pinged and its doors parted. Juli stepped in and pressed the button for the third floor.

Emerging from the elevator, she walked past the front desk, with a small wave to Ariana, the middle-aged, overworked and underpaid telephone receptionist, and headed for her cubicle, where she put down her purse and examined her computer screen. She quickly scanned the active news and checked the work assignments for the day. Nothing was going on that interested her, so she walked over to her producer's office to ask for an assignment.

"Anything doing, Mr. Raleigh?"

"Usual stuff. Really dead day." The producer was a pudgy man in his fifties in a wrinkled white shirt. He would blame his wife because she "didn't do ironing."

"So what are we covering?"

"Nothing at all on the newswire. You have your pick of the Garden Show at the Javits Center, the festival of St. Jerome in Little Italy and – this is just in – a new diet book. The author is screaming for attention."

"Your call. One's as exciting as the next."

"Yeah, it's a tough one. But let's wait. The day is young."

"Okay by me."

"We'll hope for a murder."

"Careful what you wish for, Mr. Raleigh."

"I'll call you in a bit."

Juli walked back to her cubicle. Mr. Raleigh headed for the men's room near the elevators.

Ariana took the call.

"Channel 8 News. How may I direct your call?"

"Certainly, sir. I'll connect you." Ariana buzzed Juli.

"Juli, there's a guy on the line, says a commuter train's been *hijacked*! Pick up line four. Mr. Raleigh's in the bathroom right now."

"Will do." Juli pressed the keypad on her phone and said, "Hello. This is Julianne Gables."

"Huh, Ms. Gables." The voice was deep and raspy. "My name is Shelley Bernstein. I'm with Transport International. We're alerting all the news outlets. Our CEO, Mike Snead, is being held hostage on a commuter train to Grand Central. They let all the other passengers off at Southeast and the train's been hijacked. Two guys, we found out. One has a gun on our CEO and the other has a gun on the engineer. They say they want to take the train to Washington, D.C., but of course that's crazy."

Juli could almost feel the adrenaline rush. She reacted with an unprofessional "Oh, my *god*!" before she caught herself.

Mr. Raleigh stepped out of the restroom, heard Juli's reaction, and was at her desk in an instant. Juli cupped the receiver in her hand and looked up at him.

"Someone's just hijacked a commuter train! They're holding some business exec as a hostage. Guy named Mike Snead. He runs Transport International. I've heard of this company. It's a huge conglomerate."

"That's your story. Run with it."

Juli turned her attention back to the phone and spoke as evenly as she could.

"Thank you Mr. Bernstein." Juli tried desperately to focus on the journalists' mantra she had been taught in college: What, where, when, who and why. She was missing two crucial elements: *Who* and *why*. There seemed to be another element here too: *How* could a commuter train, that was supposed to go to Grand Central, end up going to Washington?

"Mr. Bernstein, do they know who the perpetrators are?"

"No, we don't know yet. The police are trying to contact Mr. Snead on his cell phone, but there's no answer. We have no idea who it is or why they're doing this."

"You said the train was headed for *Washington*? That doesn't make sense."

"You hit the nail on the head, young lady." Mr. Bernstein's phone clicked off.

Juli sat dumbfounded, staring at her computer screen, and then began to type furiously.

Chapter 5

JULI GABLES WAS a born-and-bred New Yorker. Her fondest memories as a little girl were of her family's railroad flat in East Harlem, just north of Central Park. The rooms connected in a line, like railroad cars, so if you opened all the doors and stood in a room at one end, you could see all the way to the other side of the building.

She was diligent in school. She didn't know why, and in fact she wondered why she was different in this way from most of her friends, who didn't seem to care about school at all. Unlike boys, though, who would mercilessly tease the nerds who spent time reading and doing their homework, her friends accepted her desire to be in control of her schoolwork and were even a little envious. Just a little.

She kept a diary, making entries faithfully every day. She would report in her diary any "news" that she encountered, much as a journalist would. Her diaries had one page for every day of the year, and when the year was over, she stood the volume on her bookshelf next to the volumes of the previous years, all in a row. She kept up this routine of writing until she left for college, at which point she had completed nine and a half volumes.

She seldom read what she had written in her diaries, except for the passages in Volume IV that described a turning point in her young life. This volume was somewhat soiled from being taken down so often when she read it, usually late at night, to refresh her memory and relive the sad events.

It began on day 235 in Volume IV. These entries appeared in Juli's diary in her strong, legible handwriting:

Day 235: *Daddy came home today very sad. It was scary. I never saw him like this before. Mommy tried to comfort him but nothing she did cheered him up. Daddy said he lost his job as a porter, which I know he liked. He would be gone for several days at a time, taking trips on those trains with sleeper cars. Daddy said that the overnight trains were being cancelled because people were taking airplanes to get where they wanted to go. Daddy has worked for the railroad for pretty much all his life, so that is all he knows.*

Day 236: *Daddy slept the whole day and wouldn't get out of bed. Mommy is worried. Daddy has a small pension, but not enough to live on, so he needs to find another job.*

I am learning how important it is for a person to have work every day – especially work that he enjoys.

Day 237: *Daddy left last night while we were sleeping and has not returned yet. Mommy is frantic. She called the police but they don't know anything. She told them about his losing his job and they said he might be out on a binge. I am starting to get worried too. I didn't realize it until now, how much I love my Daddy.*

Day 238: *The police called today and said they found Daddy. They said they think he walked to the George Washington Bridge and jumped off. Someone driving by had seen him just before he jumped. They searched the river and found his body floating face down near the Statue of Liberty. What is going to happen to us now? Mommy says we have no money.*

Day 239: *Mommy learned that one of Daddy's benefits from the railroad was a life insurance policy for $100,000. Mommy will get paid soon so I can continue with school. I took off today to go to the morgue with*

Mommy and identify Daddy's body. I didn't want to look, but I did. It was horrible.

Day 240: *We went to the funeral parlor where they took Daddy. I could not stop crying. Mommy cried a lot too. Mommy made arrangements to have Daddy buried at a cemetery.*

We came home and Mommy called everybody she knew to tell them. She also told them about the funeral.

Day 241: *Daddy's funeral was today. We rode in the black limousine of the funeral parlor. We watched as they lowered Daddy's casket in the ground. I cried and cried.*

The handwriting became a little shaky on these last two days, but then it became firm again as the diary went on.

Juli's mother worked hard as a waitress to make ends meet. The insurance money could have helped, but after paying the funeral expenses, she saved the rest for Julie's college.

Juli knew it was up to her. This awareness, and also the ever-present feeling that she didn't want to let her mother down, drove her onward. She excelled in high school and matriculated at the nearby Columbia University, where she majored in journalism.

After college she applied to all the major TV news organizations but, notwithstanding her good grades at Columbia, she found it difficult to land a job. Only Channel 8, with its tiny news staff, asked her to come on board. She responded eagerly, for she knew that she lacked experience and Channel 8 would give her an opportunity to develop her skills as an investigative reporter.

Now, more than a year later, Juli had appeared in front of the camera countless times and felt comfortable reporting a news story each night – a story she had researched and written. She enjoyed her work and it showed in her performance, but she was still restless to move on to the big-time news organizations. She fit in well with the staff at Channel 8, and her producer, Mr. Raleigh, had been a kind and helpful mentor to her, and the fire that had energized her in the past still drove her forward. So when the call came in from Shelley Bernstein, she jumped at the chance to run with the breaking story.

The first thing Juli did was to investigate the Metro-North

Commuter Railroad. She found that there were three train lines, all starting (or ending, depending on your point of view) at Grand Central Station. The first, called the Hudson Line, went north along the east side of the Hudson River, passing through river towns, such as Croton-on-Hudson and Cold Spring, and continuing north to Poughkeepsie and beyond. The second, called the Connecticut Line, went north to Mount Vernon and then turned east to follow the northern coast of Long Island Sound. It passed through New Rochelle, New York, and continued on through Greenwich, Stamford and New Haven, in Connecticut, eventually passing through Providence, Rhode Island, on its way to Boston. The third line was called the Harlem Line for no good reason, since the other two the lines also passed through Harlem on their way north before branching off, west toward the Hudson or east toward Connecticut. The Harlem Line went straight up the middle, passing through White Plains, the main city in Westchester County, and eventually dead-ending in Wassaic, New York, about a hundred miles due north of New York City. This was the line with the hijacked train. Juli looked at the map and tried to figure out how this train could possibly go to Washington, D.C.

Trains between New York and Washington all passed through Pennsylvania Station, not Grand Central. Grand Central was a dead end for the three commuter lines. Once a train came there, it had to back out again. Some trains could actually keep going forward around a big loop under the station, but they still left the station going north on the same set of tracks that passed through Harlem.

Trains from Washington could continue north and finally end up on the Connecticut Line tracks at New Rochelle on their way to Boston. *That's it*, Juli thought. The hijacked train could travel south to Mount Vernon, run backward up the Connecticut Line to New Rochelle, and run forward again on the track to Penn Station and then head for Washington.

That must be the plan!

But wait a minute. Look at the Hudson Line. It branches off to the west in The Bronx, follows the Harlem River to the Hudson and then heads north again at Spuyten Duyvel. From there, the train could go south, cross the Harlem River on a drawbridge into Manhattan and run down along the old tracks on the West Side to Penn Station. Would that work? That bridge hasn't been used…well, since forever …and the old tracks on the West Side: Are they still even there?

So they'll have to take the New Rochelle route. Right? Hmmm…

"Juli! Go to Channel 2! They're sending their traffic helicopter to view the train!" The producer's voice jarred Juli back to the here and now.

Juli clicked on the TV Channel 2 news-feed icon. The newscaster described the live scene caught by the video camera in the CBS helicopter.

"Our Chopper 2 is heading north, following the Harlem Line track, to meet the hijacked train. We're looking at Chappaqua now. Mount Kisco, the next station up the line, will come into view in just a mo—there it is! You can see it in the distance moving in our direction. It's moving very fast on that straight section of track.

"It's a long train, pulled by that big gray Diesel locomotive. We've heard there are only four people on the train: The engineer who drives the locomotive, Michael Snead, the President and CEO of Transport International, and the two hijackers. We don't have any information about the hijackers yet, but they're working as a team. One of them is holding a gun on the engineer and the other has a gun on Mr. Snead.

"We do know that the hijackers want to take the train all the way to Washington, D.C. That makes no sense at all. This is only a commuter train and the tracks end at Grand Central. We have no idea why the hijackers are doing this.

"Look! There are three police cars driving parallel to the train on the Saw Mill River Parkway. I'm sure we'll see more police too. The F.B.I. has been called in, but we don't see any sign of them yet."

The camera zoomed in closer as the locomotive and the chain of cars that snaked behind it slipped, one by one, out of sight below the field of view.

"One can't help wondering which car has Mike Snead and his hijacker," the announcer continued.

Juli reduced the size of the image and left it on the lower right corner of her screen. She then called Transport International and asked for Mike Snead.

Chapter 6

PEOPLE WERE SCRAMBLING at F.B.I. headquarters in New York City. Agents were strapping on their Kevlar vests as secretaries frantically called all nearby agents on assignment in the field.

Special Agent David Price, a senior agent who happened to be in the New York Office at the time, was barking orders in the briefing room and over the phone.

"We need the S.W.A.T. team, in the van, *now!* Have them go to Mt. Vernon and wait for that train. I also want a police helicopter on standby with two armed men ready to drop. This will be like shooting ducks in a gallery.

"And one more thing. Get me the cell numbers of the engineer and that Mike Snead. I'm going to place calls to those damn hijackers."

Price pocketed the phone, strapped on his gun belt, grabbed his jacket and headed for the elevator, all in one motion.

Out at the street he jumped into the passenger seat of a waiting car, a standard gray sedan. "Mount Vernon, *fast*," he told his driver. "I used to cover this turf. Take the Willis Avenue Bridge and go up the Dewey Thruway to the exit at Route 233." The driver made a quick maneuver to cross over the highway and headed toward the FDR.

Price called the office. "Got those phone numbers yet? Yeah, hurry." He took a small pad from his breast pocket and made some notes. "Okay, thanks."

Price dialed the first number. The phone rang and rang. "Shit!" He cancelled the call.

He tried the other number with no success. "This is not going to be so easy," he thought. He looked up just in time to view the Brooklyn Bridge as his driver entered the FDR and sped north.

❀

On the train, Mike Snead was in the restroom, sitting on the can, facing Carl Collingwood's gun and talking to Juli Gables, when he heard a beep.

"Hold on! I have another call." Mike clicked the flash button and said, "Mike Snead."

"It's still me," said Juli.

"Too late then. I lost that call. When are the damn police going to show up?"

"I'm sure they're on their way, Mr. Snead. I'm surprised that the hijacker let you talk. Where is he now?"

"He's holding a gun on me. The phone rang and he told me to take the call."

"Do you know his name?"

"No."

"Could you ask him?"

"Hell, no, you kidding? I'm scared shitless."

"Could you hand him the phone?"

Mike held out the phone toward the man with the gun. "Here. She wants to talk to you." To Mike's surprise, Carl took the phone, but carefully maintained the aim of his gun.

"Hello? Who is this?" asked Carl, his voice gruff.

"I'm Juli Gables, a reporter for Channel 8. Uh… please don't hang up. I would like to ask you a few questions, if I may," Juli said as pleasantly as she could.

"I'm Carl Collingwood, Miss Gables. I've heard of you. I've seen you on the 6:00 o'clock news."

"Uh, your name again is Carl ...."""Collingwood. C-O-L-L-I-N-G-W-O-O-D."

"Oh. Thank you. I have it now. Uh, where are you, Mr. Collingwood?"

"We're on a commuter train... somewhere on the train. I can't tell you exactly."

"Oh. I understand. The police."

"That's it."

"Is there anyone else on the train?"

"Mr. Snead."

"Yes, I know. Anyone else?"

"The engineer."

"The engineer. Are you in the engine with him?"

"No."

"Well, why doesn't he just stop the train?"

"My son's up there with him."

"Your son?"

"Yes. His name is Bruce. Bruce Collingwood."

"He has a... a gun?"

"Yes. He's telling the engineer what to do."

"Oh." Juli could hardly believe the answers she was getting and paused a moment to think. "May I ask, Mr. Collingwood, what are you trying to accomplish?"

"We are going to take Mr. Snead to Washington, D.C."

"Uh, why is that?"

"Do some research, Miss Gables. And then call me back."

Carl ended the call abruptly while keeping a bead on Mike. Mike's face registered both wide-eyed surprise and mounting anger.

Carl slipped Mike's phone in his front breast pocket and pulled out his own phone.

Bleeping once, he whispered, "You there?"

"Yes."

"Any problems?" Carl's voice reflected his concern.

"No, not yet."

"We're a go here."

"Okay, Dad."

❀

Juli kept an eye on the feed from Chopper 2, which followed the train south from a view directly above and behind the last car. The image was minimized to a small square in the lower right corner of her computer display. Meanwhile, she set to work researching "Carl Collingwood," "Mike Snead," and "Transport International" on Google, Yahoo and MSN.

Nothing came up for "Carl Collingwood," but the other two inputs yielded reams of data. She started doing her homework.

Chapter 7

◆─◆‣◆‣◆─◆

As Agent Price rode north, he kept in touch with the other members of his team, to coordinate the assault. Almost an afterthought, he again tried the numbers of the engineer and Mike Snead, not expecting any answer. The engineer didn't pick up but when he dialed Mike's cell phone number, he was surprised to hear someone say, "Hello?"

"Is this Mike Snead?" he asked.

"No."

"Oh, sorry. I must have the wrong number." Price was about to end the call.

"No, you dialed right. This is Mr. Snead's cell phone."

"Then who is this?"

"Let me ask you first. Who is this?"

"Name's Price. Agent Price from the F.B.I."

"It's about time you called. I'll give the phone to Mr. Snead." Carl handed the phone gingerly to Snead with one hand while continuing to hold the gun with the other.

"Who is it?" asked Snead as he took the phone.

"It's the F.B.I."

"The F.B.I.? And you want me to speak to them?"

"Sure, go ahead. Tell them whatever you want."

Snead put the phone to his ear. "Mike Snead speaking."

"What is this? Some kind of joke?" came the reply.

"Joke? What do you mean, *joke?* Who is this?"

"Agent Price from the F.B.I. I thought you were taken hostage."

"You thought *right*, Price. This guy has a gun in my face."

"Then how is it you can talk on the phone?"

"He's being nice? How the fuck do *I* know! You're the cop. Get me out of here."

"Now, calm down, Mr. Snead. That's exactly what we intend to do."

"That's more like it. But be *careful* for chrissake! I don't want to get shot in the process."

"Where are you now?"

"We're in a restroom in the one of the cars."

"Which car?"

"In the *middle* some place. I'm supposed to memorize the car number when I get on the train?"

"Is it the same car you got on originally?"

"Yes."

"Maybe somebody remembers seeing you. We'll check that out."

"Are you planning to board the train?"

"Damn straight."

"How do you plan to do that?"

"Can't tell you. You understand why, I'm sure."

"There's this little problem."

"Oh? What's that?"

"This lunatic is going to shoot me if he hears you're closing in."

"We assume so."

"Oh, yeah? Well, then what's the plan?"

"Can't tell you."

"Shit! What am I supposed to do?"

"Cooperate. Now give the phone back to that guy with you."

"The guy with a gun?"

"Yes."

Snead held out the phone to Carl, but Carl stared at him with a smirk on his face and didn't take it. "Here, take the phone!" Snead said, annoyed. Carl just stood there so Snead put the phone back on his ear.

"He won't take it."

"Tell him I need to talk to him. I can save his life."

Snead looked at Carl. "He says he needs to talk to you. He says you're a dead man if you don't."

"Tell him there's no reason to talk. I'm not going to make any kind of deal, so it would be a waste of time."

Snead passed on the information.

"Okay, hang on. We'll get you out of there. Don't worry."

"Damn straight, I'm worried. You make one wrong move and I'm the first one to get shot. And if that happens, my friend, your career as a cop is *over*, understand?"

"I get the message."

Snead ended the call and stared, wide-eyed, at Carl.

Chapter 8

JULI WASN'T GETTING very far with her research on Michael Snead. True, she learned that Mike had a reputation for chewing up people and spitting them out. Every year he would have every manager at Transport International fire at least one member of his team. "Fire the weakest link," he would say, "to keep the fear of fire alive."

Mike practiced what he preached and routinely fired managers, no matter how many years they had devoted to "TI", as the company was called. Mike had become known as "Mike the Malevolent" within TI, but the Wall Street analysts loved him. The stock price of TI soared and remained at one of the highest price/earnings ratios in the industry.

Mike was paid handsomely by his handpicked Board of Directors – in salary, in benefits in stock and in cash bonuses. Juli had never imagined that anyone in corporate America could receive so much money in one single year, let alone over the ten-year span that Mike had been running TI. TI was a public company, so the compensation of its officers and directors was a matter of public record. Many analysts had cast aspersions on the obscene amount of money, benefits and stock that Snead received – it was far above the industry standard – but that didn't seem to affect the stock price. Investors just loved TI stock.

What was it about Snead that warranted this desperate action by a father and son?

Juli pondered the information and decided to go public with her findings, thin as they appeared to be. She thought that possibly a little jab at the big conglomerate might result in an inadvertent slip and yield some more telling information. She outlined her story, printed it out, and took it to Mr. Raleigh in his office.

"Uh, Mr. Raleigh…I have an idea," she began as she entered, speaking somewhat timidly at first because she knew this would be hard sell. Channel 8 broadcast reruns of game shows and soap operas during the day, scheduled far in advance, and hadn't wavered from this format for years. That's how they made their money – by selling commercials in the preprogrammed time slots.

Mr. Raleigh looked up and studied her a moment. "This is very *good*! Are you absolutely sure of what you're saying?"

"Oh, yes. I have verified every fact."

"So what's your idea?"

"I'd like to go on the air *now* and tell the story. Break into our regular programming. And then keep updating the story all day. Stay on the air, if necessary, and follow the train down the tracks. We'll find out why these two guys are doing this crazy thing – it's like suicide for them so they must be desperate. Maybe the cops'll stop them before they get to Washington, but then maybe they won't."

"It sure is a good story. Think you're ready?"

"Mr. Raleigh, I've been preparing my whole life for this moment."

"Then go with your gut. I'll back you up. I'll even bring in reinforcements to do the research."

Juli reacted with a surge of adrenaline and gushed, "Oh, thank you Mr. Raleigh. Thank you!" She almost reached over the desk and hugged her producer.

Mr. Raleigh lifted his phone, pressed a button and explained the procedure to his chief engineer. "We're going to interrupt our regular programming, whenever Juli's ready. Understand? Yes, *now*. And throughout the day too." Mr. Raleigh winked at Juli who still stood behind the big desk. She hurried out to prepare for the broadcast.

As the cosmetician quickly applied makeup to Juli's face and smoothed her hair, Juli sat before a mirror reviewing her script. Juli stepped into the studio and took her place behind the news desk, facing the camera as the cameraman hooked up her lapel microphone. The story had already been downloaded into the teleprompter so she could read it while staring straight into the eye of Camera 1.

The cameraman stepped back behind the camera, glanced at the video monitor and softly spoke into his headphone mike to the chief engineer in the sound booth. A little light on the bottom of the teleprompter glowed red, signaling that the camera was rolling.

Channel 8's "news jingle" played for two seconds and then faded into the voiceover, spoken live by the chief engineer: "We briefly interrupt our regular programming to bring you this special news bulletin,"

"GOOD MORNING. I'M JULIANNE GABLES AND WE ARE FOLLOWING A BREAKING NEWS STORY THAT STARTED AT 6:30 THIS MORNING WHEN TWO MEN, A FATHER AND SON, *HIJACKED* A COMMUTER TRAIN TO NEW YORK CITY. THE TRAIN ORIGINATED IN WASSAIC, NEW YORK, A COUNTRY TOWN ABOUT ONE HUNDRED MILES NORTH OF THE CITY, AND WAS SCHEDULED TO ARRIVE AT GRAND CENTRAL STATION.AT 8:31. RIGHT NOW THE TRAIN IS PASSING THROUGH WHITE PLAINS ON ITS WAY INTO THE CITY, BUT THE HIJACKERS HAVE DEMANDED THAT THE TRAIN BE SWITCHED THROUGH TO WASHINGTON D.C. HERE IS A VIEW OF THE TRAIN, COURTESY OF THE CHANNEL 2 TRAFFIC HELICOPTER.

The chief engineer cut to the video feed from Channel 2, which showed the train snaking through the White Plains station at high speed on its way south. Juli continued to speak in the background.

"ONE OF THE MEN MANAGED TO OBTAIN ACCESS TO THE DIESEL LOCOMOTIVE WITH A GUN. HE HAS THREATENED THE LIFE OF THE ENGINEER IF BOTH THE ENGINEER AND METRO-NORTH RAILROAD DON'T COMPLY WITH THEIR DEMAND.

"ALL OF THE PASSENGERS AS WELL AS THE TRAIN

CREW WERE ASKED TO DISEMBARK AT BREWSTER, NEW YORK...ALL THE PASSENGERS, THAT IS, EXCEPT *ONE*. MICHAEL SNEAD, THE PRESIDENT AND CEO OF TRANSPORT INTERNATIONAL, REMAINS ON BOARD AND IS BEING HELD AT GUN POINT BY THE OTHER HIJACKER.

"THE F.B.I. HAS BEEN NOTIFIED AND F.B.I AGENTS ARE PROCEEDING TO INTERCEPT THE TRAIN, PROBABLY AT MT. VERNON.

The chief engineer cut back to Camera 1 with Juli's head shot.

"WE HAVE NO IDEA WHY THE HIJACKERS HAVE TAKEN THIS ACTION, BUT WE SURMISE THAT THEY HAVE A SERIOUS ISSUE WITH MR. SNEAD OR HIS COMPANY THAT THEY COULD NOT RESOLVE THROUGH PROPER CHANNELS. WE ARE RESEARCHING THE BACKGROUND OF THIS HIJACKING AND HOPE TO BRING YOU OUR REPORT WITHIN THE HALF HOUR.

"WHO ARE THESE DESPERATE MEN AND WHY ARE THEY DOING THIS?

"STAY TUNED TO CHANNEL 8. WE WILL BRING YOU UP-TO-THE-MINUTE UPDATES TO THIS BREAKING STORY THROUGHOUT THE DAY.

"STAY WITH *US* AND STAY INFORMED."

Juli held her smile until the red light on the camera blinked off, and then got down from her seat and rushed back to her desk. She had a lot of work to do.

Chapter 9

———◆◆◆◆———

BRUCE WAS GETTING more and more nervous as the train got closer to Mt. Vernon. He held his gun steady, trained on the back of the engineer's head, and watched the oncoming tracks ahead of the locomotive.

It was a crystal clear October day—the leaves had just begun to turn their bright orange and yellow. Bruce would have immensely enjoyed the panoramic view through the front windshield, had the circumstances been different. Right now his fear was mounting like the pressure in a heated vessel.

Bruce was only twenty-five years old but he had already experienced many of the hardships of life. Fifteen years ago, when his father founded his aircraft company with the help and support of his mother, life was good. He soon joined his parents in working long hours, together as a team, to achieve the American dream.

Then slowly, inexorably, his father lost his will to fight. Initially there was hope of obtaining redress through the lawsuit that followed; however, his father's lawyer, who had taken the case on contingency, was overpowered by the battery of lawyers on the other side.

The circumstances were especially wearing on Bruce's mother who, after five years of watching her family face ever worsening difficulties, found that she had contracted cancer.

The ride with his mother to the hospital in the rain was the worst moment in Bruce's young life. Watching the dreary city streets pass by through the streaks of water on the side window, Bruce was overcome with a bone-deep depression that haunted him to this day, a feeling of emptiness that blocked all other emotions.

His mother had surgery that day, while Bruce and his father kept vigil in the waiting room, praying for their lifeline, Sylvia Collingwood. At long last the doctor appeared on the threshold and told them that, in his opinion, the cancer was contained and she would be fine, after a long recovery with chemotherapy and radiation.

What kept Bruce going during this period was the knowledge that, whatever despair he was feeling, his father had even less reason to be hopeful and he needed Bruce's support. When asked to take this action against the root cause of their devastation, he didn't hesitate for a second. As he had done for the past fifteen years, he accepted the responsibility and pressed on. But now here he was, and he was scared.

He stood, staring blankly out the windshield as the train passed at high speed through Hartsdale and then Scarsdale. Finally, he spoke to Jack, the engineer: "Keep going like this until Mt. Vernon. Then slow down. We're going to run backwards up the track to New Rochelle."

"Can't run backwards," replied the engineer timidly. "You have to have a person at the back of the train."

"So what if we don't?"

"They won't let you."

"We'll see about that. Call the dispatcher."

The engineer pressed the intercom. "Metro two-niner. Come in, Phil."

"Jack, we've been waiting for your call. What are we doing?" Phil's voice came over the speaker.

"Reverse up the Connecticut Line at Mt. Vernon."

"I figured."

"Says we gotta run backwards – blind."

"Whatever he says, Jack. We'll do."

"What about…you know, the cops."

"They're alerted."

"For God's sake, tell them to be careful."

"That's their business, Jack. Trust 'em."

"I don't want to piss this guy off."

"He needs you to run the train."

"I dunno. Maybe he can do it."

"Let me speak to him."

The engineer turned to look at Bruce. "The dispatcher wants to talk to you."

Bruce shook his head. "No. You talk to him. Tell him to keep the cops away."

Jack turned back to the microphone in front of him. "Says he won't talk. Says to keep the cops away."

"I'll pass it on to the F.B.I."

The train zipped through Bronxville. The next station was Fleetwood and then Mt. Vernon. Jack relaxed the throttle handle and the big Diesel engine calmed to a loud purr. The train coasted and slowed.

In front of them, Bruce could see the bridge over the tracks that brought the trains in from Connecticut. The four Connecticut Line tracks coming in from the east merged with the four Harlem Line tracks in two ways: The two right side tracks crossed over the bridge and then merged with the primarily southbound two right tracks of the Harlem line. The two tracks on the left side merged directly with the primarily northbound two remaining tracks of the Harlem Line. As the commuter train passed under the bridge Bruce could see the Connecticut Line tracks entering from both sides and leading to the switches up ahead. Surveying the scene, he froze. Men with guns, apparently policemen, lined the tracks on either side of the switches.

"Keep going," he demanded. "Don't slow down any more." The engineer did as he was told and the big Diesel roared again as the train picked up speed.

Bruce grabbed his phone from his belt and bleeped his father.

"Cops are everywhere. Gotta keep going."

"Okay. We expected that. Plan B."

"Right." Bruce belted his phone and spoke again to the engineer. "We're going to back up on the Hudson Line. Call the dispatcher."

"Wha...I thought we were going to D.C."

"Yeah, we are. Call the dispatcher and let me talk to him this time."

The engineer keyed the mike. "Metro two-niner."

"Uh, what happened, Jack? I thought you were going to stop." Phil's voice filled the small cabin area of the huge locomotive.

"Yeah, we were, but the place is crawling with cops."

"So what now?"

"He wants to talk to you."

"Who, the hijacker?"

"Here he is." Jack moved the microphone over in Bruce's direction, and Bruce stepped a bit closer.

"Hello, Phil. This is Bruce again."

"Hello, Bruce. I'm listening."

"We're not stopping at Mt. Vernon. We're taking an alternate route to Washington."

"Oh, yeah? What's that?"

"The Harlem River bridge and down the West Side."

"The Ha..." Phil looked up at the Big Board in front of him. Incredible as it seemed, there was a way. The train could back up the Hudson line tracks to Spuyten Duyvel and then he could switch it to go forward down old West Side right-of-way. But he was not about to admit it.

"Those tracks haven't been used in years."

"So what? That's the way we're going. And you're going to switch us through."

"What if I don't?"

"You don't want to know."

"Okay. Okay! I've got to get permission. This may take some time."

"You don't have any time. We're already in The Bronx."

"I don't control those switches."

"Well, I suggest you find out fast who does, and you tell him where we're going."

"*Please* take it easy."

Bruce pushed the microphone back in front of Jack and signaled him to slow the train. The branch-off to the Hudson Line was just ahead and there were no police in view.

Chapter 10

DAVE PRICE HAD ordered his agents to take their positions in preparation for storming the train. All other train traffic had been halted, and the third rail power switched off, so his men could move about freely just south of the station, Mt. Vernon West. His plan had been coordinated carefully with the dispatcher, Phil Davis. The train would stop just beyond the switches for the Connecticut Line and his men would have an opportunity to mount any or all of the ten cars. Once aboard, they would secure the cars and carefully isolate Carl Collingwood and Mike Snead. The plan was to work inward toward the middle of the train from both ends so as to surround the hijacker and take him out with a clear shot. After Carl was dispatched, they would call Bruce and tell him his father had died in the attack. They were sure that Bruce, having lost the only remaining member of his family, would then give himself up without the need to fire a further shot.

With the men in place, Price stood on the sidelines, occasionally looking north for the first glimpse of the *eye*, the single headlight in the front of the locomotive. He could see the Mt. Vernon West station in the distance and the tracks extending beyond. The station platform was empty because the local police were assisting him in keeping citizens away. He knew, however, that a couple of his agents were inside the building, out of sight, to deal with the possibility that the train would stop there.

Overhead, the police helicopter followed the progress of the train. Chopper 2 also followed the train, a safe distance behind.

Alerted by the sound, Price looked up and saw the first helicopter approaching in the distance. The locomotive eye came into view. Price keyed his phone and broadcast to his agents, "Here she comes." He held the key down to keep the channel open.

The train seemed to be slowing as it approached, but only to a point. It passed the station and continued toward the switches, coasting but not braking, until it came even with Price's position on the side of the tracks. Then, as if deciding what to do next, the engine snorted and let out a tremendous roar. The locomotive yanked on its hitch and pulled hard again on the cars behind to accelerate the train.

"Shit!" barked Price, with his finger still on transmit key of the phone. "What the fuck are they doing?"

Just then Price got a call on his cell phone. Irritated at the interruption, Price removed this phone from his belt and angrily pressed Talk. "Price!" His tone of voice said it all.

"This is Phil Davis. Metro-North dispatcher?" The last word was not a question, but was inflected upward since Phil didn't know if an F.B.I. agent knew what a dispatcher was or did.

But the mention of a train dispatcher got Price's attention immediately.

"Yeah? This is a private number. How did you get it?" demanded Price.

"I called the F.B.I. office in New York City and asked for the person in charge of the train hijacking. Some secretary patched me through. Is that okay?"

"Did she give you my name?"

"Special Agent Price, I think. Why? You *are* Agent Price aren't you?"

"So, we established I'm Price. Now what do you want?"

"That's what *I* want to know. Are you going to stop these guys or not?"

"Sure we'll stop them. We always do."

"You had better take it real easy. We don't want anyone killed or hurt on our train."

"We know how to handle this, *Davis.*" Price emphasized "Davis" as if it were a derogatory word. The whole tenor of the exchange was a signal for Davis to butt out.

"I just got a call from one of the hijackers," said Davis.

"You did?"

"Yeah. He said he wanted to keep going to the Bronx."

"Then maybe you can tell *me*, what the hell is going on?"

"They want to go down the West Side, and then switch onto the main line to Washington."

"Jesus! How can they do that?"

"No one's ever done it before. But it's possible. Those hijackers must know the system pretty well."

"Where are they now?"

"Uh, let's see…" There was a pause. "Right now they're just stopping in The Bronx."

"*What*? How the fuck are they getting over to the West Side?"

"They're backing up the Hudson Line to Spuyten Duyvel, and then going forward across the Harlem River bridge."

"Well, why didn't you say so? I'll get my men over there right away."

"Okay, but *please* be careful!"

"We'll do whatever we have to do," snapped Price abruptly, terminating the call and belting his phone. Using his walkie-talkie, he ordered his men to Spuyten Duyvel.

Chapter 11

---◆◈◆---

JULI WATCHED THE Chopper 2 feed with fascination as the train snaked through the Mt. Vernon station and continued on into the Bronx. "I'll bet they know about the West Side tracks," she thought to herself. Her intuition was quickly confirmed as she saw the train stop briefly, and then reverse direction, switching onto the Hudson Line tracks and backing west toward the Hudson River. In the distance she could see the station at Spuyten Duyvel.

Juli picked up the phone and called Transport International. After working through the self-help menu of items, she was finally connected to a company receptionist. "Transport International," she said in a singsong voice. "How may I assist you?"

"Shelley Bernstein, please."

"Just a moment, I'll connect you."

The phone rang three times and Shelley's deep voice came on the line.

"This is Shelley Bernstein. I'm sorry I missed your call. Please leave a message."

"This is Juli Gables, Mr. Bernstein. We spoke earlier about the hijacking? I have some information that may be helpful to you. Could you please call me back as soon as possible? My number is—"

Shelley's voice broke in. "Ms. Gables? I'm here. I was just screening the calls. I'm sure you understand. It has been quite a day, so far."

"Oh, Mr. Bernstein! Thanks for speaking to me. I just wanted to let you know that I've done some research, and I know how the train is going to travel to Washington, D.C. There is a way."

"You are very enterprising, Ms. Gables. As a matter of fact, we've already been informed by the F.B.I. Unfortunately, they don't think the train will get that far."

Juli was surprised to hear the word *unfortunately,* and briefly pondered what Mr. Bernstein wished to convey. Did he mean that his CEO, Mr. Snead, might be injured or killed by an F.B.I. strike at the hijackers? Or did he *want* the train to go to Washington?

"Those hijackers are very intelligent, Mr. Bernstein. I have a hunch they will get through."

"Do you know anything about them?"

"Not very much," she bluffed. She really hadn't been able to find anything on the Internet. "But I've been researching them too."

"Then you know about Hummingbird Aircraft."

"Well, yes," she lied. But as she spoke, she typed "HUMMINGBIRD AIRCRAFT" in a Google query and hit ENTER. She got 41 hits.

"Carl Collingwood is after our CEO. Between you and me, he got a raw deal."

Juli could hardly contain herself. She was just handed the key to what this hijacking was all about!

"I know," she lied again. "Do you mind if I go public with this, Mr. Bernstein?"

"It's public information. I can't stop you."

"Well, I mean… if it's sensitive, I'll respect your wishes." Juli desperately wanted to break this story, but didn't want to disrespect her source of information.

"Ms. Gables, I like your style. I hope you call me again if you have any further information that may be helpful."

"Gee, thank you, Mr. Bernstein," Juli was almost gushing now. "I will be sure to do that. Oh, just one more thing—"

"Yes?" Mr. Bernstein's voice seemed deeper now. More conspiratorial somehow.

"Do you think Mr. Snead is afraid for his life? I mean, Mr. Collingwood is going to a lot of trouble to get him to Washington. He could have just settled up with Mr. Snead and be done with it."

"Hmm. That's a very good question, Ms. Gables. Very smart. Why don't you ask Mr. Snead himself?"

"Oh? How could I do that?"

"I'll give you his cell number."

Juli quickly typed the number as he spoke. "Got it. I'll call him. Thanks so much."

"Don't mention it. But please—"

"Yes?"

"Don't tell him where you got the number."

"Absolutely not. I understand."

"Hope to speak with you soon."

"Goodbye, Mr. Bernstein."

Juli was so excited she hardly knew what to do next. "I've got to get a grip," she kept saying to herself. Then she studied the screen. The 41 Google hits were still there, superimposed on the continuous feed from Chopper 2.

She began to explore the story of Hummingbird Aircraft and learned, quickly, that Transport International – Mike Snead, she assumed – had loaned the corporation some money and when a payment was missed, it exercised an option to take over the management. Then, once in control, it put the company into bankruptcy and got rid of all the shareholders, including Carl Collingwood, in a reorganization plan. The effect was that Carl lost all his equity in the company he founded—a company worth millions of dollars—because he couldn't make a $5,000 payment on time.

She dialed Snead's number and he picked up immediately.

"Mike Snead."

"Mr. Snead. You don't know me. I'm at Channel 8 television news. My name is Juli Gables and I'd like to ask you a few questions, if I may."

"Channel 8? Did you say Channel 8?"

"Yes, sir."

"How did you get my number?"

"We have it in our system." Another white lie.

"Your *system*? What kind of system is that?"

"You know. Our information bank. Now Mr. Snead—"

"I'm sure you know this is not exactly a good time. Goodbye Channel 8, or whoever you are. Don't you ever call this number again."

Juli quickly thought how she could get Mr. Snead's attention.

"We know about Hummingbird Aircraft."

"So what? It was entirely legal. Our lawyers said so."

"You basically stole a company from Mr. Collingwood."

"That's business. I don't expect you to understand."

"Mr. Snead, is Mr. Collingwood there with you?"

"Yes, as a matter of fact, he's holding a gun to my head. Why?"

"I'm surprised he let you talk on the phone."

"Yeah. He's such a nice guy," Snead said sarcastically.

"Can I speak to him?"

"Well, that's up to him, isn't it?"

"Could you please ask him?"

Juli heard some indistinguishable voices in the background and then Carl Collingwood came on the line.

"Hello, I'm Carl Collingwood," he said—a bit timidly, Juli thought. "Who is this?"

"Mr. Collingwood, my name is Julianne Gables. You can call me Juli. I'm a television newscaster with Channel 8."

"It's nice to speak to you."

What? Juli wondered. Am I really talking with a hijacker? What do I ask him? She suddenly panicked at the situation in which she found herself, but she decided to speak to him sympathetically, like a normal human being.

"I heard about Hummingbird Aircraft. I'm so sorry."

"Don't be. It's over now."

"I understand how you must feel."

"I doubt if anybody can. But no matter. We are going to make it right."

"How are you going to do that?"

"We are delivering the problem to Washington."

"You mean Mr. Snead?"

"Yes."

"How is that going to help?"

"They'll make him testify, I hope."

"Testify to what?"

"I'm not sure. All I know is what he did to me. I assume he did it to others too. He is a criminal in disguise."

"If it's true, I'm sure that justice will prevail."

"I'm not so certain… Oops, sorry, I have to go!" There was a sudden urgency to Carl's voice and then there was silence.

Juli sat stunned for a moment, in front of her computer, with the phone to her ear. Then she quickly replaced the receiver, brought up her word processor on her computer and typed her report. Ten minutes later she was on camera again.

The news break was preceded by the Chopper 2 image of the train backing into Spuyten Duyvel station and a voice-over: "We interrupt our current programming to bring you this update of today's breaking story."

"THE MORNING TRAIN TO NEW YORK CITY FROM THE SUBURB OF WASSAIC, NEW YORK, WAS HIJACKED TODAY BY TWO MEN, CARL COLLINGWOOD AND HIS SON, BRUCE. MR. COLLINGWOOD WAS THE FOUNDER AND OWNER OF HUMMINGBIRD AIRCRAFT, A COMPANY THAT DEVELOPED A SMALL, FIXED WING AIRCRAFT, CALLED A 'PERSONAL AIRCRAFT', WHICH WAS CAPABLE OF TAKING OFF AND LANDING VERTICALLY. SHORTLY BEFORE THE INTIAL FLIGHT TEST OF THIS AIRCRAFT, THE COMPANY WAS TAKEN OVER BY A HUGE CONGLOMERATE, TRANSPORT INTERNATIONAL. THE PRESIDENT AND CEO OF TRANSPORT, MR. MICHAEL SNEAD, IS ON BOARD THE TRAIN AND IS BEING FORCED AT GUNPOINT TO TRAVEL TO WASHINGTON, D.C."

Juli's report was monitored and instantly picked up by all the other New York news desks. Within minutes the information went out to the entire nation.

Chapter 12

PRICE HAD ALL his men in place in and around the station at Spuyten Duyvel, near the western-most point in the Bronx where the Hudson River divides into two branches—the main waterway flowing due south and an eastern branch called the Harlem River. The Harlem River eventually turns south and becomes the East River, its waters returning to the mother Hudson after traversing the entire length of Manhattan. On the way, these waters pass under nine bridges including, at the end of the journey, the famous "BMW" bridges: the Brooklyn, the Manhattan and the Williamsburg Bridges.

Such an odd name, *Spuyten Duyvel*, Price thought, as he surveyed the depot overlooking the water. The name jogged recollections of reading about the early history of New York City. A history buff and avid reader, Price remained fascinated by events of the past.

According to early legend, a Dutch mail courier, Antony Van Corlear, was to deliver an important document from Manhattan Island to someone north on the upper Hudson. Reaching the northern tip of Manhattan, he found the waters in turmoil and no boatman at hand to row him across. Knowing the importance of his mission, he dove into the river and started to swim across, vowing he would deliver his document "en spijt en Duyvil"—in spite of the Devil. He drowned in the churning waters and, that very afternoon, the point on the northern bank where the Harlem River starts was named Spuyten Duyvel.

One eyewitness to the drowning, an old Dutch burgher much famed for his tall tales in the local ale houses, testified before a grand jury that he saw the Devil seize Antony by the leg and drag him beneath the waves. Even to this day, local residents claim that Antony can still be heard on stormy nights, blowing his trumpet at the howling madness of the tempestuous winds.

Near the spot where Antony jumped into the river, a large boulder called 'Shorakkopoch' marks the place where, much earlier in 1626, Peter Minuet, the colonial governor of Nieuw Amsterdam, purchased Manhattan from the Weckweesgeek Indians (or, according to some, the Reckgawancs), for beads worth at the time about 60 guilders.

Price smiled to himself in anticipation of the forthcoming raid that he was certain would result in the death of the hijackers. The major part of his job, as Chief Investigator with the Bureau, involved administration and "human resources"—handling the petty complaints of his agents—all of which he considered to be boring at best and irritating most of the time. He relished getting out in "the field" and dealing with real live situations that were constantly and consistently being created by the countless malefactors that teamed the earth. And this was just the kind of case he loved best: The Federal criminal law was clearly being broken and the lives of innocent victims were in jeopardy. This gave him and his men free license to use their weapons and, if necessary, to kill.

This time the train would *have* to stop. The train would have to reverse direction if it was going to travel to Washington, the announced destination of the hijackers. That would give his men the opportunity to board the cars at either end and then move carefully toward the middle, car by car, until they found and cornered their prey.

Price debated with himself about joining them. He wanted to be part of the action but he knew he shouldn't. As the agent in charge, he had to stay on the sidelines and direct the assault. If anything were to go wrong…. But, then, how could it? It was like shooting ducks in a pond.

Price and his men had raced through the streets of the Bronx, sirens blaring, and arrived at the station more than fifteen minutes ahead of the train. They took their positions on both sides of the tracks, but this time they took pains to stay out of sight. The four agents designated to board the train hid at each end of the station platform. Price remained outside, just below the beginning of the platform, with his walkie-talkie tuned to the common channel so he could talk and listen to all of his agents at once.

In the distance he saw the rear of the train approaching. It was moving slowly toward him, but not so slowly that someone could jump on board. Price permitted himself to briefly notice and enjoy the feeling of heightened awareness that overcame him, but then he quickly focused his mind on the police business at hand. He had trained virtually all his life for moments like this.

The rear opening in the car at the approaching end of the train, with an upside-down U-shape designed to mate with the opening at the end of another passenger car, came closer and closer and then passed by and entered the station. As each successive car went by, Price could hear the clanking of hitches and screeching of brakes. Finally the train came to a standstill, the last car even with the platform and the big gray locomotive just in front. Price could almost touch it.

"Go!" he whispered, and his agents moved out onto the platform, guns drawn, and entered the front and rear end cars of the train. One agent remained in the station building and two more were positioned on the other, open side of the train to deal with a possible attempted escape. Price kept his head low, below the level of the platform, to keep out of sight of the windows of the cars, and crouched along the side of the platform toward the middle.

"First front car clear!" called one of his agents over the open channel.

"First rear car clear," reported another.

One by one, the agents called out that the cars were clear. "How many damn cars were on this train, anyway?" wondered Price.

"They're not here!" came the call. "We're at the middle!!"

Just then, Price heard the locomotive engine growl again, and his heart sank. But the train stood still! From the corner of his eye, he saw the locomotive break free of the front car and begin to move out by itself. Standing up, he ran the few steps toward the now roaring engine as fast as his legs would carry him and, just as its speed matched his own and it was about to accelerate away, he leaped and grabbed for a ladder on the rear face of the huge machine.

Price held on tight and, with great effort, pulled himself up to the top of the locomotive as it headed due south. It was switched onto the rail line that led to the old swing drawbridge over the mouth of the Harlem River. The locomotive—with its engineer, Jack, and with Carl, Bruce and Mike on board—was on its way to Washington.

Chapter 13

—◆—

CARL COLLINGWOOD HELD his gun on Mike Snead, who sat with his back against an inside wall of the locomotive. They were in the engineer's cabin, just behind Carl's son, Bruce, who stood with his gun trained on Jack as Jack sat working the controls.

"Just *what* do you expect to accomplish?" Mike was saying, in a demanding voice, as if he were running a corporate meeting of his subordinates.

"Will you please *shut up*?" Carl complained. "We can't stand your persistent prattle."

"What are you going to do? Shoot me?"

"No, but I'll put a gag in your mouth. That will keep you quiet."

"Why are we going to Washington? Tell me *that*!"

"Mike. I've had just about enough. One more squawk and we'll have to tie you up and gag you.""You son-of-a-bitch! You're dead! You know that? You're fucking *dead*!"

Carl nodded to his son, as if by prearrangement. Carl quietly took Bruce's gun from him and stepped back to maintain control by training one gun in his right hand on the engineer and the other, in his left hand, on Snead.

47

Bruce reached into his duffel and pulled out a roll of duct tape. He started by tying Snead's ankles together. Snead objected at first but Bruce grasped his legs firmly and wrapped the tape around them several times. Then he pushed Snead over on his side and tied his arms behind him. After that, he pulled Snead into an upright sitting position again and carefully wrapped the tape around his head, covering his mouth but making sure that he could breathe through his nose. When he was done, he took back the gun from his father. They looked at each other, both visibly relieved, and Bruce took up his position again, guarding the engineer.

Jack was guiding the locomotive over the Harlem River Bridge. This bridge, situated as it was at the entry to the Harlem River, could be rotated about a central vertical axis to allow boats to pass when not in use. In years past, when a train needed to cross, the bridge could be swung into position so that its single track was in alignment with the north-south right-of-way. More recently the bridge had remained in the open, boat-free position, since trains had long since ceased to come down the West Side of Manhattan.

Under orders from the dispatcher, Phil Davis, the bridge had been swung into position so that the commuter train, now only the locomotive, could cross. It had been difficult to get the rusty old bridge to move again, but eventually it began to rotate with loud squeaking and ratcheting sounds and finally clacked into place.

Jack slowed the locomotive to a crawl as they approached the bridge. He wasn't quite sure the single bridge track aligned squarely with the old, unused track beneath the wheels of his locomotive. Looking ahead he saw the bridge was in place and the tracks appeared to mate properly, but he was taking no chances. Once on the bridge, there was a new concern. Although built to carry the weight of heavy steam locomotives, the bridge had not been maintained and had surely weakened over the years. Though constructed somewhat lighter than its steam-driven predecessors, the modern Diesel locomotive was not a lightweight. The big machine clickety-clacked over the rails, with Jack quietly holding his breath. Not until they reached the other side, and the hollow-sounding clacking noises gave way to a prominent rumble, did Jack exhale and start breathing again. He turned briefly to look back at Bruce, whose face also showed the strain.

"We made it!" he said, beaming. "That's the only place I was worried about."

"You were worried about that?" exclaimed Bruce, surprised.

"Yeah, now it's clear sailing all the way to Washington."

"What about the West Side?"

"Oh, those old tracks are okay. It's going to be a tight squeeze at Penn Station, though. Not much room in those tunnels."

"Are we too big?"

"I don't think so. They'll switch us through to the main line. We can really give her the gas."

"How fast does this thing go?"

"I dunno. Never had her at top speed, especially without any cars behind. One-twenty maybe. Maybe more. We'll soon see!"

Just then they heard what sounded like an explosion and the windshield on the "fireman's" side of the locomotive splintered into a million pieces. Glass went everywhere, assisted by the onrush of air.

Although the locomotive was traveling slowly, the 30 MPH wind that suddenly filled the cabin seemed like a hurricane.

"Holy shit!" screamed Jack.

Carl swung his gun around in the direction of the noise, but no one was there. He could find no apparent reason for the sudden breakup of the window. All he could see, through the empty window frame, were the trees and buildings of the Upper West Side as they sped by outside.

Carl moved cautiously to the window opening and peered out, leaning his head out slightly to investigate. Just as he was about to lean out farther, a shot rang out. A bullet slammed into the windowsill, narrowly missing his head.

"We've got company!" Carl shouted, stepping back into the relative safety of the locomotive cabin. "The F.B.I. has arrived."

Chapter 14

———◆◆◆———

DAVE PRICE WAS in his element. This was *Action* with a capital A. It was a bit more than he had bargained for but, hey, didn't the Bureau entice him with this kind of excitement? That's why he had signed on, more than fifteen years ago.

The first thing he did, while still on the ladder, was to key his walkie-talkie and report his whereabouts.

"I'm on the locomotive." His voice went out on the open channel to his men. "I'll get these bastards myself."

"What? You can't do it alone!" came back the voice of one of his men.

"I'll *have* to. No way that anyone else can come on board."

"You'll be without backup. Don't do it!"

"We can't let these guys get away."

"We'll get them down the line, in Washington, if we have to. They have to stop sometime."

"To hell with that. I'm going up to the roof. Check with you later."

After climbing up the ladder onto the roof of the locomotive, Price made his way toward the front, crawling on his hands and knees. In his mind he went through the options. He knew he had the element of surprise in his favor, but the locomotive seemed like an impenetrable fortress. How could he get in? More importantly, how could he disarm the two hijackers? Heck with that, how could he kill the two hijackers? They were two against one, but maybe – just maybe –if he could distract one of them, he could pick them off one by one.

The possibilities weren't great, he soon figured out. There was no way into the loc from above. The only openings through the roof were the exhaust and cooling stacks, with their giant spinning fans that he had been careful to avoid as he passed them on his way forward. There were five doors. One on each side of the engineer's cabin and one on each side of the engine, near the middle of the machine, and one in the rear.

Price quickly ruled out coming in the rear door. It was locked, he was sure, and even if he could break the lock with his gun, which was doubtful, the hijackers inside would have a clear advantage as he tried to enter.

The side doors were even more formidable. They had the same drawbacks as the rear door and were even more difficult to access from the top of the moving locomotive.

No, he would have to lure one of the hijackers up onto the roof. But how? First of all he had to get their attention. They had no idea he was there—which was a good thing, at least for now – but when he was ready he would have to make a move.

Inching forward on his stomach, and holding on tight, he got to the front of the roof where it slopes downward toward the windshield and forms the nose of the loc. Price kept to the left side of the windshield because he knew that the engineer always sat on the right. Reaching back to his belt, he grabbed his pistol and brought it forward. Then, with one swift motion he toggled off the safety, aimed it at the left windshield and fired.

The windshield shattered, and Price instinctively put his head down to avoid the exploding glass. He held his position for a moment and then, to his amazement, he saw an opportunity. One of the hijackers was sticking his head out! Quickly, he aimed again in the direction of the now broken window and fired. The bullet missed its mark and hit the windowsill.

"Damn!" screamed Price into the wind. "Damn! I'll never get *that* chance again."

Price remained clutched to the roof while thinking about what he should do next. Now that they knew he was there, the hijackers had to do something. What would *he* do if he were in their position? The rear door! If they climbed up the ladder in the rear, they would have a clear shot. Wait! What was this?

Price watched in amazement as he saw a pole rising upward in front of him. Someone was holding it out the broken window and lifting it up. It was a signal. They were trying to tell him something. There was a sheet of paper tied around the end.

Price grabbed the stick with one hand and pulled the paper off with the other. Then, letting go of the stick, he opened the folded sheet. On it, in capital letters, were the words:

TUNNEL AHEAD. SMALL CLEARANCE ON TOP. GET OFF THE ROOF.

"Holy shit!" screamed Price. Looking up, he saw the entrance to the tunnel far ahead. This was *not* a trick. Just as fast as he could, he turned around and headed back toward the ladder. However, after just a few crawl-steps on his hands and knees he saw his nemesis.

The hijacker stood on the ladder, with his head appearing just even with the roof at the back of the loc, and shouted into the wind, "Throw your gun down before you come any further!"

Price looked over his shoulder and saw the tunnel again, approaching quickly. He didn't have much time. Thinking fast, he reached back and unclipped his walkie-talkie. I don't need this anymore anyway, he thought. Maybe I can fool him. He raised the object up in the air, hiding most of it in his fist, and waved it.

"Okay, you win!"

Price threw it overboard, toward the front on the engine, so the hijacker couldn't see it.

"All right then, come on down." The hijacker waved him rearward.

Price stood up and ran toward him as fast as his legs would go. Reaching the ladder, he grabbed it and swung himself over the edge.

He slithered down to where the hijacker had previously stood, just as the locomotive entered the pitch-black tunnel.

Price waited for his eyes to adjust to the darkness. Standing on the ladder in the back of the locomotive, he could soon see enough to realize that the hijacker had disappeared into the dark interior of the machine through the open doorway in the rear.

Chapter 15

---◆·❈·◆---

PRICE WAS FIERCELY determined now, if not obsessed, with his mission to end the hijacking. All his years of training and service with the Bureau had taught him, and had reinforced his belief, that lawbreakers had to be brought to justice. If there was a crime in progress, he was permitted to use all necessary force to bring it to an end. He was allowed to be the judge, the jury and the executioner. He almost relished the thought.

Price grabbed his weapon and stepped carefully closer to the open rear door of the locomotive. He knew that, if any portion of his body entered the door space, it would be silhouetted against the light from the entrance of the tunnel behind him, so he decided to wait until the entrance receded far enough, leaving blackness in its wake. He also knew the hijacker was unaware that he was armed, which gave him a slight advantage, at least at first.

He would shoot to kill, as soon as the hijacker came into view. He had to see the hijacker before the hijacker saw him.

Slowly he formed a plan of action. Although there was little space between the top of the locomotive and the ceiling of the tunnel, and the right side of the locomotive was very close to a tunnel wall, the left side was entirely open. The tunnel accommodated two tracks and the locomotive was proceeding down the right-hand track. Price knew, or at least hoped, there was a door on the left side of the loc that he could enter and surprise the hijackers.

He holstered his weapon and started forward, inching his way along the sidewall of the rocking and rumbling machine, grasping at whatever knobs or handles there were and holding fast with his bare fingers, while propping himself up with his feet on a narrow ledge that ran the length of the locomotive. In the blackness of the tunnel he could only feel, not see, so it took him some time to ease his way along, reaching out and exploring the surface with his left hand and left leg and foot.

He occasionally slipped, but he broke his fall each time by holding fast with the fingers of his right hand. He tore the skin of his fingers and they became bloody and slippery, which made it even more difficult to hold on. He continued, however, driven by sheer willpower, moving his left hand forward, and then his leg, until eventually it bumped into something that felt like a handle. The door!

Price reached down, turned the handle and the door opened inward. He stooped and climbed through the opening. He went in, closed the door behind him and stood motionless in the dark.

Getting his bearings in the pitch black of an unfamiliar environment took a little time.

Next to him Price could hear the clacking of valves of the huge Diesel engine as it ran at half throttle, nearly coasting because of its light load. He felt about and surmised he was now in a narrow corridor on one side of the engine. Forward was the engineer's cabin and rearward was the rear door of the locomotive near which, he believed, the hijacker stood waiting.

Price grabbed his weapon and, holding it in front of him, proceeded slowly toward the rear door. The darkness was his protector, and also his enemy. He held out his left hand in front of him, as a tentacle, and held the gun with his right pointing forward.

Inch by inch, he moved. The engine was behind him now but a second engine could be heard, humming on his left. Where was that damn rear door?

He heard a sound in front of him and, suddenly, he found himself staring into the beam of a flashlight. Blinded for a moment, he paused and realized that whoever held the light could now see his weapon. He fired his gun directly toward the light source and heard the bullet career off metal with a "ping". The flashlight crashed to the floor and extinguished itself, leaving Price in total darkness again. He heard footsteps receding on the other side of the engine and, moving quietly with his left hand forward to feel any objects in the way and his right hand grasping the gun, he followed the sound.

He passed what he could tell from the sound was the open rear door on his right, and then rounded the corner to move up the walkway along the right side of the two engines – first the humming engine and then the clacking Diesel that powered the locomotive. Ahead, he knew, would be the door to the engineer's cabin. If it was locked, well…

He walked faster now, toward the front. He sensed a presence on his left, but at the same time tripped and fell forward, instinctively holding both hands out, spread eagled, to break his fall. His right hand hit bottom first, and the shock wrenched the gun away, before his entire body came crashing down onto the roughened steel walkway. Reaching quickly to retrieve his gun, Price felt a sudden pain in his right arm as a foot slammed down hard and pinned it to the floor.

"Don't move," said Carl firmly. "I have a gun to your head."

Chapter 16

———◈———

PRICE LAY MOTIONLESS for a moment and then rolled his body to the right. This time it was Carl who came crashing down, free-falling partly on top of Price and, at the same time, losing his grip on his own weapon, which went spinning off into the darkness.

The two men struggled, each trying to overpower the other, and trying at the same time to grope for the loose weapons. Price's adrenaline masked the pain in his right hand and arm, and he unleashed his full fury on Carl, who was less able to defend himself. This kind of action was what Price had dreamed about and lived forever since he had joined the Bureau.

Price managed to push Carl off him. He started swinging, slamming his fists into Carl's torso to keep him off-guard. Lying on his back, Carl held his arms and legs up to deflect the blows, but suffered several sharp thrusts to his ribs and stomach. He tried to roll over, but Price landed a jab to his jaw. Carl let out a scream.

"Stop!"

"What do you expect, you son-of-a-bitch?" Price wasn't nearly finished. He pressed his knee against Carl to keep him down, and continued hitting with renewed energy.

Defeated and in pain, Carl let his arms fall to signal his surrender, but as he did so, his right hand landed on one of the loose weapons. He grabbed it and held it up toward his adversary, just as the locomotive emerged from the tunnel and entered the lighted area of Pennsylvania Station. A faint ray of light, passing through the tiny window above the heads of the two men, reflected off the shiny surface of the pistol that now was aimed straight at Price's face. Price froze.

Slowly, carefully, Carl climbed to his feet, using his left hand for balance, while keeping the gun pointed directly at Price with his right. Price remained motionless, assuming he would die momentarily, and mumbled, "P...please don't."

"I won't shoot. Just stay right there. Don't move," came the reply. Price relaxed slightly, wondering what would happen if he made a sudden move. Why didn't the guy shoot?

Stepping back to guard against a lunge, Carl drew a breath. "Okay. Now get up – slowly – and walk that way." Carl motioned toward the door to the engineer's cabin. Price did as he was told.

"Open it," Carl instructed.

Price opened the cabin door and stepped in. He was amazed at what he saw. There, sitting with his back against a wall, tied hand and foot, with his mouth taped shut, was Mike Snead.

The engineer, on the other hand, sat in his seat looking fit, if not relaxed, and operating the controls of the big Diesel locomotive as if he were on some kind of adventurous trip. Bruce stood nearby holding a pistol with a somewhat serious, but not too serious, look on his face. Bruce looked up as soon as Price and his father entered.

"Whoa! What have we here? Dad, you look *awful*."

"It's been a rough ten minutes," Carl said breathlessly, wiping his forehead with his sleeve. "Okay," he said to Price. "Just who *are* you?"

"Special Agent David Price. F.B.I."

"Oh, yeah? Where are your men?"

"That's all I'm going to say."

Well, that's just *great*," Carl replied sarcastically. "What do you think we should do with you?"

"Look's like your call. *You* have the gun."

"For starters, we'll have to tie you up. Hope you don't mind."

"You'll pay for this!"

"I'm sure you're right. Bruce, tie him up."

Bruce gave his father his gun and set about tying Price up, the same way he had tied up Snead. When he finished, he shifted Price's position so that he and Snead sat side by side, but not so close that they could touch or assist each other.

"What about his mouth?" Bruce asked.

"Let him talk," Carl looked at Price inquisitively. "Maybe he'll say something important. Oh, and take the tape off Mike's mouth now. He's got the point, I'm sure."

Bruce reached down and ripped the tape off Snead's mouth. Snead snarled, but didn't say a word.

Just then Snead's cell phone rang. Bruce reached into Snead's pocket and took it from him. Opening the flap, he put the phone to his ear and asked, "Who's this?"

"This is Julianne Gables from Channel 8 News. Is Mr. Collingwood there?" came the cheerful voice. Bruce's eyes rolled.

"Here, Dad, it's for you." He held out the phone, at arm's length, to his father with one hand, while taking back his gun with the other.

"Hello?"

"Mr. Collingwood? I just want you to know that I checked out your story. That was a terrible thing they did to you. I want to help you get the word out."

Chapter 17

❖◈❖

JULI GABLES HAD done her homework. She had entered dozens of key words, such as "Hummingbird Aircraft" and "Transport International" into the search engines of Google, Yahoo and MSN, and reviewed reams of information. She used the LexisNexis database to retrieve court decisions involving Transport International, and found that this company had been sued innumerable times, and always won.

Hummingbird Aircraft Corp. vs. Transport International, Inc. was particularly revealing. This case had proceeded through the civil justice system at a snail's pace, and had generated no less than thirty-six pretrial motions. Plaintiff's motions were all to seek the court's aid in stopping the defendant's stalling tactics, and to give them access to critical information they were entitled to. Plaintiff's attorneys were forced to file motion after motion to compel discovery. They also moved for sanctions against the defendant for failure to produce documents. They sought to obtain court orders to allow them to conduct depositions of important witnesses and even to compel witnesses to answer key questions—questions that had been blocked by the defense attorneys— and after being ordered by the court to answer, the witnesses suddenly developed amnesia and just "couldn't recall" any facts that were helpful to the plaintiff.

Even then, most of the motions were filed by the defendant's attorneys. These were requests for court intervention designed to keep the plaintiff's attorneys reactive rather than pro-active. It also vastly increased the cost of the suit for Hummingbird. Transport International had hired no less than three law firms to bombard the plaintiff with frivolous and sometimes almost bogus motions. The court's decisions were invariably in favor of plaintiff, but that was not the point. These motions had the intended effect of wearing plaintiff's attorneys down as they struggled to get the facts to make their case. The plaintiff's attorneys were simply outnumbered and outclassed.

The case went to trial before a jury composed entirely of people from middle-class backgrounds. As Juli studied the makeup of the jury, she created flesh-and-blood characters in her imagination from the brief descriptions on the page.

Most notable was a man named Joey Graziella, a senior manager in an electronics firm. He had attended Brooklyn Polytech and earned a bachelor's degree in electrical engineering before joining a small high-tech company that made parts for the military. The company was sold to a larger aerospace firm and Joey moved up the ladder, year by year, to a very responsible position. Juli thought of him as short and stocky, with a two-day growth of beard, a Brooklyn accent, and a fairly hot temper.

On the female side, Juli focused on a woman named Betty Falmouth, a mother of five children, ages three to eleven. She was a homemaker – how else could she have handled the family household? Her husband, Bob, was a construction worker who had to attend to the kids while Betty was on jury duty. Juli imagined Bob must have given Betty an earful whenever she came home from court at the end of the day. Bob would complain bitterly he had lost his wife's services, but there was nothing Betty could do about it. In fact, Juli thought, Betty probably enjoyed getting out of the house, but she would never admit it. She would tell her husband she was doing her duty as a citizen.

The jury included a nicely balanced ethnic mix. There were three Latino members, two African-Americans and one person of Asian descent. The rest, including Joey and Betty, were of European descent. Why she had singled out Joey and Betty, Juli didn't know. Those two just stuck out as strong individuals and, in Juli's mind at least, they were probably vocal and self-aware – the kind of personality that can sway a jury. It was just a hunch, but Juli knew she had the gift of intuition.

She started by phoning Graziella and reached him in his office.

"Graziella!" His voice was gruff and loud. Yes, he was vocal all right.

"Hello, I'm Julianne Gables, with Channel 8 News?" Juli inflected the last three words upwards, as if asking a question.

"Channel *what*?"

"Channel 8." Juli got that question a lot.

"I didn't even know there *was* a Channel 8. Y'mean on TV?" Graziella *did* have a trace of a Brooklyn accent.

"Yes, that's right, I—"

"I don't watch much television. What's this about?"

"I'm covering the hijacking of the commuter train today. Have you heard about it?"

"Yeah, it's all over the news. Some guy and his son. It's ridiculous. They didn't catch 'em *yet*?"

"No sir. It's still going on. The train is on its way to Washington."

"What on earth? Why?"

"Well, that's what I'm calling about. I think it has something to do with a lawsuit called <u>Hummingbird Aircraft versus Transport International</u>."

"Yeah, I remember that. A year or so back, it was."

"You were on the jury?"

"Yup."

"Can you tell me about it? I'd just like to ask a few questions."

"Lady, I don't have much time. What's this case got to do with the hijacking, anyway?"

"The hijacker was the owner of Hummingbird, and the CEO of Transport is on that train."

"Holy shit! Well that guy got screwed, that's all I can say."

"How's that?"

"They 'bout stole his company, and when he sued he got *bupkus*."

"That's why I'm calling, as a matter of fact. What happened?"

"Beats me. Jury didn't buy his story. But I did. I know how tough it is in the real world out there."

"The jury thought he was lying?"

"Not really. There was just this question. The attorneys for Transport kept harping on it.

Did he really have any technology, or was it all smoke and mirrors."

"That's what the jury thought?"

"Well, one of them did, and then—"

"And then what?"

"That woman! She couldn't stop talking. I think they went along with her just to shut her up."

"What woman?"

"Geez, I forget her name. Some lonely housewife, you know the type—"

"Betty Falmouth?"

"Yeah, that's *it*! I called her Betty Boob. She had such big boobs, ya know what I mean?"

"I'm sure she appreciated that."

"She was a piece of work, that one. Listen, I gotta go. Another call's coming in."

"Oh, and one more question—"

"What's that?"

"Do you know what Transport did with the Hummingbird aircraft technology?"

"Far as I know, they buried it! Bye." The phone clicked off, leaving Juli listening to a dial tone.

Chapter 18

———◆———

JULI DIALED DIRECTORY assistance for "Falmouth" in the Westchester/Putnam County area. The operator found a new listing for "R. Falmouth" in Chappaqua at 47 Cherry Tree Lane. Juli thanked her and quickly dialed the number.

"Hello?"

"Is this Betty Falmouth?"

"With whom am I speaking?"

"I'm Barbara Fitzpatrick. I'm studying law at NYU and working on this project," Juli lied. She had a feeling that mention of Channel 8 News might scare Betty away.

"Who?"

"Please call me Barbara."

There was some noise in the background and Juli thought she heard "Shut up. I'm on the phone!"

"I'm sorry. Just the kids. Always acting up, you know. You are?" "Barbara Fitzpatrick, a law student, and—"

"Oh, I thought you were someone else. Sorry. What can I do for you?"

"May I ask you a few questions?"

"About what? You're a law student?"

"About a case you were involved in. <u>Hummingbird Aircraft versus Transport International</u>."

"Oh sure, I remember that. I was on the jury."

"Do you remember who won?"

"Of course. Transport International. Hummingbird didn't have a case."

"They didn't?"

"Heck no. You can quote me. Transport were the good guys on that one."

"I understand that you were quite an influence on the other jurors in the Jury Room."

"Really? Who told you that?"

"Another juror."

"Oh? Who was that?"

"Joe Graziella."

"I should have known. He's a troublemaker, that one."

"Well, was it true?"

"What?"

"That you convinced a number of jurors to change their minds and find for the defendant."

"Listen Miss, whoever you are. This is ancient history. Why are you asking me these questions?"

"As I said, I'm a law student. I'm doing research on juries, how they go about reaching a decision."

Just then, over the phone, Juli heard a slamming noise in the background, and a dog started barking. "I'm sorry I have to go. We just bought this new house and the painters have arrived."

"Well, thank you, Ms. Falmouth. You've been very helpful."

"Goodbye Miss—"

"Fitzpatrick. Barbara Fitzpatrick. I may be in touch again soon."

Juli hung up and immediately contacted the Town Hall in Chappaqua to find out when Robert and Betty Falmouth purchased their home, and how much they paid for it. The secretary refused to give out this information, so Juli went online with the local multiple listing service. Scanning through the houses in Chappaqua that were recently sold, she found it, on Cherry Tree Lane, picture and all. The house had been listed for sale over a year ago for a shade over a million dollars. She printed the page.

Chapter 19

———◆———

WHAT TO DO next? Juli decided to go to the mountain itself: Transport International. She called the only person there that she knew, Shelley Bernstein.

"Pick up. Pick up," she pleaded as she heard the phone ring and ring without an answer. After four rings, the recorded voicemail message began to play, and when it ran its course and the beep sounded, Juli cleared her throat and spoke with urgency in her voice. "Mr. Bernstein, it's me, Juli Gables. At Channel 8. If you're there, could you pick up? I have something very important to tell you—"

"Hello, Juli. This is Shelley Bernstein. Call me Shelley, everyone does." The deep voice was unmistakable. "What's up?"

"Mr. Ber – er, Shelley. I've been investigating the Hummingbird case. I just want to check a small fact before I go public with it."

"Oh? What's that?"

"I've found out that one of the jurors, a Ms. Falmouth, was instrumental in convincing the jury to find in favor of Transport International."

"All right. That's true. Anything else?"

"Uh, yes…" Juli found it difficult to continue, but she pressed on. "Ms. Falmouth is a homemaker and her husband is a blue-collar construction worker. Yet they were just able to purchase a million-dollar home."

There was a pause. Juli held her breath. What would Mr. Bernstein say? Obviously he would not like the implication.

"I'm very impressed, Juli. Just follow the money," came the deep voice. It seemed even deeper than before.

"What?"

"You heard me. That's all I can say."

"Oh, I heard you, but—" The phone clicked off,

Juli sat stunned in front of her computer. Shelley Bernstein hadn't denied that a payoff had been made!

How could she "follow the money?" What money was it, anyway? What could she do? She had a tiger by the tail but didn't know how to bring it under control.

She went to the web site of the Securities and Exchange Commission. Within seconds she obtained the records of Transport International, but the maze of numbers and accompanying gobbledygook meant less than nothing to her. All she could understand was that the corporation had total sales of 23 billion from its various operations, including those of its subsidiaries in more than a dozen countries around the world. She scanned the list: All the main countries of Europe, Asia and the Middle East, as well as Bermuda. What to do? What to do?

Juli buried her face in her hands and thought. Looking up, she stared at her printer. There was a single sheet of paper in the tray. She took it out and stared at the picture of the Falmouths' house in Chappaqua. She reached for the phone and dialed a number.

"Holmes Realty!" answered a pleasant female voice. "How may I assist you?"

"Hello. My name is Barbara Fitzpatrick." The name worked before, so why not use it again? "I'm interested in a house that you're listing. At 25 Cherry Tree Lane? Can you tell me if it is sold yet?"

"Just a moment. I'll check." There was a short pause, and then the receptionist came on the line again. "Yes it did. The new owners closed on that house just one week ago."

"Oh, darn! I loved that house. Can I speak to the broker who handled this sale? Maybe he can suggest something similar."

"That's a good idea. I believe it was Peter Holmes himself. Let me connect you."

There was a longer pause.

"Peter Holmes." The agent's voice was calm, confident. After all, this was Chappaqua, where the Clintons lived.

"Mr. Holmes, I'm Barbara Fitzpatrick, and I'm calling—"

"Call me Peter."

"Okay, uh, Peter. I'm Barbara. I understand you sold the house on Cherry Tree Lane."

"Yes, that's right. Were you interested in that home?"

"Yes. Very much. May I ask what it sold for?"

"That's a matter of public record, so yes, it sold for $955,000."

"It closed already?"

"Just last week. To a nice family from the Bronx."

"The Falmouths, right?"

"Yes, that's right! Do you know them?"

"As a matter of fact we do. I'm afraid I was not completely honest with your receptionist, Peter. You see I'm calling from The New York Bank for Savings. The Falmouths moved out of their home in the Bronx without keeping up with their mortgage. In fact, they hadn't made payments for almost a year and their property was in foreclosure."

"That's odd. Are you sure you have the right people. Bob and Betty Falmouth? They said they previously lived in an apartment."

"Oh, I'm sure they would say that. They owed our bank over $85,000, as well as back taxes. How were they able to purchase this new home for nine-five-five?"

"Frankly, I thought it odd. They paid cash. That's almost never done."

"Paid cash? Do you remember what bank they used?"

"Yes that was strange too. It was an offshore bank. The Falmouths did it by fund transfers."

"Did your fee come out of that transaction?"

"As a matter fact, it did. We received a fund transfer too."

"Could you tell me where it came from?"

"Just a minute, please. I just received our bank confirmation in the mail. Yes, here it is. The fund transfer came from the International Bank of Bermuda."

Chapter 20

———◆◆◆◆◆———

Juli barged into Mr. Raleigh's office while he was on the phone and placed a paper on his desk with one word: URGENT! Mr. Raleigh wound up the call and faced her.

"Okay, what is it?" he barked, annoyed at the interruption.

"Mr. Raleigh. I'm sorry to bother you, but you've *got* to hear this."

Juli began by explaining what had happened to the train, who the four people were who were now on the locomotive and what she had found out about Carl Collingwood's company, Hummingbird Aircraft. She then told Mr. Raleigh what she had learned about the Falmouths: How Mrs. Falmouth had swung the jury against Hummingbird and, shortly thereafter, her family had moved from an apartment in the Bronx to a million-dollar home in Chappaqua with funds that came from a bank in Bermuda, the same small country where, oddly, Transport International had a subsidiary.

"Can I go public with this, *please*?" she begged.

"Go public with *what*?"

"Possible jury tampering."

"No way! You *don't* have my permission to say *anything*. If you so much as hint that Transport International is involved in a scandal, we'll be sued for slander so fast our lawyers won't have time to go to the bathroom."

"Don't you think Transport could have gotten to the jury?"

"What *I* think won't count for shit when a lawsuit is involved."

"But what if it's true? You can't be sued for telling the truth."

"You can be sued for sneezing in the wrong place. Whether you win or lose is another matter, and I don't even want to go down that road."

"What would it take to convince you that we've got a story?"

"*You've* got a story. Don't bring me, or Channel 8, into this. The only way I'll let you say *peep*, is if Transport admits they made a payment."

"Okay, let's try!"

"What?"

"Let's call Transport International."

"Are you crazy? They won't admit to anything."

"It won't hurt to ask, will it?"

"No, but—"

"Here, let me dial the number." Juli went around behind Mr. Raleigh's desk, pressed the "speaker" button on the phone, and dialed the number.

Mr. Raleigh rolled his eyes as Shelley Bernstein's voicemail message filled the room.

"Mr. Bernstein? Shelley? It's me again, Juli. Could you pick up, please?"

"Hello, Juli. I've been waiting for your call. How did you make out?" came the deep male voice.

Mr. Raleigh almost fell of his chair when he heard this. He stared at Juli in amazement.

"I followed the money, like you said."

"You found the trail?"

"Yes."

"And where did it lead?"

"It led to Bermuda."

"Is that so?"

"Yes, and Transport International has a subsidiary in Bermuda."

"That's true."

"But I can't connect the dots in Bermuda."

"Oh. That's too bad."

"So, I'm stuck."

"Maybe I can help."

"Could you?"

"Off the record."

"Absolutely."

"You won't reveal your source."

"Never."

"All right then. Transport has an account with the International Bank of Bermuda."

"Yes?"

"Account number 95267842."

For the second time that day, the phone clicked off abruptly.

Mr. Raleigh just sat stunned, frozen in his chair, as Juli dialed another number.

"Holmes Realty!" came the perky voice.

"Peter Holmes, please. I just spoke to him a few moments ago. Could you—"

"Peter Holmes. Is this Barbara?"

"Yes, Peter. I just have a quick question. Could you tell me the number of the account in Bermuda that paid your commission?"

"Just a sec. I had the statement. Oh, here it is. Yes, it gives the account number at that bank in Bermuda. Is that what you want?

"Yes." Juli held her breath.

"95267842."

Mr. Raleigh nodded as Juli finished the call. "All right. Go!"

"Oh *thank you*, Mr. Raleigh! You won't regret this." Juli leaned down and gave him a peck on the cheek.

"I hope not. Oh, but by the way—"

Juli braked briefly as she sped out the door.

"Yes?"

"Who the hell's Barbara?"

Chapter 21

AT 9:00 AM on Monday, Channel 8 was scheduled to present a cooking show. Instead, the viewers who tuned in weekly to learn a new recipe were treated to a breaking news story which, they would learn later, reverberated throughout the country like the aftershock of an earthquake.

At the top of the hour, the image of the creaky old Harlem River bridge filled the screen and there, within the lattice-work, crossing gingerly, was the gray locomotive, heading south on the unused, rusty tracks. As the locomotive reached the other side, the camera in Chopper 2 zoomed in an odd sight: A man lying on top of the engine holding on for dear life with one hand and wielding a gun with the other.

Juli's head appeared on the screen, superimposed on this background, and began to speak.

GOOD MORNING. I'M JULIANNE GABLES AND WE'RE CONTINUING TO FOLLOW THE BREAKING NEWS STORY THAT STARTED AT 6:30 THIS MORNING WHEN TWO MEN, A FATHER AND SON, HIJACKED A COMMUTER TRAIN TO NEW YORK CITY. THE TRAIN ORIGINATED IN WASSAIC,

NEW YORK, A COUNTRY TOWN ABOUT ONE HUNDRED MILES NORTH OF THE CITY. THE TRAIN WAS HEADED FOR GRAND CENTRAL STATION BUT THE HIJACKERS DEMANDED THAT IT BE SWITCHED THROUGH TO WASHINGTON D.C. THAT MIGHT SEEM IMPOSSIBLE, BECAUSE GRAND CENTRAL IS A DEAD END, BUT METRO NORTH FOUND A WAY. WHAT YOU SEE ON THE SCREEN, COURTESY OF THE CHANNEL 2 TRAFFIC HELICOPTER, IS A VIEW OF THE LOCOMOTIVE AS IT MAKES ITS WAY DOWN THE WEST SIDE OF MANHATTAN ON ITS WAY TO PENN STATION. THEY LEFT THE REST OF THE TRAIN— ALL TWELVE CARS—AT A STATION CALLED SPUYTEN DUYVEL IN THE BRONX.

WHY WOULD THE TWO MEN DO SUCH A THING? WHY WOULD THEY RISK CERTAIN CAPTURE, AND MAYBE THEIR LIVES, TO COMMANDEER A TRAIN?

WE HAVE LEARNED THAT ONE OF THE MEN, CARL COLLINGWOOD, WAS THE FOUNDER AND OWNER OF HUMMINGBIRD AIRCRAFT, A COMPANY THAT WAS TAKEN OVER BY TRANSPORT INTERNATIONAL. TRANSPORT PUT THE COMPANY INTO BANKRUPTCY TO GET RID OF COLLINGWOOD'S SHARES OF STOCK, AND COLLINGWOOD LOST EVERYTHING.

COLLLINGWOOD SUED TRANSPORT TO GET HIS STOCK BACK, BUT AFTER A LENGTHY TRIAL, THE JURY FOUND IN FAVOR OF TRANSPORT.

THE PRESIDENT OF TRANSPORT, MICHAEL SNEAD, WAS ON BOARD THE TRAIN WHEN IT WAS HIJACKED. ALL THE OTHER PASSENGERS AND THE TRAIN CREW WERE ALLOWED TO DISEMBARK AT BREWSTER, LEAVING ONLY SNEAD AND THE LOCOMOTIVE ENGINEER AS HOSTAGES.

IT SEEMS THAT COLLINGWOOD IS TAKING SNEAD

TO WASHINGTON, TO FACE WHAT HE HOPES WILL BE
AN ANGRY GOVERNMENT, FED UP WITH CORPORATE
CORRUPTION.

Juli paused for a moment to allow the message to sink in, and then
continued.

OUR INVESTIGATION HAS REVEALED THAT
COLLINGWOOD WAS CERTAIN TO WIN HIS LAWSUIT.
WE LEARNED, HOWEVER, THAT TRANSPORT PAID A
HANDSOME SUM OF MONEY TO ONE OF THE JURORS,
BETTY FALMOUTH, TO INFLUENCE HER VOTE. MS.
FALMOUTH WAS SO EFFECTIVE IN CONVINCING
SEVERAL OTHER MEMBERS OF THE JURY TO CHANGE
THEIR VOTES THAT THE JURY EVENTUALLY FOUND IN
FAVOR OF TRANSPORT. THIS SHOCKING STORY HAS BEEN
CONFIRMED BY A RELIABLE SOURCE.

WE'LL BE FOLLOWING THIS STORY THROUGHOUT
THE DAY. STAY WITH *US* AND STAY INFORMED.

In the background, the locomotive could just be seen entering
the tunnel to Penn Station. The camera zoomed in to a man in the
back, climbing down a ladder from the roof, just as the locomotive
disappeared into the dark opening.

Within minutes, the telephone switchboard at Ariana's front
desk lit up like a Christmas tree. ABC, CBS and NBC, as well as all
the local New York print media, were on the line to ask for detailed
information. The *New York Post* readied a special edition with the
front-page headline: "GO CARL GO!" The *Daily News* chose the
headline "CEO SHAME," with a picture of Mike Snead getting out
of a stretch limo.

Chapter 22

CARL COLLINGWOOD WAS not feeling so well after the furious beating he had received at the hands of the F.B.I. agent. So when Juli from Channel 8 News called, he handed the phone back to Bruce to respond to her questions.

"Hi, this is Bruce Collingwood. I'm Mr. Collingwood's son," offered Bruce, after putting the phone to his ear with his left hand. With his right, he kept his gun steady, trained on Jack, the engineer.

"Hi Bruce. This is Juli Gables. May I ask a few questions?"

"About what?"

"Oh, I'm sorry. I work for Channel 8 News. Your story is all over the news right now. We know what happened to your father. Everyone is rooting for you."

"Really?" Bruce was incredulous.

"Yes, but you have to be careful. There are going to be some forces that will try to stop you. Try to kill you, even."

"Oh! My dad told me it won't be easy for us, but—"

"Why are you doing this?"

"To help my dad."

"Not too many guys would do such a thing for their dads."

"My dad needs me. He couldn't do this alone."

Juli felt a sudden flood of empathy. Her father had been pushed to the limit too, and she would have done anything, anything at all, to help him if only he had asked her.

"I know," she said softly. "How old are you?"

"I'm twenty-five."

"I am too."

"You're a reporter?"

"Yes."

"You know what happened to Dad?"

"Yes. It must have been really tough."

"It was awful. He was so depressed."

"What will you do when you get to Washington?"

"It depends."

"Depends on what?"

"If anyone will listen."

"Well, I'm listening. If you tell me, I'll put it out there."

"It's complicated."

"Well, let's get started!"

"Okay. Where do you want to start?"

"How about when your Dad lost his lawsuit."

"You know about that?"

"More than you can imagine."

"God, it was *awful*. Dad was so sure he could win. We were all set to celebrate. But then the jury came back and found for TI. It was like they slugged him with a baseball bat."

"What happened then?"

"It was scary. I never saw Dad like that before. Mom tried to comfort him but nothing she did would cheer him up. Dad not only lost his job, which I know he liked, but his dream too. He was going to be like Henry Ford, and build a car, a car that could fly! Before this happened he would stay at the office for several days at a time, working all day and sleeping on the floor whenever he could, while he and his men worked on the project. They called it the 'Personal Aircraft.'

"Dad said he had to make a test flight by a certain date or Transport International would call in the loan. He was making payments on the loan, but there were deadlines. He was so close, but then he missed a payment and they put the company into bankruptcy. Dad had worked on this project on and off pretty much all his life. It was his dream, even when he was a kid.

"At first Dad just slept all day and wouldn't get out of bed. Mom was worried. Dad had saved a little bit of money, but not enough for us to live on, so he needed to find another job.

"We were even afraid Dad would commit suicide. He left one night while we were sleeping and didn't return for days. Mom was frantic. She called the police but they didn't know anything. She told them about his losing his job and they said he might be out a binge

"Then a few days later the police called and said they had found Dad on the George Washington Bridge. Someone driving by had seen him standing on the edge, and they called it in. We found out later that he had a million-dollar life insurance policy and he was going to jump off so the money would go to Mom.

"When Dad came home again he was different from before. He had always been determined, but now he was bitter. He wanted to get back to where he was before but there was no way he could. He first thought the appeal might succeed, but when that failed he lost all hope of finding justice the normal way. He knew that Mr. Snead was crooked, but there was nothing he could do about it. No one was listening. No one seemed to care!

"Then about six months ago he hit upon this way to get the attention of the government. He said he was going to *deliver* Mr. Snead to Washington, so that they would investigate him and his company."

At this point, Bruce's voice began to waver. Juli's heart went out to him, but she said nothing and let the moment pass. After a short pause Bruce went on, firmer this time, and continued the story.

"I wanted to help my dad so much, and he finally me let in on his plan. It was just him and me. No one else knew, not even Mom.

"We took turns following Mr. Snead and learned where he went on weekends. He has a farm in Millbrook and it's a pretty long commute, so he stays in his apartment in New York during the week. We also learned that he took the commuter train from Dover Plains every Monday morning. There aren't many trains in the morning from that far up, so he always took the one at 6:40. It was pretty easy to figure out what to do then."

"How did you figure you could get him to Washington with a commuter train to New York City?" Juli queried, sympathetically.

"We knew that, with a Diesel engine, you could go just about anywhere. We figured out a couple of different ways."

"I know now too. All of New York knows."

"Really?"

"Yes. I don't suppose you hear a helicopter overhead."

"No, it's kind of noisy in here."

"Well there's at least one, and everyone is watching your progress."

"I don't know if that's good or bad."

"That's good. You want everyone to know what you are doing. But it may be scary. The F.B.I. will try to stop you."

"They already did," replied Bruce, looking down at Agent Price, tied up and squirming.

"They'll try again. Believe me."

"I figure they will."

"Tell me one more thing, Bruce."

"Sure, what's that?

"Do you know why your dad lost the lawsuit?"

"We figured they had better lawyers."

"No, it wasn't that."

"Why then?"

"Mr. Snead and his company bribed the jury."

Bruce almost dropped the cell phone. He just stood glaring at Mike Snead.

"Metro two-niner. Jack, this is Phil at dispatch. Come back."

The engineer adjusted his headset. "Metro two-niner. This is Jack."

"Jack, put this call on the speaker. I want everyone there to hear it."

"Roger that." Jack pressed a button on the dash.

"*They are coming to get you with another Diesel.*"

Everyone heard this, even Juli. Just then, from somewhere behind them, they all heard the forlorn blast of a Diesel locomotive. Forgetting it was off-hook, Bruce jammed the phone into his breast pocket.

"Jack," Carl commanded, "I want you to see how fast this engine can go."

Chapter 23

———◆◆◆———

SITTING AT HER computer, Juli could see the video feed from overhead in Chopper 2. Down below, the gray locomotive in northern New Jersey was speeding down the main line on the right-hand track. About a quarter mile behind, in the left-hand track, a black locomotive was coming up fast and, at the rate it was going, it would soon pull even with the gray. The gap between the two locomotives was quickly closing.

Or was it? As Juli watched, the gray locomotive slowly accelerated. It appeared that its speed would soon match that of the black one, and that it would pull away.

Inside the gray machine, Jack edged the throttle forward as he watched the speedometer slowly climb: 50...60...70...80...85. The wind whistled through the broken left windshield as the Diesel engine thundered in the background. The locomotive whizzed past station after station along the line.

"Is that it?" shouted Carl. "Can't we go any faster?"

"I'm afraid to!" Jacked shouted back. "This is an old engine. It'll blow a gasket!"

"I'll take that chance. Give me all you've got!"

Jack moved the throttle lever all the way forward. "Okay, don't say I didn't warn you! Hold your breath and hold on tight!" The speedometer moved slowly up to 90, kept climbing and then seemed to hover at 92. Behind them, in the engine room, the engine roared above the clacking sound of the valve tappets on the cylinder heads. Black smoke, caused by incomplete combustion at this maximum power, blew out the cooling tower above the engine and left a contrail in the air behind the locomotive.

As Juli watched, she could see the gray locomotive holding its distance from the pursuing black engine and then, or so it seemed, the distance increased. The gray locomotive was widening the gap between the two engines!

"We can't keep going like this!" Jack screamed over the deafening roar. He alternated viewing the track and signals ahead with scanning a row of temperature gauges on the dashboard in front of him. One of the gauges had climbed into the red zone.

"See this!" he shouted, pointing. "One of the bearings is *overheating*."

Carl looked at the gauge and then stared at Bruce with tears in his eyes. They both knew that their ride to Washington would soon be over.

Carl leaned down so Jack could hear. "What's the next station?"

"I'm not sure. Metropark, I think. It's in Edison."

"How fast can you stop?"

"Without a train behind me? I can stop on a dime."

"Okay, slow down easy."

Jack gave a sigh of relief and eased off the throttle. The big Diesel behind him in the engine room quieted slightly and seemed relieved too. The temperature gauge on the dash stopped climbing, but still hovered in the red zone.

Far up ahead, the station came into view.

"Keep going as long as you can. When we get to the station, hit the brakes."

"What if we overshoot the platform?"

"Don't! Bruce and I are going to jump off."

"It's gonna be hard to judge when to brake."

"Give it your best shot."

"Okay! Have a nice stay in Metropark."

The station was fast approaching. Carl motioned to Bruce, who nodded. They opened the side door to the cab and braced themselves.

Meanwhile, the black locomotive had nearly caught up to the gray engine and was moving in parallel alongside, only an arm's reach away. The two doors on the side of the locomotive, facing the neighboring tracks with the gray engine, had been removed. F.B.I. agents stood in the openings with their weapons ready. One of the agents held what looked like a bazooka, aimed directly at the side of the gray engine. Then, just when the black engine came up even with the gray one, the main line tracks spread apart to make room between them for the Metropark station platform.

Suddenly, Jack pulled back on the throttle lever and hit the brakes, hard. The gray locomotive's wheels locked and skidded over the steel track, shooting out sparks like fireworks.

The black locomotive rocketed ahead before its engineer realized what had happened. Then he, too, hit the brakes and the F.B.I. agents who were standing in the doorways went tumbling forward, losing their balance and letting go of their weapons as they reached out to grab for support.

Back at Channel 8, listening and watching the race unfold, Juli put her calls on hold, slipped her cell phone into her purse, and again ran into Mr. Raleigh's office.

"Mr. Raleigh, I need a car and a cameraman *now!*"

"We don't have either."

"I've gotta get out there! To follow Carl and Bruce."

"Follow? Where?"

"Listen!" Juli took her cell phone out of her purse, put it on speaker and dialed the office number.

"Ariana, it's me, Juli. I have Bruce on hold on the other line. Can you patch it through to me on this cell phone?"

"Sure. Easy. Here it is."

At first only heavy breathing could be heard from the cell phone. Then Carl's voice came over the speaker. "Over this way, Bruce! Let's take that road—"

"My God, you can listen in?" Mr. Raleigh mouthed the words.

Juli nodded affirmative and held the phone to her chest to cover its microphone. "Bruce left his cell phone on. We can hear everything."

"Here. Take my car." He reached in his pocket for the keys. "You'll have to run the camera yourself."

"I want to take George. He can do it."

"George? Who's George?"

"The security guard. Downstairs? When you come in?"

"A security guard for a cameraman? I don't—"

"You have a problem with that?"

"No. Go!"

Juli grabbed a camera that lay on a table in the corner and headed out the door. "Thanks, boss. You won't regret this!" In a few seconds she was descending in an elevator, thinking of what she would say to George.

Chapter 24

―――――◆×◆―――――

"*Mo*? A cameraman?"

"You can do it, George. I know you can. Here, take the camera."

"Geez, Juli. I don't know—"

"Take it!"

"Who's gonna cover this desk?"

"George, I need you, *now*!"

"Well, pretty lady, since you put it that way, what are we waiting for?"

George grabbed the camera and followed Juli as she raced out the door.

Juli found Mr. Raleigh's car in his designated spot, and the two climbed in. Juli started it up, headed out into the street and zoomed her way through the traffic on the West Side toward the nearby Lincoln Tunnel. George feigned fright by the wild experience as she darted this way and that to get around the equally aggressive yellow cabs.

"Good golly, Miss Molly!" George pretended to duck down.

"You're chicken!"

"*Puck, puck, puck!*" George made a chicken sound. "I don't want to end my career as a cameraman so soon!"

"Okay, okay. I'll be careful. But let me tell you: We've got a shot at interviewing those guys who hijacked the train! If we don't get out there, we'll be kicking ourselves tomorrow."

"That would be *good* news: I mean that we're *still kicking* tomorrow."

They slipped inside the tunnel, following the car ahead in the semi-darkness in silence until they broke out into the daylight again.

From there it was clear sailing over the eastern spur of the New Jersey Turnpike. As Juli drove, George held the camera on his lap and examined all the buttons.

"I think I've got this thing figured out," he said eventually. "Okay, my lady. Just what do you want me to do?"

"Follow me around and I'll tell you what to shoot. Hold the camera real steady. That's the key."

"I'll stick to you like fleas on a dog."

"But if you see something and I don't, feel free to shoot some footage."

"Got it."

"You do good, and it'll make me look good."

"My lady," George winked, "I'm gonna make you a *star*."

"Now we've got to think about where we're going. Ever heard of Metropark?"

"Who, *moi?* I've never been out of *New York*."

"Okay, smarty-pants. How do we get there?"

"Uh, maybe this thing?" George motioned toward the GPS navigation system on the dash.

"Well, I'll be." Juli's jaw dropped. "Thank you, Mr. Raleigh!"

George reached forward and started playing with knobs on the console. In a few seconds he had a map on the screen; in a few more, he had a "Directions Lady" telling them where to go: "*Take the next Exit.*"

"Geez, George. I could never work those things."

Juli took Exit 11, marked Woodbridge, and followed the ramp over a bridge to face a row of tollbooths.

"*After the tollbooths, bear right.*"

She headed for the booth on the far right and slowed to pay the toll. To her surprise the sign read, "EZPass Toll Paid."

"Thanks again, Mr. Raleigh!" Juli sped on. She kept to the right and entered the Garden State Parkway North. "So where's Metropark?"

"Right there!" George pointed to the left as they drove by, passing under the railroad bridge as they went. Just then the Directions Lady broke in with the advisory: "*Take the next exit.*"

Juli pulled out of the Parkway traffic at Exit 131a, marked by a blue sign that said "Metropark." They drove back over the Parkway and followed the commands of the lady in the console.

As the station came into view, they could see the two Diesel locomotives, standing still but very much alive, giving off heat from their cooling towers while idling at the station platform. The black Diesel had moved over to the same track as the gray one, and stood in front of it. A police car blocked the entrance to the parking lot, while an officer stood by and waved them away.

"Where is everybody?" Juli wondered aloud. She stopped the car on the side of the road and she and George got out, George holding the camera perched on his shoulder. Overhead they heard the loud sound of a nearby helicopter beating the air.

"That must be Chopper 2!" Juli shouted over the noise as they walked toward the policeman, who at the moment was frantically shooing traffic away from the station lot.

The noise from the sky became louder and George pointed the camera at it, just in time to record the fast descent of a police helicopter as it dropped like a stone and then feathered just before touching down. The big black machine landed on its skids in the middle of the parking lot, not 100 feet from where Juli and George were standing, and waited with its blades turning rapidly while David Price and two dark-suited men with guns ran toward it from the station area. A side panel on the 'copter slid rearward as they approached, revealing another man with a shoulder holster in the open doorway. The three runners climbed aboard and the door closed, all in a split second, while George kept the camera rolling. The helicopter increased its roar and then lifted off, heading upward and beating away in the northerly direction.

"I got it on tape!" George crowed. "Let's follow them!"

"No, not yet. I don't think they know where Carl and Bruce went."

"Do we?"

Juli took her cell phone out of her purse, pressed "speaker," and held the phone upwards in front of her. She and George listened intently to the sounds of running and heavy breathing. Carl's voice broke in.

"We've got to slow down, Bruce. I . . . I can't go on."

"Okay. Let's just walk. We're far enough away, anyway."

"Let's take this side road." Carl was still panting. "Lots of trees. They can't see us from the helicopter."

"Let's just stroll along, like we belong here."

Juli held her thumb over the microphone and looked at George with a knowing smile.

"Now we just have to figure out where they are!"

"Why don't you ask them?"

"We can't let them know their phone is on."

"They can't have gone far."

"But in what direction?"

"Where there are trees."

"This way? That way?"

"We need more clues."

As if on cue, the phone sounds broke in again.

"What's that?" came Bruce's voice.

"Some kind of monument," Carl answered.

"Let's just keep going."

"No wait! I want to read what it says."

"We have time for this?"

"We've got all the time in the world. Let's face it, Bruce. They're going to catch us sooner or later."

"Yeah, Dad. I guess you're right." The sadness in his voice was palpable.

There was a long pause. Juli thought for a second that her phone went dead.

"Bruce! Come here! Look at this!!"

"What, Dad?" Bruce's voice did not pick up on his father's wonder.

"This is where Thomas Edison had his lab! This is where he invented the light bulb, the phonograph, the movie camera, all that stuff! The tracks for the very first electric train, they must have run over that way. Edison used to live in a rooming house nearby. It must have been somewhere down there!"

"Yeah? You sure? This place is *historic.*"

"It's hallowed ground for inventors."

"So where's the lab?"

"Henry Ford had it disassembled, piece by piece, and sent it to Detroit for a museum."

Juli and George raced to their car and took off, rear tires squealing. "That way!" George pointed to Wood Avenue, going north, as he brought up the navigation map and zoomed in on Menlo Park, New Jersey.

Chapter 25

———◆◆◆———

CARL AND BRUCE stared in awe at the modest monument that marked the spot where Thomas Edison had worked with his little loyal band of research engineers nearly one hundred and fifty years earlier.

"This is where it all started," Carl told his son.

"The electrical age." Bruce knew what it meant to his father.

"Yup, and then came Henry Ford's automobile."

"And the Wright Brother's aircraft."

"They changed the world." Carl gave a sigh. "Too bad we won't have a chance to do that too."

As they were talking, a gray car had quietly driven up and stopped just across the road from where Carl and Bruce were standing.

"Maybe you will!" came a young woman's voice from an open driver's-side window.

They turned to see the woman bounding out of the car and coming across the road toward them, followed by a man with a video camera on his shoulder. The red light was on; the camera was rolling.

"Hello. I'm Juli Gables. We spoke on the phone." Juli held out her hand.

Dumbfounded, Carl took Juli's hand as Bruce looked on. "I . . .I'm

Carl Collingwood and this is—" Carl tried to pull himself together to make a proper introduction.

"We know who you are. You are both heroes in my book."

"You know us?"

"The whole of New York City knows you now. Probably the whole country."

"What?"

"You're all over the news, Mr. Collingwood. This country owes pioneers like you our deepest gratitude. But as soon as you develop something good, you're exploited."

Still startled and confused, Carl managed to say, "Uh, how did you find us?"

"With this!" Juli held up her cell phone and spoke into it. "Hi, Bruce." Her voice came out of Bruce's breast pocket.

Amazed, Bruce pulled out his phone. "It's still on!" Embarrassed, he switched it off and put it back in his pocket.

"You're darn lucky you left it on, so we could get to you before the police. Mr. Collingwood, may I call you Carl?"

"Yes, of course."

"Carl, you have just about three minutes to tell your story to the media before the F.B.I. descends from their helicopter in the sky. Go!" Juli stepped aside and let George zoom in on the father and son.

"Well, okay. How do I start? My name is Carl Collingwood and this is my son, Bruce." Both he and Bruce looked directly into the camera's eye, slightly self-consciously at first. "For about five years now I have been developing a flying car. I call it a 'Personal Aircraft' or 'PAC', for short. It can take off and land vertically and cruise at about one hundred miles an hour. It's fuel-efficient and has a range of more than two hundred and fifty miles. A good way to beat the commuting traffic."

Bruce, clearly proud of his father, continued the narrative. "About two years ago, Dad received a loan from Transport International. It looked like a good deal at the time, but there was a catch: If Dad missed just one deadline, they could take over the company. Dad worked night and day until the aircraft was almost ready to test fly. He missed a loan payment and they kicked him out. Not only that; they put the company into bankruptcy and took away his stock. Like it was all planned in advance."

"I'm sure it was," added Juli. "What they didn't plan on, though, was that you would file a lawsuit."

"I had nothing, but I found a good lawyer who took the case on contingency," Carl recalled. "I suppose they were surprised that any lawyer would fight against them. They had about a hundred lawyers on retainer, and they did everything they could to wear my lawyer down. But he kept going, God bless him. But we didn't win."

"You did win." Juli said calmly. "We have evidence that Transport International got to the jury."

As they spoke, the beating of helicopter blades could be heard above the treetops. Everyone looked up, including George's camera eye, to see the big black helicopter descending over the Edison Monument. The door on the left side of the craft slid rearward and a rope dropped down from the doorway opening, its end almost touching down on the grassy area in front of the monument where Edison's laboratory once stood.

Special agent Price and two armed men appeared in the opening and, one by one, they slid down the rope to the ground in front of Carl and Bruce. Both Carl and his son held up their hands.

"Turn that camera off!"

"We're from Channel 8 News," Juli announced. "George, you keep that camera rolling."

"Sure thing, Juli. Nothin's gonna stop this li'l ol' camera."

"We're the F.B.I. I said *stop*!" Price nodded to his men to draw their weapons.

"What are you goin' to do, man? Shoot us?" George panned in for a close-up of Price's head. Anger was welling up and showing in his face.

"What are you two doing here?"

"We're recording this moment for history," Juli replied, as sternly as she could.

"Well, record this: We're taking these two men to jail."

"I don't think so."

"What? Are you going to stop us?"

"Yes. And all we have is a camera."

"Do you know these men hijacked a train?"

"Everyone knows that, thanks to the media. Do you know *why*?"

"Ma'am, what difference does it make?"

"It's because the F.B.I. hasn't been doing its job."

"Yeah, like we were supposed to know these perps were going to decide to hijack a train."

"No, not that. You were supposed to uncover a million-dollar bribe from an offshore bank."

"Come again?"

"Don't you have people who watch when large sums of money change hands?"

"Yeah, so?"

"They must have missed when Mike Snead paid off a juror in this man's lawsuit."

"Watch it, lady. You can't just go making charges like that. How would *you* know?"

"It took me about a half hour to find out."

"Okay, enlighten me."

"I suggest you check with your people in Bermuda. The money came from a TI subsidiary there."

"I'll do that. Meanwhile, I'm taking these hijackers in."

"Where are you taking them? New York?

"That's where they hijacked the train, lady."

"Isn't that a Federal crime?"

"What if it is?"

"The F.B.I. has jurisdiction everywhere."

"So?"

"Can't you take them to Washington?"

"I guess I could do that. That's where my office is."

"How are you going to do it?"

"Do what?"

"Take them to Washington."

"A car is on the way."

"How about using a Diesel locomotive?"

Chapter 26

———◆◆◆———

"GET IN THE chopper and head back to the station," Price commanded his two agents. The men, who had been standing by with their guns drawn, did as they were told. They both grabbed the dangling rope and held on tightly as it was drawn up by winch on the roof of the helicopter. When they reached the open side door, they jumped in and the helicopter floated away in a southerly direction and disappeared over the treetops.

Price ordered Carl and Bruce into the back seat of Juli's car and squeezed in after them. Juli drove while George, in the front passenger seat with the camera on his lap, removed the videotape and replaced it with a new one.

As they rushed back to the station, Juli called in to Channel 8 and asked Ariana to break into the boss's call.

"Juli, make it quick. I've got CNN holding on the other line. They want a feed!"

"We won't disappoint. Have a news van meet us at Metropark and we'll pass you the tape."

"It's on the way. Should be there in two minutes."

In the back seat, Price was calling his man at the station. "Where's Snead?"

"He's waiting for a ride back to New York. Company chopper's coming."

"Good. I want to talk to him."

Everyone converged on the station lot, nearly at once. A bright blue helicopter with TI painted on the side began its descent. Behind and above it was the black police helicopter. It hovered in the air, waiting its turn to land.

Juli drove into the lot and continued on toward the station platform, with a white TV van right behind her. The van, complete with a rooftop satellite antenna, belonged to the local TV station, WTNJ.

As soon as Juli stopped the car, George jumped out of the car with the videotape in hand and ran back to the van.

"Hurry, man," he said breathlessly and handed the tape up to the driver. "Send this quick to Channel 8."

"Yeah, Bro. What's on it?" The driver had a drawl and a wide friendly grin. His Afro almost doubled the size of his head.

"No time to explain. Just help a poor brother, *please.*" George placed his hands together in a praying position.

"No prob. Catch ya later."

Relieved, George ran back to the car and grabbed the camera, just as Mike Snead emerged from the station and strode in the direction of the waiting helicopter, idling quietly, blades still turning. George followed him with the camera and zoomed in to show his slightly snarling face.

Snead's short walk was intercepted by Price, who simply stepped out of the car as Snead passed by. George panned around in a wide shot to pick up the surroundings, with the chopper in the background, and then zoomed in again on the talking heads.

"Just a minute, Mr. Snead." Price began, politely.

"No time, Price. As you see, I've got a helicopter waiting."

"I have a few questions."

"Not now. Call my office and make an appointment."

"Mr. Snead, you're the CEO of Transport International, are you not?"

Snead ignored Price and kept walking toward the helicopter.

"Stop, Snead!"

Snead continued on without replying. Juli, Carl and Bruce got out of the car and watched the confrontation.

"I said *stop*! This is the F.B.I.!" Price reached for his weapon and assumed the crouching position with the weapon pointed straight at Snead's back. Clearly Price was not used to anyone ignoring him.

"So what are you going to do, shoot me?" Snead shouted over his shoulder. He had almost reached the helicopter, when he turned around and stared mockingly at the crouching Price. "I've got nothing to say. And by the way, you'd look awfully silly on the 6:00 o'clock news shooting an unarmed man. President of a Fortune 500 company. This whole ridiculous scene is being videotaped by that black bastard back there."

With that parting shot, he turned back to the helicopter and walked up the three small steps of the entry ladder into the open door. The sliding door closed automatically as the engine increased its whine and the rotor blades picked up speed. In a few seconds he would be gone.

Carl ran over to Price, who stared helplessly at the departing helicopter.

"Mr. Price, tell your helicopter pilot to fly directly over this one."

"What? Are you crazy? They'll crash."

"No! Trust me. I know the technology. Your chopper will force theirs to the ground."

Price eyed Carl skeptically, but keyed his mike. "Four-two-one, Commander. Fly directly over the TI chopper."

"Directly over?" came the reply.

"You heard right. Directly over. Do it, now!"

The big black helicopter, hovering off to the side, moved forward into the open airspace above the departing helicopter. What happened next made even George's jaw drop as he struggled to keep the camera steady.

The rotating blades of the smaller helicopter increased their speed and seemed to rotate freely beneath the downward rush of air from the larger machine immediately above it. The helicopter's engine screamed in pain, at a higher and higher pitch until, with a loud snap, it suddenly stopped became silent. And then, as if by magic, with its rotor blades still spinning freely, the helicopter settled slowly down to the ground and stood with its skids frozen to the tarmac, while its blades whirred fast at first but eventually wound down and stopped. For the first time since its arrival, the helicopter was completely motionless. Having done its work, the police helicopter flew away, leaving the scene strangely silent.

The side door of the TI helicopter opened, the little ladder dropped down and out stepped Mike Snead. It was supposed to have been just a regular day at the office, but it wasn't turning out at all the way he had planned.

Chapter 27

———◆◆◆◆———

GEORGE TOOK OUT the second tape and handed it to his friend in the van.

"Wow, Bro! You should get a Pulitzer or somethin' for that shot!"

"Who? *Moi*?" George grinned. "Stick around. There may be more!"

"I'm stayin' right here. As long as there's action."

Juli, who had almost forgotten she was the journalist on the scene, adjusted her clothes, and patted her hair down.

"Let's do a newscast, George."

"Atta girl! Stand right there," George pointed to a spot on the parking lot. "We'll shoot you with that helicopter in the background."

Juli took her place in front of George. With camera rolling and staring straight at the little red dot, Juli summarized the facts of the commuter train hijacking, leading to the race of the Diesel locomotives and the subsequent capture of Carl and Bruce. Finally she explained the stand-off between Price and Snead, culminating in the battle of the helicopters.

AND NOW MIKE SNEAD HAS BEEN FORCED TO RETURN

TO FACE AN INVESTIGATION. HE WILL HAVE TO EXPLAIN HIMSELF TO THE F.B.I. AND TO THE COUNTRY.

THIS IS CHANNEL 8 NEWS. STAY WITH *US* AND STAY INFORMED.

When Juli finished, George panned over and zoomed in on Snead. Price, who had been speaking to the home office on his cell phone, turned to Snead and said simply, "I'm taking you in for questioning."

"I've got nothing to say."

"You have a right to remain silent. Anything you say may be used against you in a court of law." Price ran his mentally-recorded speech with a weary sigh.

"And I want my lawyer present."

"You have a right to be represented by an attorney. If you can't afford one, we'll have one appointed for you," Price allowed himself a smirk. Snead scowled back.

Then, right in front of the running camera, Price unhooked a set of handcuffs from his belt and snapped them over Snead's wrists.

Snead clearly had difficulty keeping his temper, but he managed to get in a parting shot.

"I'll have your job for this, you bastard."

"Okay, let's go." Price ignored the remark and marched Snead back toward the station.

"Where are they going?" the van driver queried George as he climbed out of the cab to get a closer look at the suit in handcuffs.

"Washington, and I'm going too!" George lifted the camera off his shoulder, held it in one hand while he took the videotape out of the back with the other, and then passed the tape to his new friend.

"Here, Bro," said the driver of the van. "You're gonna' need these." He handed George four new blank tapes. "We already transmitted your other tapes. We'll get this one right out. See you on TV!" George gave him a high-five as he ran toward the station, loaded down with the camera and the four new tapes.

When everyone had clamored aboard the black locomotive, the engineer, Jack, released the brakes with a loud hiss, announced their imminent departure by a brief toot of the whistle and called in for permission to use the main line to Washington.

Chapter 28

———◆✦◆———

THE HIGH SCHOOL audience sat entranced, hanging on every Shakespearian word from King Henry VI, Part Three, that their fellow classmates enacted before them. Though one of many in the cast, "Mike Sneak" or just "Sneakie", as he was disrespectfully called, played the lead: Richard, Duke of Gloucester, plotting his way to be King Richard III. He had worked hard to learn the part, and now he was in his glory. He had become Richard, and Richard had become him. His favorite moment was in Richard's self-awakening; standing there alone on stage pressing through his very personal, private fears of failure and announcing his rebirth as the future Machiavellian King:

> "…I'll drown more sailors than the mermaid shall;
> I'll slay more gazers that the basilisk;
> I'll play the orator as well as Nestor,
> Deceive more slyly than Ulysses could,
> And, like a Sinon, take another Troy.
> I can add colours to the chameleon,
> Change shapes with Proteus for advantages,
> And set the murd'rous Machiavel to school.

Can I do this, and cannot get a crown?
Tut! Were it further off, I'll pluck it down."

As he walked off the stage and heard the audience roar its approval, he smiled. He was an actor, and in acting he would find his way in the world. As a chameleon could change its colors, he could act his way through life, fooling others into thinking he was someone he was not. His deep feelings of inadequacy only fanned his burning desire to be a *player* and to play to win. He would show them!

If his fellow classmates only knew what thoughts passed through his mind at that moment, it would surely shock them. But right now they admired and adored him. "Mike Sneak" was history. From that moment on, they called him a respectful "Mike." "Mike the Meanie" began to be heard now and then from his enemies and, eventually, this moniker morphed into the awesome "Mike the Malevolent."

Chapter 29

"Metro-Central, this is the Chief on Metro two-niner out of Wassaic."

"Jack, you're back! Where the *heck* have you been?"

"I, uh, stopped at Metropark to go pee."

"Whassa matter? Toilet stuffed on that old locomotive?"

"Somethin' like that. Windshield's broken. A few bullet holes in the side. I'm on another locomotive right now, heading for Washington."

"What! You get your ass back here. That engine too."

"Nope. I'm on an adventure, and I'm gonna ride it to the end."

"They'll have your job, Jack! I can't save you, you know."

"Phil, I'm not asking you for a favor. After what I've been through, I'll take my chances with the suits."

"Well, then, all I can say is *bon voyage* and enjoy the ride. Contact Amtrak right away, though. They're waiting for your call. 105-1010."

"10-4, my friend."

Jack punched in the numbers.

"This is Jack Springer. Engineer on locomotive 541 at Metropark. Request an open track to Washington, D.C. "

"We hear you, Jack. What happened to our engineer?" came the return call.

"He'll call in. He's taking my old locomotive back to Metro-North."

"And you think you're going *where*?"

"Washington. Union Station."

There were loud guffaws in the background. Then the supervisor came on the line. "Now you hear this, whoever you are on locomotive 541. You can't just borrow one of our Diesels and drive it wherever you want to go. We are sending the police down there right now. If you move that locomotive so much as an inch, you'll spend the rest of your life in jail!"

"The F.B.I. is right here with us. He says we're going to Washington."

"You carrying that scumbag from TI?"

"Yup."

"Whyn't you say so! Okay, you're clear right through to Union Station. The track's good for one hundred fifty miles an hour."

"I'll bet this engine's never gone so fast."

"So try it out."

"Maybe I will. But if we blow a gasket, it's *your* machine."

"We'll take the chance. Take that S.O.B. to jail!"

"10-4."

Jack turned around in his right-side driver's seat to face the crowd: Carl and Bruce, Juli and George, and Price and Snead. "We're good to go. Brace yourselves. This is going to be a *ride*."

With that, Jack gave a long blast of the Diesel horn and started to roll out. After he cleared the station, he thrust the throttle lever forward and the huge Diesel engine behind him let out a deep, satisfying growl. The big locomotive shuddered and quickly picked up speed.

George opened the small side window and pointed the camera lens out the opening. He wasn't sure what he expected to see and record, but he had a sense that something interesting was coming into view.

At the next station, Metuchin, George saw a few people on the station platform smiling and cheering as they passed by. When they rode through New Brunswick, he saw even more people staring at them and waving wildly. Many were at the station but, oddly, many stood along the right-of-way. George squeezed the trigger on the camera to catch the action.

By the time they left the outskirts of New Brunswick, the locomotive was roaring through the countryside at a fast clip. Jack kept the speed under one hundred miles an hour because he was unfamiliar with the track and with the lights, but to the passengers standing in the cabin, it seemed a lot faster.

Outside, as the engine traversed green farmland, occasionally people could be seen waving to them. Two enterprising youths held up a banner with the hastily written words *Go Carl Go!*—the headline from the New York Post. Some had purposely stopped their cars and had gotten out to better see and be seen. George kept the camera running, sometimes even in slow motion to capture the enthusiasm of the people cheering them on.

Nearing Trenton, Jack slowed and gave several blasts on the horn to warn of their approach. To the amazement of all on the locomotive, as they looked forward down the line they could see crowds lined up on both sides of the tracks, behind the protective fences, waving frantically. Some held signs with messages of hope, like "Save the SkyCar," but some had messages of hate: "Kill Snead."

Jack eased off further and coasted through the Trenton station, blowing the horn again in concern for the people who jammed the platform, shouting and cheering wildly.

Watching the spectacle from behind Jack's seat, Mike allowed himself one simple utterance. "Shit!"

Chapter 30

"Now that we're stuck together on this locomotive," suggested Juli, after Trenton was behind them and Philadelphia was still half an hour, and Washington still two hours away, "why don't we get to know each other?"

"Not a bad idea." Price was immediately interested. "What do we talk about?"

"Let's start with Mr. Collingwood's case against Transport International."

Price looked at both Collingwood and Snead. "What do you think?"

Carl made a pained face and threw up his hands to convey, "It's hopeless. You'll never get Mike Snead to agree."

"I'm not saying anything without my lawyer present," Snead said emphatically. He then held out his handcuffed hands. "Price, take these damn cuffs off *now*! Do you think I'm going to jump out of this moving train? This is *bullshit* and you know it."

"Sure, give me your hands." Price unlocked the handcuffs while taunting his prisoner. "What's wrong with a little dialogue? Afraid you might spill the beans?"

"Yeah. I'm invoking the Fifth Amendment."

"That was a civil case, stupid. No possibility of incriminating yourself."

"Okay, so tell me why I should say anything?"

"You see those people out there? They think you're a crook. This is a chance to redeem yourself in front of a camera."

"Videotape our little get-together here? You out of your mind?"

"That's a problem for you?"

"No." Mike Snead paused to think about it a moment. "All right, maybe I'll do it. But there's one condition."

"What's the condition?"

"If I don't like it, I'll destroy the tape."

"I don't *think* so, Snead. Whatever goes down in this locomotive is for the public to see."

"Then forget it. I'm not interested."

"All right then. We'll go ahead without you."

"That's ridiculous!"

"We'll see about that. We'll start by putting Collingwood in front of the camera." Price motioned for Carl to take the empty driver's seat on the left side of the locomotive cabin. "Just for fun, I'll swear you in so you'll promise to tell the truth. Bruce, you pretend you're the lawyer for the plaintiff and take your father through his testimony. Juli, you be the lawyer for the defendant and cross-examine him. I'm going to role-play judge *and* jury."

"Hold it! Hold it," Snead interrupted. "I used to act in school plays when I was back in high school and college and I can't resist having a little fun. Okay, count me in."

"All right. Juli is your lawyer. You can choose to testify for the defense—or not—it's up to you."

"Now, if I'm to record all this for posterity, I'm going to need a little cooperation here."

George stood back so his camera lens could take in the entire scene, including the "witness chair." The track ahead and the scenery speeding by on both sides were visible behind this seat and through the windshield. "Just act natural and forget *moi*, your cameraman."

George looked through the viewer and adjusted the zoom. "When I say *cut*, it means you *stop* what you're doing. I'll have to change the tape. Okay, I'm ready now. Let's go: camera, action!"

"Are the parties ready?" asked Price, the judge.

"Plaintiff's ready," replied Bruce.

"Defendant is ready," said Juli.

"All right. Let's hear your opening statements."

Bruce stood tall before the judge and stated his case. "The plaintiff, my father, has worked for many years developing and patenting a vertical take-off-and-landing aircraft that would carry four people for short distances, up to three hundred miles.

"He wanted it to be used like an automobile: it would be easy to control and almost as fuel-efficient over these short distances. It would not have to go very fast to save people a lot of time, compared to driving an automobile: just one hundred miles an hour would do, because it could fly directly to the destination and land.

"Dad had a dream. He knew if he figured out the right configuration for the aircraft – a configuration that worked—others would follow and he would start a whole new industry. Kind of like Henry Ford did with the automobile.

"When he thought he was ready, he quit his job and founded a company with his own money. He assigned all his patents to the company, hired a few good people and started to build the first prototype. I guess he thought it would be easy to interest others in investing money once he was committed like that, but at first he found no one else who shared the dream.

"This was a tough time for all of us in his family, but we did what we could to help. My mother and I both got jobs and somehow we kept going. All of the family money went into the business, and then some. We were deeply in debt.

"Then one day, Dad came home all smiles and said that a big company, Transport International, was interested in investing in his company. They were willing to put in up to ten million dollars. It was almost too good to be true. As it turned out, it was—too good to be true."

Bruce paused to reflect on where he was going with this opening statement.

"Dad kept fifty-one percent of the stock and gave TI forty-nine percent, in return for a line of credit up to ten million dollars. They said they wanted to structure the deal as a loan, not a stock purchase, for accounting purposes. Dad had to make periodic payments on the loan, and also finish the prototype and test it successfully by a certain date.

"Well, Dad and his men worked really hard to meet the deadline. They never came home before midnight and toward the end they worked all night, but they didn't make the prototype in time. Dad also missed one payment on the loan. He didn't think it was important and just forgot about it; he was so busy getting the aircraft ready for the test flight.

"The next day – the day after they were supposed to finish and test the aircraft – he got a letter from Transport International exercising their right to take an additional two percent of the stock, giving them a majority ownership of fifty-one percent.

"That same day they voted in a new Board of Directors and fired Dad."

Bruce paused again. This time there were tears in his eyes and he had to get a grip on his emotions before he could continue.

"All of this was probably fair, if you want to call it that. We found out later that Transport International was betting—and hoping—that Dad wouldn't make the deadline and they had the letter all ready a month in advance. But whatever they did with the company, Dad would keep a forty-nine percent interest.

"But instead of finishing the prototype, they put the company into bankruptcy and asked the court to cancel all of Dad's shares. They made deals with all the companies that supplied parts and services to the company so that they got paid, *only if* they went along with the plan. All of them did, and the court approved taking all of Dad's shares away. He lost everything."

With that, Bruce concluded, barely audibly, with "Thank you, your honor," and stepped aside.

Price, the judge, invited Juli to step forward. "All right. Let's hear the defendant's opening statement."

Juli began, "Everything my client has done was perfectly legal. What happened to the plaintiff was surely unfortunate, but that was the luck of the draw. It might have turned out better for the plaintiff, and we wish it did, but the defendant was not required to bail the plaintiff out.

"Your honor, even if everything that counsel for the plaintiff alleges is true, there would still be no liability to my client."

"Is that all?" asked Price.

"Yes, your honor." Juli gave a little nod and stepped away from the camera view.

"All right. Counsel for the plaintiff, call your first witness."

Chapter 31

CARL COLLINGWOOD CAME forward and sat down on the pretend witness chair.

"Do you swear to tell the truth and nothing but the truth?" Price asked.

"Yes, I do."

"All right, counsel. Ask away."

Bruce stepped forward again and began.

"Dad. Do you recall the contract you had with TI?"

"Yes, I do."

"What was your understanding of this contract?"

"TI was going to fund the development of the aircraft for a forty-nine percent interest in my company. There were benchmarks we were required to meet and interest we had to pay, but that was pretty much it."

"You mean you were to pay interest on a loan and also give up forty-nine percent of the stock?"

"Yes, that was the deal."

"What was the interest rate?"

"Eighteen percent, as I recall."

"Eighteen percent interest *plus* nearly half the stock in your company?"

"Yes."

"If you missed an interest payment, then what?"

"The penalty was another two percent of the equity."

"Weren't those terms a bit onerous, in your mind?"

"It was the best that I could do. I needed to get that loan."

"Weren't you upset when you had to give up the two percent and lost control?"

"Yes, but I figured I had shown the way, so the new management would be able to finish the project and make a success of the company. I still had a forty-nine percent interest which would become very valuable if the management did their job well."

"What happened next?"

"Well, Transport used the bankruptcy law to take away my forty-nine percent interest in the company."

"So you lost that too?"

"Yes, I ended up with nothing."

"That's all I have, your honor."

Price looked at Juli. "Do you wish to cross-examine?"

"Yes, your honor. I have a few questions."

"Go right ahead."

"Mr. Collingwood"—Juli played the charade in a formal tone, just like a lawyer would—"how much money did you actually borrow from Transport International?"

"We ran through about six million dollars."

"Was your prototype finished and ready to test?"

"No, not quite. I figured we needed another month."

"Whatever happened to the prototype after you left the company?"

"I don't know. I don't think the new management ever finished it."

"So you spent six million and the aircraft never flew. Is that correct? Yes or no?"

"Well, yes, but—"

"No further questions, your honor."

"Any questions in redirect?"

"Just one, your honor," Bruce replied.

"Go ahead."

"What's to prevent you from starting over and building another prototype?"

"I can't. The patents belong to the company."

"The plaintiff rests."

"Mr. Collingwood," said Judge Price, "I have one further question."

"Yes, sir?"

"Why did you hijack the commuter train?"

Carl thought for a moment, trying hard to figure out the right answer. "I guess I didn't think it through. I just thought if I brought Mike Snead to Washington, and put him in the spotlight, he would crash and burn."

Chapter 32

———◆◆◆◆◆———

PRICE TURNED TO Juli. "Counsel for the defense, call your first witness."

Mike Snead was called to the stand and sworn in as a witness. Snead settled comfortably into the engineer's seat on the left side of the locomotive and shot a conspiratorial smile at his acting attorney. Meanwhile Jack, in the right-hand side engineer's seat, had negotiated the big machine through the Philadelphia area and now pushed the throttle forward to proceed on toward Washington with increased speed.

"Mr. Snead"—Juli stood to one side as George zoomed in on his face—"Why did you put Mr. Collingwood's company into bankruptcy?"

"We wanted to get rid of his stock interest. It was as simple as that."

"Did you ever think you may have broken the law?"

"No, we were very careful about that. Everything we did was cleared in advance by our in-house counsel. And eventually the bankruptcy plan was approved by the court." Snead's voice was cheerful, charming, even.

"Do you think what you did was fair to Mr. Collingwood?"

"My dear...may I call you Juli?" Snead addressed Juli slightly condescendingly, but cordially and conspiratorially, as if she were his real counsel for the defense. "I have been a businessman for a long time. It's a real honest-to-goodness jungle out there. Your competition is continually plotting against you, your customers are demanding more and more, and the real world is constantly mounting surprise attacks from the underbrush. But if you're resourceful, you *can* succeed. And if you succeed, the game is actually *fun*.

"The rules of the game are the huge, complicated body of laws, rules and regulations that our governments are constantly turning out. These are the restrictions that we are careful to abide by. We hire high-priced lawyers to continuously tell us what we can and cannot do and even our lawyers are wrong sometimes.

"When you ask a businessman whether what he does is 'fair,' he doesn't really understand the question. We do not ever think about whether something is 'fair' or 'unfair.' Fairness has nothing to do with the rules of the game, so it is simply not an issue with us.

"So, Juli, you may ask me any question you want and I will answer it. You are a smart young lady, and I would like to have you join our organization sometime when you've had your fill of being a crusading journalist. We can use good people like you. But just don't ask me to tell you what is *fair*. That is not a fair question.

"All right, Mr. Snead. Are you aware that Mr. Collingwood sued Transport International to get back his stock interest in the company he founded?"

"Yes, indeed. I am aware of all lawsuits brought against our company. We take them very seriously."

"Are you aware that one of the jurors in the lawsuit received a large sum of money from the Bermuda subsidiary of Transport International?'

"I am not only not aware of such a thing; it never could have happened. We have very tight controls over our money."

"Mr. Snead, to be absolutely clear: Do you deny that Transport International bribed one of the jurors in Mr. Collingswood's lawsuit?"

"Yes, I do. Most emphatically."

"No further questions." Juli looked disappointed, but nodded to Judge Price.

"Bruce, would you care to cross-examine?"

"Yes, your honor. I have a few questions, if I may."

"Go right ahead."

"Mr. Snead, have you ever lied on the witness stand?"

"I resent that insinuation, young man. Of course not."

"After you took over my father's company, did your company continue to develop the Personal Aircraft?"

"No, we did not."

Bruce paused to ponder this answer. "Let me get this straight: After you invested six million dollars in developing the aircraft, you did not continue?"

"That's right."

"Why not?"

"We thought that your father, Mr. Collingwood, would fail."

"You did?"

"Yes."

"Then why did you invest the money?"

"We viewed it as a kind of insurance. We wanted him to fail, but we had to be sure."

"I don't understand."

"If he succeeded, your father's aircraft would have derailed our strategy."

"What strategy was that?"

"We were developing a new amphibious vehicle for the military. If your father's VTOL aircraft could perform as intended, this project would have been dead in the water. So you see, we had to take your father out – take him out completely – to give us free reign to sell our own project to the government."

"*Cut!*" shouted George. "Hold that thought, Mr. Snead, while I put in a new tape."

The judge and counsel stood there, stunned, as George stopped the recording and replaced the videotape with a new one.

"All right. Camera, action!" He placed the camera back on his shoulder and pressed *record*.

Chapter 33

———◆◆◆———

BRUCE CONTINUED WITH his questioning. "You mean you were willing to spend up to ten million dollars to kill my father's project?"

"Yes, that's right."

Bruce was almost in tears. "But what if my father had succeeded? What then?"

"We figured that was a long shot, but if he succeeded we would have benefited too. Remember, we had forty-nine percent of the stock and we would have received all our money back, with interest, on the loan we floated."

"Either way you would have won," Bruce said, almost to himself, in disbelief.

"Bruce, you have to understand how the game is played." Snead leaned toward Bruce, as if to whisper in his ear. "A lot of people don't."

"I . . . I must admit, I don't understand."

"It's about developing a winning strategy to make money, no matter what that may be."

"It's not about developing new ideas and new technology?"

"No, not at all. If we could make the same amount of money by buying and selling foreign currency, we would just as soon do that. And it would be a lot less hassle."

"So it's all about the money?"

"Well, not exactly." Snead gave a sigh as if to signify that the young man facing him was out of his depth, but he continued. "The game of business is all about *power*: power over people. A corporation today is very much like a fiefdom of medieval times. We often say that the corporation is run for the benefit of its shareholders, but that is just a fiction. The managers of a corporation are like the kings and dukes in olden times. They play the game for their *own* benefit.

"And if they can make the corporate shareholders happy along the way, so much the better. They are then allowed to take home higher salaries, more stock options and even greater bonuses at the end of the year. But believe me when I say, we are addicted to the game and we would play it even if we received no financial reward at all. It's heady stuff."

"I…I have no more questions."

George zoomed in for a close-up of Snead, just in time to catch a wry satisfied smile. He cut quickly to Price, who stared at Snead and said simply, "I'll reserve my decision on this until I hear from my agents in the field."

Juli raised her hand to get George's attention and faced the camera for one last segment. George took the cue and starting recording again, first with a full view of Juli and the engineer, Jack, in the background, and then progressively closer toward a final tight shot of Juli's face.

THERE YOU HAVE IT. RIGHT HERE ON A TRAIN TO WASHINGTON, YOU'VE SEEN AND HEARD THE HIJACKERS, CARL AND BRUCE COLLINGWOOD, AND THEIR HOSTAGE, MICHAEL SNEAD, UP CLOSE AND PERSONAL.

CARL IS AN INVENTOR AND ENTREPRENEUR WITH A DREAM OF GIVING EVERYONE THE GIFT OF FLIGHT. IF HE WERE SUCCESSFUL HE WOULD HAVE STARTED A NEW INDUSTRY AND WOULD SURELY HAVE CHANGED THE WAY WE LIVE.

MIKE IS THE CORPORATE EXECUTIVE AND BUSINESS LEADER WHO TOOK A CHANCE ON CARL, BUT PULLED THE PLUG WHEN CARL COULDN'T DELIVER ON TIME.

FOR MIKE, THIS WAS JUST ANOTHER BUSINESS DECISION
OF THE KIND THAT HAS MADE HIS CORPORATION,
TRANSPORT INTERNATIONAL, ONE OF THE LARGEST
AND MOST PROFITABLE COMPANIES IN AMERICA.

YOU BE THE JUDGE: DO YOU SIDE WITH THE
INVENTOR WHO DARES TO DREAM, OR WITH THE
CORPORATE EXECUTIVE WHO GETS THINGS DONE?

THE FACT REMAINS THAT CARL AND HIS SON BRUCE
HAVE HIJACKED A TRAIN. THIS IS A SERIOUS FEDERAL
CRIME FOR WHICH THEY WILL HAVE TO PAY THE
PRICE.

ALSO, MIKE IS BEING TAKEN IN FOR QUESTIONING
ON A CHARGE OF JURY TAMPERING. THIS IS JUST AS
SERIOUS A CRIME SINCE IT STRIKES AT THE HEART OF
OUR JUDICIAL SYSTEM AND THE RULE OF LAW.

DO YOU HAVE AN OPINION ON THIS? DO YOU THINK
WHAT THE CORPORATION DID TO CARL WAS FAIR? DO
YOU THINK THAT FAIRNESS SHOULD PLAY A PART IN
CORPORATE DECISIONS? LET'S HEAR YOUR VOICES!

AND STAY TUNED. WE HAVE YET TO SEE WHAT
WILL HAPPEN WHEN A CONGRESSIONAL COMMITTEE
ON CORPORATE CORRUPTION THROWS A SPOTLIGHT
ON THE INTERNAL WORKINGS OF TRANSPORT
INTERNATIONAL.

THIS IS JULI GABLES FROM CHANNEL 8 NEWS,
WITH THE F.B.I. AGENT, DAVID PRICE, WITH CARL
COLLINGWOOD AND HIS SON BRUCE, WITH MIKE SNEAD,
AND WITH OUR ENGINEER, JACK, IN A ROARING DIESEL
LOCOMOTIVE ON ITS WAY TO WASHINGTON, D.C.

STAY WITH *US* AND STAY INFORMED."

Juli held her smile for a moment until George stopped the recording and gave her the high sign.

"I think I'm in love!" George quipped, "You did good, my lady."

"You did good too. I think I'll keep you as my cameraman *forever.*"

"Who, *Moi? Yes!* I like this job."

George put down his camera and proceeded to give Juli a big bear hug.

"George, behave!" Juli resisted, but not unkindly. "We have to get your tapes to Mr. Raleigh, right away." She quickly took out her cell phone and called in to headquarters.

"Mr. Raleigh? It's me, Juli. We have two tapes we want to send to you immediately. Where are we? Uh, I don't know. Just a minute."

Juli covered the phone with her hand and leaned over to Jack. "Where are we?"

"Coming into Baltimore. Be there in about fifteen minutes."

"We're coming up on Baltimore," Juli repeated, into the phone. "Okay, great! We can do that. Bye, Mr. Raleigh!"

"Jack, can you stop for just a second at the Baltimore station? We want to hand down a couple of tapes to a messenger on the platform."

"Sure, I can do that. Open that side door when I slow down and you can reach them out."

"Will do. Thanks."

The locomotive coasted as it approached the Baltimore station. The station platforms on both sides of the tracks were jammed with people waving hastily written signs, while shouting and cheering.

Juli spotted the messenger, opened the engineer's door and leaned out, holding the two tapes with one hand while supporting herself with the other. The messenger stretched out his hand as far as he dared in the path of the oncoming locomotive. In an instant, the tapes were passed, from Juli's hand to his. The messenger grabbed and held them protectively to his chest as the engine slipped by.

"Mission accomplished, Jack. Let her rip!"

Jack pressed the throttle forward and, with a satisfying roar of the Diesel engine, the locomotive picked up speed again. Only a half hour to go before the next course of events would unfold and be recorded as another chapter in the news.

———◆◆◆———

Chapter 34

JACK CAREFULLY MONITORED the train signals that flashed past, and slowed the locomotive as it approached Union Station. The main-line tracks from Baltimore branched out on both sides, one by one, into multiple parallel tracks as the station came into view, forming an industrial jungle of switches, tracks, signals and overhead electric power lines.

All the occupants of the locomotive pressed closer to the two windshields and strained to see the cavernous entrance to the station and the end of the line. It was difficult at first to tell which track would lead them in because of the many switches and crossovers in their path, but soon they noticed they were being shunted to a far right side of the station. The platforms on both sides of their track were jammed with people screaming and waving banners. Uniformed police were on hand to control the crowd and TV cameras were everywhere, with newsmen and newswomen holding microphones, connected like umbilical cords to their cameras.

Jack pulled back the throttle to a fast idle and allowed the locomotive to coast until its speed eventually dropped to a crawl. He edged the big machine cautiously forward into the station building, moving down the track toward its dead end, while crowds of people followed on both platforms, shouting and waving as they ran alongside. A few banged on the steel wall of the locomotive in their exuberance. Jack braked to a stop just ten feet short of the end stop and shut down the Diesel engine. There was an audible "shush" from the press of people as they held their collective breath, expectantly. TV cameras trained on the locomotive doors on both sides waited for someone to emerge. For a brief moment, the area was almost quiet.

The front door on the left side of the locomotive opened inward, and George stepped out onto the platform, followed by Juli. Juli remained near the doorway and surveyed the crowd while George pressed forward and joined the other TV crews in recording the news event. George scanned the boisterous crowd with his camera, recording the TV crews that were in his field of view while they recorded him, and eventually panned back toward the locomotive and zoomed in on Juli and the open door behind her.

Next, framed in the doorway, David Price appeared, and the already noisy crowd let out a huge roar. Price stood for a moment to take in the facing sights and sounds and then stepped forward into the parting press of people, pulling on the wrist of another man behind him, handcuffed to his own. Tethered by the cuff, Carl followed dutifully with a stoic face, masking his emotions, while the TV cameras zoomed in for a tight shot. Next came Bruce, right behind his father, with tears in his eyes. Seeing all this, the crowd exploded with angry shouts of disapproval.

"You've got the wrong man!"

"Get Mike Snead!"

"Let Carl go!"

And then the crowd began to chant, sporadically at first but eventually in unison: "We want Mean Mike! We want Mean Mike! We want Mean Mike!" followed by simply, "Mean Mike! Mean Mike!"

Price held up his free hand to signal silence and the crowd calmed for a moment. Five TV journalists, including Juli, held out microphones to catch every word.

"My name is David Price, Special Agent of the F.B.I., based here in Washington, in charge of an anti-terror strike force. We happened to be in New York on assignment when we got the call that a commuter train was hijacked and that Michael Snead, CEO of Transport International, had been kidnapped.

"I have arrested Carl Collingwood and his son, Bruce, for perpetrating this crime. I'm taking them into custody.

"As for Mr. Snead, our office has fully investigated the allegations that have been made against him and his company for jury tampering and we have found them groundless. My office informed me by phone, just a few minutes ago, there is absolutely no evidence that Transport International paid any amount of money to any juror."

Juli couldn't believe her ears. She stared at George, who gave her a sympathetic look.

"So where is Snead now?" asked another female reporter.

"I'm right here!" announced Snead, suddenly standing at the doorway of the locomotive. The crowd gasped as if a magician had suddenly appeared.

"Let him through. Let him through." The police officers pressed the crowd back and opened a path to an exit door leading to the lobby of the station. Snead took his cue from the officer in charge and started in that direction.

Just then a man shot out from the crowd and stood in front of Snead, blocking his path. The police made a grab for the man, but before they could reach him, he thrust forward and held out a manila envelope. Since Snead made no attempt to take it from him, the man touched Snead's jacket with the envelope and let it drop to the cement floor. "This is a subpoena to appear and testify before Congress at ten o'clock tomorrow morning."

"You bastard!" replied Snead, and reached down to pick up the envelope. The police grabbed the process server and pulled him out of the way, clearing a path for Snead to exit.

Snead turned briefly to look at Carl and Bruce. They stood next to Price, strangely subdued after their bold action of the last few hours, ready to pay the price for what they had done. "I hope you rot in jail, both of you!" snarled Snead. "That's where criminals like you belong."

Chapter 35

AFTER PRICE TOOK Carl and Bruce into custody and the crowd began to disperse, Juli and George found a quiet corner of the station. Juli called Mr. Raleigh on her cell phone. "Ariana, it's me," she said sheepishly.

"Uh-oh, Juli. Good thing you called in. Boss is on the warpath."

"He was watching?"

"You kidding? We're all watching. It's the biggest news story here since Al Sharpton died and went to heaven."

"Al Sharpton...died?"

"No, dearie. That's just an expression."

"Could you put me on with Mr. Raleigh?"

"Sure, but watch out. Wouldn't want to be in your shoes right now."

"It's that bad?"

"Yeah, sorry to tell ya. But I promise not to listen in. Here goes..."

Juli was on hold for less than a second when Mr. Raleigh's voice boomed over her tiny cell phone.

"Juli! What the hell did you get us into?"

"Uh, you mean about the jury tampering?"

"Yes *that* and about the lawsuit that Transport International is *certain* to file against us for libel and slander."

"Well, I—"

"*Damage control!* We've got to do damage control right away!"

"Okay, but—"

"You have got to go on camera and apologize, *right away!* Set the record straight. Tell 'em it was a mistake you made. There was no jury tampering. The TI is as clean as the drifting winter snow."

"If that's what you want."

"*Want?* I don't want any of this. I want this problem to go away."

"Do you really think TI is that innocent?"

"What the *ef* do I know? Sometimes you gotta just do what you gotta do."

"Yes, but I don't think they're so innocent."

"What's this, Juli? Now you're giving me *static*, after I let you put out that story and it blew up in our faces?"

"No, I mean, *yes!* I stand by that story."

"Juli, this is a direct order. You go on camera and retract, or you're *fired*! That cockamamie cameraman you have, too. What's his name? The *security guard?*"

"George."

"Yes, *George.* His shots of you aren't half bad."

Juli paused a moment and glanced at George, who was changing the tape again.

"All right, Mr. Raleigh. I'll do it. You can even fire me, if you want, but you have to let George keep his camera job."

"What choice have I got? Now go on camera and tell them, Juli, that it was all a mistake. And then transmit that video to me, pronto!"

"Yes, Mr. Raleigh. Right away."

Juli snapped her cell phone shut and started combing her hair, angrily pulling at the comb.

"We got a problem?" George asked.

"Nothing I can't fix." Juli fussed, making herself ready. "How do I look?"

"Fabulous, my lady. What's this about?"

"Boss wants me to say I made a mistake."

"On camera?"

"Yeah, on camera."

"I don't think you should."

"Okay, smarty, I'll bite: Why not?"

"Because you did the right thing. And you *know* they bribed a juror."

"I don't know that for sure. F.B.I. says they didn't."

"If you go on camera with that, those sleazebags are off the hook and the Collingwoods will get the max."

"If I don't, we'll both lose our jobs."

"The boss said that?"

"Yes, he did."

"That sucks! Just when I thought we had something good going."

George reflected for a moment and then turned to face Juli. "You don't have to take a fall for me, pretty lady. Do what you think is right."

"I don't know what is right, George. I don't know." Tears were welling in Juli's eyes.

"Yes, you do. And so do I."

"Are you sure it's all right with you?"

"Well, not really, but what the hell. I can always be a security guard."

"I admire you, George. You know that?"

"Let's get you on camera before I change my mind." George placed the camera on his shoulder and aimed the lens at Juli.

Juli held up her hand, palm toward the camera, signaling George to hold off. "What do I say now?"

"Explain what just happened back there when we arrived at the station. And then tell them you have it on a reliable source that TI bribed a juror."

"Okay, George. Here goes. Roll the camera."

Just then Juli's cell phone beeped a tune. Juli pressed the green button and took the call.

"Hello? Is this Juli Gables?" Juli heard an unmistakable deep voice.

"Mr. Bernstein, I mean, Shelley?"

"Just in case you're thinking of selling out...*don't*."

Juli was about to say something when she heard a *click* and the phone went dead.

Chapter 36

———◆❋◆———

KEVIN RALEIGH SAT in his office and brought up the latest video from Juli on his computer screen. He was hoping, at best, to relieve his embarrassment and, at worst, his fear of a lawsuit, due to the missteps and misstatements of his unseasoned and naïve young journalist, Julianne Gables.

"Juli agreed to eat humble pie, so why am I nervous about this video?" he wondered to himself, half aloud. "Well, here goes." He clicked the "Play" button on the screen.

It was a shot of Juli from the waist up. She looked gorgeous, as if she had just stepped out of a beauty parlor. She also appeared flushed with excitement, as though she had been through an ordeal and was pleased with the outcome. But when he heard her monologue, Kevin almost fell off his chair.

GOOD EVENING, EVERYONE. THIS IS JULIANNE GABLES, BROADCASTING FROM UNION STATION IN WASHINGTON, D.C., WHERE JUST A FEW MINUTES AGO I ARRIVED ON A LOCOMOTIVE ALONG WITH JACK, THE ENGINEER; DAVID PRICE, SPECIAL AGENT OF THE F.B.I.;

MICHAEL SNEAD, CEO OF TRANSPORT INTERNATIONAL; AND CARL COLLINGWOOD AND HIS SON, BRUCE, THE COMMUTER TRAIN HIJACKERS FROM NEW YORK CITY. AGENT PRICE HAS JUST TAKEN CARL AND BRUCE COLLINGWOOD INTO CUSTODY, WHERE THEY WILL BE ARRAIGNED AND REQUIRED TO PLEAD EITHER 'GUILTY' OR 'NOT GUILTY.' IT IS DIFFICULT TO SEE HOW THEY COULD PLEAD 'NOT GUILTY' IN THIS CASE BECAUSE THE EVIDENCE AGAINST THEM IS SO OVEWHELMING. HOWEVER, WE WILL HAVE TO WAIT AND SEE HOW THIS STORY UNFOLDS.

WHEN HE ARRIVED AND STEPPED OFF THE LOCOMOTIVE, MIKE SNEAD WAS ISSUED A SUBOENA TO TESTIFY BEFORE A CONGRESSIONAL COMMITTEE INVESTIGATING CORPORATE CORRUPTION. IT IS BELIEVED MR. SNEAD WILL STAY IN WASHINGTON AND WILL TESTIFY TOMORROW BEFORE GOING BACK TO HIS HEADQUARTERS IN NEW YORK.

MEANWHILE, THIS REPORTER HAS DISCOVERED THAT TRANSPORT INTERNATIONAL HAS PAID A JUROR APPROXIMATELY ONE MILLION DOLLARS TO FIND IN FAVOR OF TRANSPORT IN A LAWSUIT BROUGHT BY CARL COLLINGWOOD. MIKE SNEAD HAS DENIED THIS AND THE F.B.I. COULD FIND NO EVIDENCE OF WRONGDOING IN THEIR INVESTIGATION, BUT WE STAND BY OUR FINDINGS, WHICH CAME FROM A RELIABLE SOURCE.

JUST PRIOR TO BEING TAKEN INTO CUSTODY, CARL COLLINGWOOD APOLOGIZED TO MIKE SNEAD IN FRONT OF THE HUGE CROWD AND THE TELEVISION CAMERAS HERE AT THE STATION.

The camera cut to Carl and Bruce Collingwood, who stood forlornly next to David Price, surrounded by the boisterous crowd with the locomotive in the background. As Mike Snead walked by Carl he could be heard, saying: "I'm sorry, Mike." The person for whom the apology was meant—Mike Snead—walked on by without so much as an acknowledgment of either Carl's or Bruce's existence.

WHAT'S THE MATTER, MIKE? DON'T YOU HAVE A HEART? DID YOU REALLY PAY OFF A JUROR SO YOU WOULDN'T LOSE THE LAWSUIT?

STAY TUNED. THERE IS SURELY MORE TO COME IN THIS DAVID AND GOLIATH STORY. THIS IS YOUR REPORTER, JULIANNE GABLES, SIGNING OFF FROM CHANNEL 8 NEWS.

STAY WITH *CHANNEL 8* AND STAY INFORMED."

"Signing off *from* Channel 8 News?" Raleigh thought. "Doesn't she usually say, "*For* Channel 8 News?"

Raleigh quickly lifted the phone on his desk and followed through on his threat to fire Juli and George. He phoned human resources and ordered that they be terminated "for cause." When inquired about the cause, he said "For insubordination."

Chapter 37

THE CONGRESSIONAL INVESTIGATING committee room was wired wall-to-wall for the media. Television cameras stood on dollies in every corner, a microphone was strategically placed on the long bench in a position facing every committee member's chair, and several microphones stood erect on the witness table in front of the bench.

Cameras rolled as the committee members strode in, single file, and took their seats. In order they were Abraham Israel, Democrat from New York; William Freeman, Democrat from Louisiana; Betty-Sue Richards, Republican from Texas; Philip Rogers, Republican from Montana; and Albert Weizenegger, Republican from California. The committee chairperson, the Honorable Ms. Richards, took her seat at the center of the table and, after a brief confidential chat with her assistant, called the meeting to order with a sharp bang of her gavel.

"I call this meeting to order. Before we get down to the business at hand, it seems to me we should sum up the purpose of this investigation. I want to emphasize that we are finders of fact—not a judge and jury. I know there are those in the audience who think we should condemn those whose actions we find distasteful, and reward those we find deserving.

"That is not our role or our purpose. We are here to seek the truth—to find out if legislation is needed to curb some practices which are legal today but, we believe, are unjust or improper.

"To carry out this mission, we need to explore the inner workings of the large organizations in this country. We must place ourselves behind the scenes on the Boards of Directors, the managing members and the trustees of these organizations to find out what truly goes on when no one is watching.

"Our first witness this morning will be Mr. Michael Snead, President and CEO of Transport International Corporation. TI is one of our major suppliers of transportation equipment to the military." Ms. Richards turned to the Sergeant-at-Arms. "Mr. Henne, would you please swear in Mr. Snead?"

"Do you swear to tell the truth, the whole truth, and nothing but the truth, so help you God and under penalty of perjury?"

"Yes, I do, Mr. Henne."

"Welcome, Mr. Snead." Ms. Richards began the questioning. "Would you state your name and address for the record?"

"Michael H. Snead, 133 Old Farm Road, Millbrook, New York."

"What is your occupation, Mr. Snead?"

"I am the President and CEO of Transport International. We make just about every type of vehicle that moves: on land, on the sea and in the air. Our total annual sales are close to twelve billion dollars."

"Are you also a director of the company?"

"Yes, I am. I have also recently been elected Chairman of the Board."

"And what is the total compensation you receive for your work for the company?"

"Figuring the value of stock options, together with salary and bonus, it would be approximately thirty-seven million dollars."

"I mean in one year, Mr. Snead."

"That *was* the compensation for last year, Ma'am." This remark produced a collective snicker in the background.

"That does not include any perquisites, does it, Mr. Snead? Health benefits, company car, tickets to baseball games, that sort of thing?"

"No, that's pretty small stuff, though."

"Any other perks you haven't mentioned?"

"Can't think of any."

"Use of the corporate jet for personal business?"

"Well, yes, that's true. I never fly commercial."

"Expense account for entertainment?"

"You got me there. I'm on an expense account pretty much full time."

"Use of an apartment, paid for by your company?

"Well, yes. In New York City."

"Mr. Snead, conservatively, how much would you say you cost the company each year?"

"Cost the company?"

"Well, if you add everything up, what does it come to?"

"Oh." Snead and rolled his eyes and thought for a moment. "Close to fifty million dollars, I would say."

"Fifty million, for just your services alone." This was a statement rather than a question.

"Yes."

"Every year?"

"Well, it does tend to go up every year." There was a soft chuckle in the room.

"Don't you think that's a bit excessive?"

"The board doesn't seem to think so."

"Well, who picked the members of the board?"

"I did." There was another chuckle, this one louder than the first.

"How much does each director get paid?"

"About a million dollars a year."

"You mean your company pays them a million dollars each year to vote you a compensation package worth about fifty million?"

"That's right. But they vote on other things too." By this time the room was beginning to burst with laughter. Congresswoman Richards banged the gavel twice and the room became quiet again.

"Let me get this straight," Congressman Freeman broke in. "You receive about thirty-seven million dollars a year, give or take a million or two, and you still charge the company for all those living expenses— for an apartment in New York City, for travel and entertainment, whatever—that a normal person would pay out of his own pocket?"

"That's right, sir."

"You don't have any pangs of guilt about this? I mean with so many people in this country below the poverty level?"

"I've earned it, don't you think?" retorted Snead. The room burst out in a roar of laughter and Chairperson Richards gaveled again.

"Don't your shareholders complain?" Freeman wanted to know.

"They haven't yet. As long as the stock price keeps going up, they're happy as clams at the bottom of the ocean."

"How has the stock been doing lately?"

"Our stock price has been climbing steadily. You should *buy* some." Snead looked at Freeman with an innocent face, as if he were simply giving him a stock tip, and again the answer caused a reaction in the room.

"Why do you think that is?"

"That's a difficult question. Some might say it's because our sales keep going up. Others say it's just a self-fulfilling prophecy—the stock goes up because it goes up. Of course, we say it's because the company is well managed." This attempt at levity resulted in a few titters.

Congressman Israel jumped in next: "Okay, let's take the first reason you gave. Why do the sales go up each year?"

"To be honest, Congressman—"

"We wouldn't want it any other way, Mr. Snead." A smattering of laughter. *Gotcha!*

"I was going to say," Snead began again, annoyed. He wasn't used to this ribbing from *anyone*, not even a Congressman from New York. "When we need to, we simply raise our prices."

"Don't your customers object?"

"Not *our* customers, Congressman. They're the U.S. Military." The room virtually exploded with laughter. *Gotcha back!*

"What do you sell to the Military?"

"Anything they ask for, we develop and sell to them. Ground transportation equipment – tanks and trucks of every size. Boats and ships—not the big ones, but up to medium size. Winged aircraft and helicopters, and engines for all of these. Communications equipment too. We're a big outfit."

"Your company partial to the military?" It was Congressman Rogers's turn now.

"Yeah, we never a met military general we didn't like." Snead paraphrased a famous quote from Will Rogers. This quip brought out a few more titters, but from this point on the room remained strangely quiet.

"Maybe that's because they have deep pockets."

"It's because they like us, sir. We deliver a top-quality product."

"Let's explore this a minute, Mr. Snead. Have you ever given our generals a ride on your corporate jets?"

"Yes, sir. We have."

"How often would you say? Once or twice a year?"

"We take them wherever and whenever they want to go."

"You *what?* They don't fly on military aircraft?"

"Of course they do. But we take them and their families to places like Aspen for skiing or Bermuda for vacation."

"Bermuda?"

"We have a subsidiary there."

"How in God's name do the generals justify that? It's not business; it's personal!"

"Oh, we make sure that it's business, sir. We give them presentations about all our new developments."

"*Your* new developments? You make it sound like no one else has any developments." Congressman Weizenegger broke in because he couldn't contain his frustration. "What about the competition?"

"Congressman, we really have no competition. We are working hard to become the prime source of transportation equipment for the U.S. Military."

"And what happens when another company develops a good product?"

"We do whatever it takes to beat that other company in the marketplace."

"And what if you can't?"

"Trust me, we eventually prevail."

"There are a lot of smart people in my state of California. You mean to tell me that no one else ever has a bright idea?"

"It takes more than a bright idea to come up with a military product."

"Suppose someone, or some company, approaches you with a next-generation product. What do you do?"

"Well, we ignore them at first. Usually they self-destruct. They don't have the staying power."

"What about Carl Collingwood?"

"Collingwood. I admit, he was a problem."

"A problem?"

"His aircraft—it was a new approach. The generals were asking for it."

"So you invested in his company—what's it called—*Hummingbird Aircraft*?"

"There are more ways than one to skin a cat."

"Then you made sure he failed."

"Let's just say that we 'derailed' his project. We had our own competing project to protect."

"You think that was right?"

"Hey, that's business."

"You know what I think?" Congressman Weizenegger asked, rhetorically. "I think our government should take another look at that Personal Aircraft of Mr. Collingwood. Could be that TI didn't give it a fair shake."

Chapter 38

SPECIAL AGENT PRICE sat in his office in the Hoover Building, watching the TV feed from the Congressional hearing room and wondering if possibly, just possibly, he should have brought Snead in for questioning. He quickly dismissed the thought because he knew that Snead and his lawyers would have simply denied the allegation of jury tampering and would have left no traces of criminal activity. Those damn corporate suits, they always cross their t's and dot their i's. There was no catching them in their nefarious schemes.

Price's cell phone beeped. The screen showed a number, followed by "J Gables."

"Hello, this is Price."

"Mr. Price, it's me, Juli Gables."

"I know who you are, Ms. Gables. How can I help you?"

"I was wondering…could my cameraman George and I come visit you at your office, maybe even today?"

"What's this about?"

"Well, I have some, uh, information that may be of interest to you. It concerns Mr. Snead."

"I know you alleged that Snead bribed a jury. You made a serious charge, Ms. Gables, and I believe you did so without evidence to back it up."

"I would like to explain. There is more to it than you know."

"All right, I'll see you, but just for a half hour. And I'm not going to waste my time on any unsubstantiated allegations. If that's what this turns out to be, the meeting will be over before it starts."

"What's a good time for you?"

"Well, when do you suggest?"

"How about now?"

"What do you mean *now*? Where are you?"

"Down here in the security desk of your building. You just tell the guard it's okay, and we'll be right up."

Within minutes, Juli and George were ushered into Price's office.

"Thanks for seeing us on such short notice."

"The door is always open. I like your aggressive style. Both of you, I mean it. You're good reporters."

"Well, thank you for the compliment. George and I can use a little boost right now. We lost our jobs."

"You did?"

"Yes. We got fired. Our boss was worried about a lawsuit over what I said."

"Should he be?"

"We think not."

"Okay, I'm listening."

"There's this guy in TI. He tells us things—"

"You have a *mole* in the company?" Price looked at them incredulously.

"Well, not exactly a mole, but.…. I'm not sure what he is. We call him *Deep Voice*."

"*Deep Voice*? Like *Deep Throat*?"

"He really has a deep voice. We didn't make this up."

"Okay. So when did you speak to this Deep Voice?"

"We've spoken to him several times. The last time was yesterday."

"What did he tell you?"

"He doesn't really *tell* us anything. He just sort of *confirms* what we already know."

"That's not much of a help then, is it?"

"Oh, yes, it is. It helps a lot!"

"I can't see how."

"Do you want us to show you?"

"You mean you can talk to him *now?*"

"Sure. He takes my calls. When he's not busy, that is. Then I leave a message and he calls back."

"Well, I'll be damned! Here, use my phone. Try calling him now."

"I can't call from your phone. I have to use my cell phone."

"Let me get this straight. This man, Deep Voice, will speak to you any time you want, provided you use your cell phone?"

"Caller ID. The call's got to come from me."

"Okay, I'll bite. So call him. Call him now."

"I can't."

"You can't? Oh, so why not?" Price was beginning to see a pattern here.

"Because the security guard down in the lobby took my cell phone."

Exasperated, Price lifted the phone on his desk and called security.

"John, this is Agent Price. A few moments ago you sent up a couple of TV reporters. Yes, they're the ones. You took their cell phones, right? … Only one? Okay, well get that damn phone and bring it up to my office, right away."

Within a few moments the phone was delivered.

"Now *call*," ordered Price, holding the phone out to Juli.

Juli took the phone and dialed the number. As the call was going through, she pressed the button for "speaker." The familiar deep voice picked up. "Juli?"

"Yes, sir. It's me."

"Am I on the speakerphone? I hear noises in the background."

Juli pressed the "speaker" button a second time. "Not anymore."

"I've got to be careful, Juli. You must know that."

"Yes, I do. I'm sorry."

"All right. How can I help you?"

"I don't know. I'm stumped again."

"Didn't I tell you? Follow the money."

"But that's in *Bermuda*."

"So? It's very nice there this time of year." The phone clicked and
Juli stood there, with the dead phone in her hand.

Chapter 39

"WHAT DID HE say?" Price was clearly impressed.

"He said... he said to go to Bermuda and follow the money."

"Seems like good advice to me. Who is this guy? What's his name?"

"You're not supposed to know that. I can't tell you."

"Then give me his number."

"I... uh, can't tell you that either."

"Why not?"

"Because then you'll send your gumshoes after him to investigate and you'll blow his cover."

"Well, how do you expect me to investigate this at all? I've got no information to go on. So TI has a company in Bermuda. That's legal. And we checked out where this juror, this Betty something, got her money to pay for her house. That was legal too. I can't send agents out to some foreign country with scratch to go on."

"We can go. George and me."

"You?"

"Sure. We're out of a job, remember?"

"What would you do there?"

"We're civilians. We're entitled to go there and snoop around."

"Think you would find something?"

"Can't do any worse than you did. You found nothing. *Nada*."

"Watch it young lady. That hurts."

"Well, we have Deep Voice. You don't."

Price reflected on this a moment. "You've got a point. I suppose I could put you under contract, as a consultant."

"I want George with me."

"No problem. From what I gather about the TI organization, you'll *need* a bodyguard."

"When do we start?"

"Is tomorrow morning soon enough?"

"How much do we get paid?"

"Standard scale is five hundred dollars a day."

"For each of us?" George was listening intently now.

"Affirmative."

"Plus our expenses?"

"Yup."

"For one whole month?"

"We'll start with that."

"Deal."

Chapter 40

———◆◆◆———

JULI AND GEORGE hopped the very next Delta Shuttle back to New York City. They hadn't had a good night's sleep or even a change of clothes since the day before, so they were eager to get home as fast as they could. They were running on adrenaline, though, and weren't the least bit tired. They couldn't stop talking about their good fortune.

"I couldn't have done it without you," Juli acknowledged as they left the aircraft and walked single-file through the narrow passageway into the airport lobby. "George, you've been just amazing!"

"*Moi?*"

"*Oui, vous.*"

"You and the Lord gave me a shot," George replied with all due humility. "I didn't want to screw it up, pretty lady."

"I wish you would stop calling me that."

"Calling you what?"

"Pretty lady. In the first place, we're business partners, and in the second place, I know I'm not especially pretty."

"In the first place, you *are* pretty, so you had better get used to it. In the second place, I want my *business partner*"—George gave a little wink as he said this—"to know how I feel about her."

"Let's not get too personal. We have a job to do."

"I can't help how I feel."

"You're getting through to me, George. I've got feelings too."

"You do?"

"I do."

"Yeah! This is the luckiest day of my life!" George grabbed Juli in a bear hug and planted a big kiss on her lips, right there in the lobby. Everyone nearby turned to watch, and a few bystanders even clapped in approval.

"There's lots more where that came from," George said as the two came up for air.

"Unfortunately for both of us, we need a good night sleep tonight," Juli said as she took hold of his hands in hers and squeezed them. "Whatever you have in mind has got to wait. Just hold the thought, okay?"

"I guess. We've got to catch a plane in the morning."

"Bright and early."

"I'll be there. I'll borrow a suitcase from my mom."

"You don't have a suitcase?"

"Nope. Never got to go anywhere."

"You live with your mom?"

"Yup. She's my first pretty lady."

"How quaint is that! George, the more I learn about you the more I like you."

"*Moi?* Hey, what you see is what you get." George left her standing in the busy lobby as he trotted off to the bus stop with his camera in hand.

The next afternoon Juli and George sat together in the rear of the plane, holding hands, on an American Airlines flight, destination Bermuda. No two people who had ever flown were more excited and enthusiastic about what lay ahead. The world was a wonderful place that people should enjoy. Now, if only some of those people could put aside their greed and lust for power

As the aircraft pushed back from the gate, George, who sat in the window seat, turned his head to Juli and whispered, "Thank you." From then on, lost in their own thoughts, neither said another word to the other for the rest of the flight.

Two hours later, at 7:30 in the evening, American Airlines Flight

1444 from JFK approached the island of Bermuda. The two investigators took turns staring out the side window, marveling at the lush green of the fauna and the pink of the sandy beaches that extended outward in a westerly direction from the airport on this fish-hook shaped jewel in the Atlantic ocean.

Finally, Juli and George both returned to an upright position in their seats and joined hands as the plane made its final approach and descended out of the azure blue sky toward the runway. They were about to embark on a whole new adventure.

---◆›◈‹◆---

Chapter 41

As Juli and George stepped off the aircraft and walked down the steps that had been rolled up to the cabin door, the enormity of what they were about to do suddenly weighed heavily on them. Where were they going to stay? How were they going to get around? Did they have enough money in their pockets? And after that, how were they going to get any information about TI's Bermuda subsidiary, let alone confidential inside information that TI guarded like the crown jewels of England?

"Do they take U.S. dollars here?" George said aloud, although more to himself than to Juli. He had never been, nor had he even thought about going to a foreign country. Thanks to the F.B.I., he and Juli had each received one hundred dollars cash in temporary duty pay, as well as an emergency passport, before leaving the Hoover Building. At the end of each week they were to receive a paycheck in the mail.

"Bermuda dollars," said a fellow passenger, who was also disembarking.

"What?"

"Bermuda dollars. They're worth exactly the same as U.S. dollars."

"Oh. Well, thanks. Where do I get them?"

"Go to the currency exchange after you get through customs," said the bystander, shaking his head. Young people today, they just don't plan ahead.

After retrieving their luggage, George and Juli waited in line and, when their turn came, they approached the customs officer who stood behind a podium.

"Well, here we are!" George greeted the officer, beaming at him from ear to ear.

"Honeymoon?" asked the officer politely, while at the same time glancing through George's and Juli's passports.

"Uh, no...its—" George began.

"Yeah, you guessed right. It's our honeymoon," Juli cut him off as she secretly kicked him in the foot. "Is it that obvious?"

"I can always tell," said the officer, with a wink at Juli. "Have a great time."

After the customs officer handed them back their passports, the couple entered the airport lobby and looked around for a place to change their money.

Juli spotted a booth with the word EXCHANGE above it in large yellow letters.

"That must be it," she said, tugging George in that direction.

When they walked up to the booth they were greeted by an attractive dark-skinned woman with a sing-song voice. "How much would you like to exchange?"

George and Juli glanced at each other. "Heck, lets do it all," they agreed and emptied their pockets. Together they had nearly two hundred dollars.

The pretty attendant looked at George and asked, "You on your honeymoon?"

"Uh, yes. Yes we are."

"Well, honey, shame on you. This amount of money won't get you very far here in Bermuda. That's the cost of about one dinner."

"Well, I have a credit card." He lied.

"Is that so? You'll still need more cash than that to get around. Got money waiting at the hotel?"

"Uh, no."

"Where are you staying?"

"We don't know."

"Oh, is someone picking you up then?"

"No, should they be?"

"Just a minute, please." The young lady picked up a phone at the booth and dialed a number. Within seconds, three policemen appeared out of nowhere and surrounded them.

"Now, just a minute, officers. Just because we don't have a lot of money to spend here, it's no reason to call out the National Guard." George protested defensively, holding his hands up.

"We would like you two to come with us," said one of the officers.

"What for?"

"Just come with us."

Juli and George had little choice but to follow the officers through a frosted glass door to a small office off the lobby. The room was Spartan, furnished with only a table and five chairs.

"Have a seat," the senior official said cordially. "We received advanced notice that you were coming. We have everything set up. First of all, here is some cash for each of you."

The officer handed two envelopes across the table. "That's $5,000 Bermudian dollars for each of you. Don't use a credit card, *ever*. Your whereabouts can be too easily traced. When you need more cash, call me at this number and I'll have it delivered to you." The officer handed each a business card.

George and Juli accepted and held their envelopes extremely gingerly, as if they contained vials of nitroglycerine. George focused on his envelope, his eyes widening, and then returned his attention to the officer. Juli, on the other hand, simply nodded matter-of-factly and dropped her envelope in her purse.

"Now for accommodations," the officer continued, "we have arranged for you to stay at the Fairmont Southampton Resort. I am sure you will find it comfortable. Everything is paid for. Charge everything to your room."

George did his best to stifle a little involuntary sound.

"And by the way, I hope you don't mind. You'll both have to stay in the same hotel room. Tell everyone you're on your honeymoon."

With this, George couldn't help from bursting out, "That does it!" Everyone stared at him. "Somebody pinch me awake, please!"

"It's all right, George. It's not a dream." Juli put her arm around his shoulder. "We need to have money if we're going to do our job."

"But, a *honeymoon*? Everybody's talking about a honeymoon!"

"There are a lot of honeymooners here. Its kind of a tradition," the officer broke in.

"It's your *cover* while you're here in the island."

"Oh, right! Of course." Juli immediately understood.

"We'll work with you every step of the way."

"You will?"

"I can assure you, you'll have our complete cooperation."

"We will?"

"You're very well connected."

"Oh, yeah? With who?"

"With the Federal Bureau of Investigation."

Chapter 42

A FEW MINUTES later Juli and George were on their way to the hotel, via a Bermuda taxi van, courtesy of the Bermuda Police Department.

George and Juli handed their bags to the taxi driver to load into the back of the miniature van and then climbed in. "Well, I'll be... There's a lot more room inside this thing than it looks like on the outside," said George.

The driver, a wiry and lively native islander with a porkpie hat, took the right front seat behind the steering wheel and started the engine. Before putting the van in gear, though, he looked over his shoulder and grinned at his passengers. "You two ready?"

"We're ready."

"All set then." The driver switched on the radio to an island tune, setting the mood, and set the van in motion. "Here we *goooo...*"

"Hey, watch out!" George shouted, pointing to another van coming in the opposite direction. "You'll hit that guy!"

"Not to worry. You're in Bermuda now. We drive differently, but it's safe. You'll see."

The driver maneuvered the van expertly through the airport traffic, keeping to the left-hand side of the road. After crossing a long bridge, he followed the twists and turns in the narrow highway on the left side of the single unbroken line that divided the road in half. The left side of the road! Especially at the roundabouts, of which there were several, George had to close his eyes briefly to calm his nerves.

As they sped along, both he and Juli noticed the greenery, with its flora and fauna, which bounded the road on either side. The island was lush with cultivated vegetation, with every square meter of land carefully cared for and utilized. Every so often they got a glimpse of the sea, through the bushes and trees, in its blue-green splendor, extending out to the horizon.

After about a half hour of high-speed driving, the driver slowed and turned right into the access road to the Southampton Resort. As he followed this driveway up the hill, Juli and George felt the urge to open their senses at the beauty and fragrance of the flowers and foliage that surrounded and guided their path.

"Wow! What a place!" George exclaimed.

"You've got that right," agreed Juli, staring out the window as their van approached the white portico and stopped in front of the entryway.

Two hotel attendants, who stood at attention in white uniforms, immediately went into action. One opened the door for Juli and George and escorted the two guests into the lobby, while the other took the bags and suitcases from the van driver and loaded them onto a brass-trimmed dolly. Never having been catered to, George felt a bit uncomfortable. He could just as easily have been one of the bellhops himself.

Sensing what George was thinking, Juli whispered in his ear, "I don't feel like I belong here, either, but let's go with the flow."

"I'll try my best." George faked a smile for the check-in girl.

"Good afternoon. May I have your names please?" she said sweetly.

"Uh, Mr. And Mrs. Gables," George blurted out. "George Gables."

The girl punched a few keys on the computer and a look of recognition spread across her face. "Oh, yes, Mr. Gables! We've been expecting you. I see you'll be staying in one of our nicest honeymoon suites. I'm sure you will find it very comfortable. And as part of a prepaid package, all of your meals, and even your drinks are included. Just charge everything to your room."

Juli smiled at the clerk and asked, "Could you please confirm our check-out date?"

The girl glanced at the screen. "Check-out is…Hmm . . . it doesn't say. That's odd. Just a minute please, I'll have to check." She lifted the phone, pressed a couple of numbers, then spoke to some higher-up authority. After listening a moment, she replaced the receiver. "We have you down here for at least a month."

George and Juli looked at each other in disbelief. "It's all paid for?" Juli asked, just to be sure.

"Apparently so. You're going to have a great honeymoon!" The girl beamed back at what she assumed were newlyweds. "I'm so jealous!"

George put his arm around Juli, partly for show, but partly because he felt like it. Juli responded by snuggling close and winked back at the girl. "I can't wait to get started!"

Chapter 43

GEORGE AND JULI took the elevator to the top floor and found their suite at the end of the hall. George put the card-key in the slot and opened the door. As they walked in, they were greeted by bright sunlight and by the fragrance of fresh cut flowers that had been placed at strategic places throughout the suite: flowers on the small conference and dining table, flowers on a cocktail table in front of the sofa, flowers on the end tables on either side of the sofa, flowers on the kitchen counter, flowers on the two bedside tables and even a long stem rose carefully laid on each pillow on the king-size bed.

George and Juli eyed each other when they saw the one, and only one, bed.

"Now, George. Don't get any ideas, just because this is supposed to be our *honeymoon*."

"Who? *Moi?* Ideas?"

"I know. I shouldn't have to say anything. I trust you, George."

"You can trust me with your life. We're F.B.I., remember?"

"Darn straight. We're partners, right?"

"Right! Partners it is."

"And we're here to do a job, right?"

"Right! So what's the plan?" George pushed his honeymoon thoughts aside, at least for the time being.

"First off, we're going to need some wheels to get around."

"You mind riding a motor scooter?"

"Those little things? Aren't they dangerous?" Juli looked dubious.

"They're all over the place. We've gotta blend in."

"I guess you're right. Last thing we need is a big fat SUV."

"It'll be fun, riding around."

"Not too much fun, I hope. Remember we're here to check out that company that belongs to Transport International."

"Know where to find them?"

"No, and I don't think it'll be easy."

"Uh, why don't we just look them up in the phone book?"

"Organizations like that try to hide from the public."

"Really? How can they do any business then?" George pulled open a desk drawer and took out a phonebook. He thumbed though the "T's" but found no entry for Transport International. "Well, I'll be… There's no entry! So what'll we do?"

"Don't know, but we've gotta get in there somehow. See what they're up to."

"Well, the good news is that they don't know who we are and they're not expecting us."

"That's right, but we'll need a good cover."

"Got any ideas?"

"Maybe. We're on our honeymoon, remember?"

"*Moi?* Forget our honeymoon? So?"

"So, we're tourists! Bermuda is doing its best to promote tourism."

"I follow you so far. But what's your point?"

"Okay, here's what I read on the way down on the plane: Bermuda's economy used to be based primarily on tourism, but over the years tourism declined to the point where now only ten percent of the foreign revenue comes from that source."

"So, where's the other ninety percent come from?"

"From *foreign corporations*, like Transport International."

"I don't get it. What's the problem with that?"

"The problem is, the corporations are mainly U.S. corporations that use our laws to avoid taxes and launder money. Bermuda's entire economy could collapse overnight if our government changed a few laws, closing some loopholes."

"I still don't get it. What's that got to do with us?"

"It's called the power of the press. If we let people know that we're down here on a dream vacation – our one and only honeymoon – and we threaten to go to the news media to expose one of those offshore companies – think Transport International – as a tax fraud, we have a double whammy.

"First of all the tourist business will be jeopardized, because of all the publicity. And then, horror of horrors, our U.S. government will take a good hard look at the tax incentives they have given to Bermuda companies that have ties to firms doing business in the U.S."

"And the Bermuda government would panic!"

"You got it! Now, about our cover . . . " Juli explained her idea.

George broke into a wide grin. "I like! Let's *do* it."

Chapter 44

———⊷✦⊶———

JULI AND GEORGE went down to the lobby and inquired about renting a motor scooter.

"There's a scooter rental right on the premises, around the back of this resort."

"Can we walk there?" Juli wanted to know.

"Sure, or if you would like to try one of our trolleys, they come by every ten minutes or so."

"We come from New York and we're used to walking everywhere," George said.

"Good idea!" replied the concierge, eyeing the couple with a twinkle. "It's a very romantic walk, along the garden path."

George winked back. "We're on our honeymoon."

"I know."

"You do? How is that?"

"Been here a long time. After awhile you can tell by the look."

"And we look the part?"

"You've got 'Just Married' written all over you."

George and Juli looked into each other's eyes and smiled knowingly before leaving, hand in hand.

After a five-minute walk they arrived at the scooter rental kiosk and looked over the row of scooters. The attendant approached them as they were deciding on a color.

"You from the States?"

"Yup. From New York."

"Most people from Stateside pick a bright color."

"How about from Bermuda?"

"Everything in Bermuda is sort of a teal color, or pink. Like that one there," the attendant added, pointing.

"We'll take that one," Juli said decisively.

"You're honeymooners, aren't you?"

"Yeah, how'd you guess?" George was used to this now.

"You've got that look. Anyway, our honeymooners usually pick red."

"We'll stay with pink. Gotta please the lady, ya know," George explained.

"Good policy, fella. Gimme your credit card and driver's license and I'll do the paperwork."

"We, uh, want to pay cash."

"No credit card? I'll need one for security. In case you crash or trash the scooter."

"How much is one of these scooters?"

"Couple of thousand dollars, why?"

"Here's a couple of thousand," replied George, fishing into his pocket for the money envelope and starting to count out that amount in one hundred dollar crisp new Bermudian bills. "Will that be okay?"

"No problem! Most folks don't have that kind of cash," the attendant acknowledged. "By the way, my name's Mike." He held out a friendly hand, first to George and then to Juli, to break the ice. "I'll refund all the money you have left over after the rental." He went into his little one-room shelter to write up the transaction. A minute later he poked his head out and spoke. "I forgot to ask: How long do you want it for?"

Juli and George looked at each other, not knowing what to say.

"Okay, how long is your honeymoon?" Mike added helpfully.

"We might need it a whole month," volunteered George.

Mike stared at George, impressed. "Your honeymoon that long? Wow, lucky guy!"

George wondered if he had said the right thing. "We, uh, might bring it back sooner. Is that okay?"

"Hey, buddy: knock yourself out!" Mike winked at him. "You only get one honeymoon, right?" He disappeared into the shelter again and came back in a minute holding the completed contract. "I show your deposit right here," he said, pointing with his index finger. "Sign here and you're on your way. Oh, here's your driver's license back."

George signed the paper and turned his attention to the green machine. "Need a lesson?" asked Mike.

"Yeah, I do," conceded George.

"Easiest thing in the world to drive. Here let me show you."

Mike climbed on the scooter and pressed a button to crank the engine. It started instantly and hummed. "This here's the rear brake," he said, demonstrating with his left hand on the handlebar. "On the right is the gas and the front brake. It's got an automatic transmission so that's all there is to it." Mike got off and offered the controls to George. "There is only one thing that you're going to find difficult—"

"Uh, what's that?"

"You got to drive on the left side of the road. If you don't, you die!"

"That shouldn't be too hard."

"Well, people have trouble with that. You'll see."

George sat down in the driver's seat and Juli stretched her leg over and sat behind him. "Ready, Juli?"

"Ready as I'll ever be," she replied, putting her arms around George's waist and hugging him tightly. "Don't forget to go left. *Go left. Go left.* I'll keep saying it in your ear until its drilled into your brain."

"Okay, here we go!" George released the brakes and gave the scooter a little gas. The machine jumped forward, wobbled a bit, and they were off.

Chapter 45

GEORGE TURNED LEFT onto the southern coast highway, from the access road of the Southampton Resort. Proceeding along left side of the road felt awkward at first so he kept the speed down to a slow twenty-five miles an hour. Traffic soon backed up behind him but, rather than increase his speed, he hugged the left edge of the road and allowed the cars and vans to pass on the right. A few minutes later, a public bus passed them with a *whoosh*.

Eventually George felt more comfortable and allowed himself to speed up a bit. The fresh, warm breeze on his face was exhilarating. Both he and Juli, holding fast behind him, felt energized as they passed by breathtaking views of the ocean, interspersed with tiny communities of little white houses decked out in flowers.

In about fifteen minutes they arrived at a roundabout, with more than a dozen signs indicating the directions to the various different villages on the island. George became suddenly confused and slowed nearly to a stop. "Go left. *Go left*!" Juli shouted in his ear. "Don't stop now! Keep going! But go left! Take that road!" she said, pointing with one hand at a sign that read "Hamilton," and holding tight with the other.

"Whew! That was awful!" George admitted, after they had managed to get through the encircling traffic and were traveling along safely in the left lane on the road to Hamilton. "I don't know what I would have done without you!"

"I'll do what I can. I want to live too!"

In just a few more minutes they arrived in Hamilton. "Boy, this is a really small island. Everything is so close!" George shouted over the noise of the scooter, without turning his head.

"Slow down now. Watch out for pedestrians," warned Juli, looking ahead over George's shoulder. "We're almost there."

George allowed the scooter to wind down as they cruised along Front Street. To the left was the harbor, with several boats tied up along the dock, and on the right were one glitzy shop after another. George pulled over and stopped at the end of a long row of scooters facing Triminghams, a fancy department store.

"Wow, this is nice!" remarked Juli as she climbed off and looked around. George held the scooter steady for her and then pulled the scooter backwards onto the kickstand.

"We made it!" he said, relieved.

"Now we need to find the Bermuda Tourist Bureau." Juli reviewed a small sheet of notepaper she fished out of her pocket. "It's at twenty-nine Front Street. Can't be far."

"Ready or not, here we come."

Juli and George walked back along Front Street in the direction they had come, until they found a small office building bearing the number *twenty-nine* in large gold letters.

A young girl at a reception desk looked up from reading a magazine. "May I help you?"

"Yes. I'm Shurin and this is my husband, Iman. We would like to see the person in charge here. We have a complaint."

"A complaint? What about? This is the Tourist Bureau, and—"

"We *know* it's the Tourist Bureau. We want to speak to your boss."

"It's just that—"

"That no one ever complained before? Well, guess what? We have a complaint! Now are you going to let us speak to your boss or do we have to go to the Prime Minister?"

"Just a minute, please." The receptionist glared at Juli, but didn't lose her composure. She quickly lifted the phone and pressed a button. "Mrs. Stone? I have a couple of, uh, *tourists* out here who say they have a complaint. All right then, I'll tell them." The receptionist glared back at Juli again. "Mrs. Stone will meet with you."

"Who's Mrs. Stone?"

"She runs this Tourist Bureau."

A tall, well-tailored woman appeared a moment later and introduced herself. "I'm Marjorie Stone, Executive Director of the Bureau." She held out her hand to Juli and George in turn. "Won't you come in?"

The couple followed her to her small office and she signaled for them to sit in the two side chairs. Mrs. Stone took her place behind the big desk. "Can I offer you tea? It's not exactly four o'clock, but—"

"No, thank you, ma'am," Juli began. "My name is Shurin. This is my husband, Iman."

"Unusual names," Stone commented.

'My husband's parents named him after Don Imus—you know, from 'Imus in the Morning'? They call him the 'I-Man.' Our last name is 'Love'."

"How sweet! You're tourists here?"

"Yes, we're on our honeymoon, and—"

"Your honeymoon! You'll find that Bermuda is just the place. Your name fits very well, by the way."

"I know. Everyone says that. And I'm just getting used to it—the name, I mean. Anyway, we have a complaint. A request really."

"Oh, I'm sure we can fix that!" gushed Mrs. Stone.

"We hope so. It's about a certain company here in Bermuda."

"What about it?"

"For one thing, we can't find the company at all."

"Well, then, its identity is probably confidential. What's the name?"

"We don't know the name, but it's a subsidiary of a U.S. company called Transport International."

Mrs. Stone suddenly dropped her bubbly demeanor and eyed Juli suspiciously. "Why do you want to contact them?"

"They owe us money."

"That's not possible."

"Oh? Why not?"

"They don't do any business, other than with their parent company."

"That's not what Mike Snead told us. He's the president of TI."

"I know who Mike Snead is. What did he tell you?"

"He said that five hundred thousand dollars would be transferred to our account from their subsidiary in Bermuda. Well, the money never came."

"He said that, did he? Now why would he do that?"

"I can't tell you. Let's just say we did him a favor."

"So why don't you go back to Mr. Snead with your complaint?"

"We think it's just an administrative error. They don't know our account number, so we want to meet with them and straighten it out."

"To tell you the truth, Surin Love, or whatever your name is, I don't believe one word of what you're saying. And anyway, I'm not going to give you the name and address of this company. I told you, its confidential. Now, I hope you have a very nice honeymoon."

Mrs. Stone arose from her seat and started walking toward the door to lead George and Juli out. George took the cue and got up to leave, but Juli stayed put in her seat and announced in a loud voice: "If you don't tell us where the company is, we'll go to the *police!*"

"And what will you tell them?"

"Now that's none of your business, is it?"

"Perhaps not. But there's one thing I do know. The police won't give you the time of day."

"We'll just have to see, won't we?" With that, Juli got up out of her chair and walked determinedly out of the office. George followed her, pretending to be miffed at the treatment they received from Mrs. Stone.

Mrs. Stone closed her office door behind them and quickly went back to her desk. Picking up the phone, she dialed a number from memory and waited for someone to answer. "Hello, Walter? This is Marjorie Stone. I just want to alert you. A young couple were in here a moment ago inquiring about you. They said they're on their honeymoon . No, they don't know, and I didn't tell them anything."

Chapter 46

———❖———

Outside, Juli and George looked at each other's mock-serious faces, trying to stifle their smiles and then spontaneously burst into laughter, both at the same time.

When she was able to catch her breath, Juli blurted out, "Did you see her expression when I told her our names?"

"From then on it was all down hill. She wasn't buying anything you were saying!"

"Was I really that bad?"

"You were so bad, you couldn't have fooled a ten-year old kid, or even *me*. And I wanted to believe you."

"I guess I need more practice with this undercover stuff."

"Next time, let me try."

"Be my guest. By all means."

"So where do we go from here?"

"Every time I get stuck, what do I do?" asked Juli rhetorically.

George and Juli looked at each other and answered the question in unison: "Call Shelley!"

Juli whipped out her cell phone and dialed the number. After three rings, Shelley picked up with a deep "Hello, Juli."

"We're in Bermuda, Shelley. But we can't seem to find your subsidiary here."

"Frankly, I'm not surprised. We keep our presence pretty well hidden."

"So what do we do? We're at a dead end."

"Can't talk. But see Maurice at the Bank of Bermuda."

"Thanks, Shelley. Bye." Juli clicked off.

"That was short," George commented with concern.

"But to the point. We've got a name. Let's go."

"Where to?"

"Bank of Bermuda. It's got to be around here somewhere."

George and Juli headed back in the direction of their scooter and saw a policeman, directing traffic from a booth at the intersection. They waited for the light to change and then crossed over to his station. They walked hand in hand, so as to look like the honeymooners they were pretending to be.

George looked up at the officer and asked directions to the bank.

"There are several branches. You know which one?"

"We want the main office," Juli volunteered.

"That'd be on Church Street. Just two blocks up that way." The officer pointed.

Within minutes they were on Church Street, a major business area of the city, it turned out, and found the bank. They walked in and looked around the dark, cavernous hall that doubled as a lobby and workspace for bank officers. They stepped up to the reception desk.

This time George took the lead. "Hi, my name's George," he addressed the young girl behind the desk. "Do you have an officer here named Maurice?"

"No, I don't think so. Let me check." She looked down at her intercom list. "No, nobody here by that name."

"There must be somebody. Are you sure?"

She checked again, carefully. "No. Sorry."

"If you were looking for somebody—anybody—at the Bank of Bermuda, whose first name is Maurice, where would you look?"

"Well, the first thing I'd do is check the company phone book."

"Isn't that where you just looked?"

"No, sir. This is the intercom list for people on this floor."

"Do you have a company phone book?"

"Yes, its right here." The girl picked up a small phone book on her desk.

"Could you look there?"

"Uh, sure. Hmm, there are a lot of names. Do you have a last name? No wait. Here is a Maurice Dubois. He's the manager of the St. George's branch."

"St. George's what?"

"Branch."

"St. George has a branch?"

"No, it's in St. George's."

"St. George's what?"

"Branch."

"What did you say your name was?"

"George."

"You two are honeymooners, aren't you?"

"Yeah."

"I can tell."

"Everyone says that. Why?"

"Your mind is always on something else."

Having cleared that up, George and Juli walked back to their scooter. On the way they purchased a roadmap of Bermuda and studied it.

"They named a whole town after me!" kidded George.

"And they made you a *saint* too."

"*Moi?* A saint? I don't think so."

"Neither do I," Juli teased. "Now how do we get there?"

"It's near the airport. We'll head over there, on the same road we came in on, and turn off before we pass the airport. The road should run right into it."

"Okay, saddle up, pardner. Let's ride!"

Chapter 47

———◆◆◆◆———

IN HALF AN hour they had crossed the causeway and were scooting along Kindley Field Road. When they reached the Swing Bridge, they turned left, crossed over the bay and followed the highway, past Fort George Hill, into the town of St. George's.

A few minutes later they were in the center of the village, at Kings Square. "There's the bank!" shouted George above the sound of the motor. He headed into a scooter parking area, switched the motor off, and they both dismounted.

This time they had a better reception at the bank. When they entered and asked for Maurice Dubois they were immediately ushered into his corner office. Dubois came out from behind his big desk and greeted them warmly.

"No. Don't tell me. Let me guess. You're honeymooners, right?"

"I don't believe it," George responded, shaking his head. "We must have it written on our foreheads."

"What can I do for you?"

George took the lead this time. "First of all, my wife, Juli here, and I would like to open an account."

"That's easily done. Do you have a passport with you?"

"Yes, here it is." Juli fished her passport out of her pocket and gave it to Dubois.

"You don't want a joint account?"

"No, just Juli," George replied.

Maurice took some papers out of his credenza and filled in some of the blanks. "I'll need your signature in several places, Ms. Gables. I have marked them with an 'X'. Do you want your statements sent to the home address listed here on your passport?"

"Yes."

"Well then, just sign in these places and that's all there is to it. How much will be your initial deposit?"

"Will $100 Bermuda dollars be enough, just to start the account?"

"Certainly. Do you have cash?"

"Yes." Juli took out five twenty-dollar bills and was about to hand them over, when George said, somewhat nonchalantly, "We understand that you handle the accounts of Transport International."

"Yes, as a matter of fact, I do."

"Well, the president, Mike Snead, asked us to open an account here. He said he would transfer some money into this account."

"Do you know Mr. Snead?"

"Yes, we do."

"I assume you heard about that kidnapping in New York?"

"Oh yes, it was horrible. It was on TV and in all the papers."

"Terrible thing, wasn't it?"

"Poor Mike! It must have been awful for him."

"I agree. Anyway, I've done this before for Mr. Snead, but I don't yet have any instructions from him yet to transfer money. I'll have to call the subsidiary here in Bermuda. Instructions like this usually come from them."

"Go right ahead. I'm sure you'll find everything in order."

Dubois hit a few keys on his computer to bring up the account information for the subsidiary. He started to place the call when Juli interrupted him.

"Oh, before you call them, why don't we open the new account. Here's the hundred dollars."

"Good idea. First things first."

Dubois got up from his desk and went over to one of the tellers with the account information and the one hundred dollars. Just as soon as he left the office, George quietly stepped around the desk so he could see the screen.

"It's here!" he said, excitedly.

"Write it down, quick!"

George grabbed a pen and wrote the name, address and phone number on a slip of paper. When Dubois returned both George and Juli were sitting calmly in their seats.

"Here's your deposit receipt for the hundred dollars, and here is the package for your new account, with a book of starter checks. Now let's call TI." Dubois again reached for the phone.

Again Juli interrupted him. "If you don't mind, we would like to wait until someone at TI calls you and authorizes the transfer. We don't want to seem too anxious, if you know what I mean."

"I understand completely. We'll let you contact Mr. Snead, or someone in his organization, to arrange for the transfer. I'll wait to hear from you."

The couple politely thanked Dubois, got up and walked out of the bank into the bright sunlight. They strolled across the square back to their scooter, climbed on and drove away without looking at the slip of paper, just in case Maurice decided at that moment to look out the window. As a matter of fact, that is just what Maurice did.

He picked up the phone and dialed the number on his screen. "Walter, hello. This is Maurice at the bank. There was a honeymoon couple in here who claimed that you were going to transfer some money to them. They opened an account for that purpose. No, of course not. They have no idea where you are located, or even the name of your company."

Chapter 48

━━◆❖◆━━

WHEN THEY GOT to the edge of town, George pulled over to the side of the road and braked to a stop. Holding the scooter steady with his feet on the ground, he removed the slip of paper from his shirt pocket and showed it to Juli. His fast scribble was nearly unreadable but she could make out the name, address and phone number. "Good job, George! But now what do we do?"

"First, let's find this place. Then we'll make a plan."

"Good idea. Maybe it's time to visit a gas station and ask directions. We do need gas, don't we?"

"Not much," George replied, glancing at the gas gauge. "This thing is really good on gas."

"So? We should put in a couple of gallons anyway. You never know when we might need a full tank."

"You mean like for a getaway?"

"Whatever. There's a gas station just up ahead. Let's try there."

George revved the scooter engine, causing the machine to lurch forward a bit unsteadily, and headed toward the station. Once there, both he and Juli got off and looked all over for the fuel inlet.

"It's gotta be here someplace!" George said, getting more and more frustrated.

The gas station attendant walked out from his booth to resolve the situation. "Can I help you?"

"Yeah! Where the heck do you put the gas in this thing?"

The attendant lifted the seat, which was hinged in the back, and revealed the gas inlet.

"Geez, thanks. Who would have thought?"

"No problem. Get a lot of requests for that. 'Specially from honeymooners like you."

"Yup, we're honeymooners. You guessed it right."

"I can always tell."

George started filling the gas tank while he was talking to the attendant. "By the way, do you know where we can find this company?" He handed the attendant the slip of paper.

The man squinted at the scribbled writing and gave it back. "Y'know what this is?"

"Well, yeah. I think so."

"You've been invited?"

"Not exactly."

"Then you don't want to go there."

"Why not?"

"The place is a fortress. It's guarded twenty-four-seven."

"Really? Why is that?"

"Who the heck knows? They must be in tight with the politicians, ya know what I mean?"

George finished pumping the two gallons of gas and paid the attendant.

"Thanks for the warning. But you never told me where the place was."

George and Juli mounted the scooter and George pressed the button to start the engine.

"It's easy. It's about the southernmost point of the Island. You go back to the airport and go around it. Keep heading south on Coopers and it runs into Mercury Road. It's right at the end of Mercury. Can't miss it. But they won't let you in."

"Thanks a lot. Whenever we need gas, we'll stop in."

"Name's Rudy. What's yours? "

"George. And this is my bride, Juli." Juli gave him a great big smile. "See you, Rudy!"

"Hope so. Good for business, ya know what I mean?"

George headed back toward the airport, crossed the Swing Bridge and turned left on St. David's Road, following it around the airport until they merged with Coopers Road. Eventually, just as Rudy had said, they found Mercury Road. It was a narrow dead end street that ran from the airport out to a point of land that jutted into the ocean. Turning left onto Mercury they saw, facing them at road's end, an iron gate with a sign that read: *FINANCIAL MANAGEMENT, LTD. Private Property. Keep Out.*

Mounted on both pillars on either side of the gate, a video camera followed the motor scooter as it approached the gate, stopped for a moment, and then made a U-turn and headed back in the direction from whence it came.

Chapter 49

"OKAY, NOW WHAT'S the plan?" George wanted to know. He had driven the scooter back on Mercury Road and stopped near a rear entrance to the airport.

The airport property was surrounded by a cyclone fence and the rear entrance was monitored by a gate and a guard house displaying a large sign that said *General Aviation*. Looking through the fence, George and Juli could see quite a number of small single-engine aircraft, as well as a few twin-engine corporate jets on the tarmac.

"I haven't a clue. Maybe it's time to call Shelley again."

"Let's do it. We don't even know what we're looking for."

"I hate to bother him. But it's as if he *wants* us to find something."

"I agree. But what could it be?"

Juli dialed the number and put the phone to her ear. In a moment, Shelley's unmistakable voice came on.

"Sorry I couldn't be much help the last time you called. I was in a meeting. How did you make out?"

"We found your subsidiary on Mercury Road."

"Very good! Don't tell me how. I'm sure you had to bend the rules a bit to find it."

"So what do we do now? We have no idea what we are supposed to find here."

"Our subsidiary, where you are now, is the base of Mike Snead's power. He has a man there, named Walter, who is above the law. If Mike runs into any kind of problem, and that happens more often than you might think, Walter makes it go away."

"How does he do that?"

"Whatever it takes. Money, muscle, even murder. Mostly money, though. Vast amounts of money."

"Why are you telling *me* this? Why don't you go to the police?"

"I need this job. And it's a good company if you discount that it's rotten at the core. You, Juli, have the ability to cut out the rotten core. That's what I want you to do."

"Me? I'm just one person." She glanced at George. "Well, really two. George and me. We're a team." She winked at George and he winked back.

"You have more power than Mike, even. You can bring him down."

"Power? I don't have any power."

"Yes, you do. You have the power of the *media*."

"Oh, that! Well I guess I forgot to mention, we lost our jobs at Channel 8. We're not media any more."

"Yes, you are. If you make a documentary about what goes on there, believe me, it will get on the news and people will take some corrective action."

"Maybe so. That is, *if* we can get stuff on tape."

"I'll help you with that. Trust me. I know the weak links and I know where the bodies are buried."

"Well, for starters, how do we get into the compound? It's like a fortress in there."

"Two answers to that: You have to come in by sea, and you have to come at night."

"By sea and by night. How do we do that?"

"Rent a boat, of course! Start using your resources. You're young and you're on a honeymoon. There's nothing you can't do. Just don't involve the local police. Anything you tell them will get right back to Walter."

"We'll call the F.B.I."

"They can't do anything if the crime is committed in Bermuda. Anyway, they can't investigate without a warrant, and they can't get a warrant without probable cause. Believe me, TI knows how to cover its tracks so that everything appears legal and aboveboard. There's only so much the F.B.I. can do. If you get caught spying, they can't help you. In fact, they'll deny any knowledge of you."

"I know. Agent Price made that pretty clear. But there's one thing I just don't understand: If you want *media*, why don't you call in *60 Minutes* or some heavy hitters like that?"

"That won't work. Everything they do has to be on the record. They can't expose lies. Remember when Bill Clinton went on *60 Minutes* and said he never had sex with Gennifer Flowers? Everyone at CBS knew he was lying but they had to air the segment anyway and Clinton was able to fool the whole country. He even got elected."

"So *we're* your only hope?"

"I don't see any other way. You may think it's a pretty thin thread, but you're up to the task. I know you are. I've been watching you."

"Well, I'm glad you're so confident, because I sure am not."

"Oh, and one final thing."

"What's that?"

"Please be careful. That Walter is ruthless. He stops at nothing. I mean *nothing*."

"Well, thanks. You just boosted my confidence some more."

"Just want you to know what you're facing. Now get in there. Good luck!"

Shelley ended the call. Juli stared at her phone and then eased herself down on the scooter seat and put her face in her hands to think about what she had just heard.

After a minute, George, standing there, uttered an impatient "Well?"

Juli looked up at him and replied, "We've got a heck of a job to do," and went on to explain what Shelley had said.

"No prob, pretty lady. I'm ready for anything. But let's start in the morning if it's all right with you."

Chapter 50

GEORGE AND JULI rode the scooter back to their hotel in silence, except for the occasional *"go left"* that Juli whispered in George's ear when he seemed to be uncertain about which way to go. George switched on the single headlight and taillight to make the scooter more visible to other drivers.

Tired as they were from the long day, the ride awakened all their senses, with the cooling sensation of the wind on their faces, the ever-changing, pleasant smells of the flowers alongside the roadway as they passed and the comforting hum and soothing vibration of the scooter motor.

When they returned to the Southampton Resort, George and Juli took turns in the bathroom, each taking a shower and dressing for dinner. When Juli finally emerged after nearly an hour, dressed in a sapphire satin sheath that accentuated her curves, George had to do an honest double-take. "Indeed, my lady, you do look gorgeous!"

"Why you look just dashing yourself," responded Juli. "Will you be my date for the evening?"

Standing tall, George graciously offered her his arm, and led her proudly out the door of their suite, down the flights of the sweeping, semi-circular staircase to the hotel lobby, and from there to the main dining room. The *maitre'd* eyed them both with a welcome smile, bowed deferentially, and led them through the maze of tables in the restaurant to a quiet, oak-paneled area near the rear, far from the entrance to the kitchen. There they took their places at a table for two with a white tablecloth that that bore a colorful bouquet of local flowers and a small candle.

George ordered a bottle of California Chardonnay – Juli's preference – from the wine steward and, while they were waiting to be served, they perused the menu.

"Since we're not paying for this, why don't we go all out? Have whatever our hearts desire," suggested George.

"I've never done that before. It seems sinful, but maybe just this once—"

"I'm sure Mr. Snead doesn't think about his charges when he dines at a restaurant."

"But he's not exactly the role model we want to emulate," Juli reminded him.

"I don't think we're in any danger of doing that. Not the way *we* grew up."

"Okay, let's throw caution to the wind."

"Just this once."

Juli raised her glass and proposed a toast, "To Mike Snead!"

"Mike Snead!" George echoed. "A real *dude*!"

Before they knew it, George and Juli had finished their meal and had emptied the bottle of wine.

"Would you like desert?" George asked.

"I don't want anything to break the mood. Let's just call it a night."

"Fine by me." George signaled the waiter for the check and charged the meal to the room.

"How much is it?"

"You don't want to know. That will definitely break your mood."

"Not if my rich uncle is paying."

"Your uncle?"

"Uncle Sam."

"Oh, yeah, well even Uncle Sam must have a limit." George leaned over and whispered, "I've never seen a bill this high in my whole life!"

"Then, don't tell me," Juli giggled. "I'll pretend we're on a date."

"Or on a honeymoon."

"Yes, that's even better."

George stood and helped Juli to her feet.

"I'm a little wobbly from the wine," she confessed.

"Me too. But we don't have far to go, thank goodness."

Within minutes, George and Juli were fast asleep on their king-size bed.

Chapter 51

—◆◆——

THE NEXT MORNING George and Juli raced through a huge breakfast at the hotel café before heading to the information desk in the lobby. "We want to charter a boat and rent the equipment to go scuba diving," George said enthusiastically. Juli beamed her brightest smile at the uniformed concierge.

"You two on your honeymoon?" the man asked.

George was getting used to this honeymoon question, and this time he actually had a true answer. "No, we're here on our first date."

"Very funny. You couldn't fool anyone."

"About that boat?" Juli said.

"You have a lot of options. How deep do you want to dive?"

"How deep?"

"You can stay on top of the continental shelf and dive among the coral reefs or, if you go out just a couple of miles toward the southeast, the bottom of the ocean drops off suddenly. It's really an abyss down there if you like that sort of thing."

"Uh, I think we'll stay in the shallow waters."

"Ever dive before?"

"Nope. We're from New York."

"Figured as much. I know just the guy for you. He runs a scuba diving school right out of this hotel."

"Does he give private lessons?" Juli asked, wanting to avoid meeting too many strangers.

"Sure, but it's much cheaper to join a class. He teaches you the basics here in our swimming pool and then takes you out on his boat."

"Can we charge it to our room?" asked George, winking conspiratorially at the concierge. "My rich uncle is paying the hotel bill."

"I'm sure we can arrange that," replied the concierge with an acknowledging wink back. He knew how expensive these honeymoons could get.

George looked at Juli, who nodded. "We'd like a private lesson."

"Okay. Let me make a call." The concierge lifted the phone. "When would you like to go?"

"Right away." George looked at Juli again, and again she nodded in agreement.

The concierge dialed a number and spoke to someone briefly. Looking back at George he asked, "Two this afternoon okay?"

"Perfect."

The concierge repeated the answer into the phone and then asked, "How long do you want him for?"

"The rest of the day. Evening too."

"I'll check."

A minute later the concierge hung up and said, "It's all set. The guy's name is Harry. He'll meet you here at 2:00."

That afternoon George and Juli stood in the lobby waiting for Harry. At about 2:15 a weather-beaten man with a crumpled captain's hat walked in and looked around. George waived his hand at him and called, "Here we are!"

"Hi, I'm Harry Reed," he said with a pleasant grin.

"Mr. Reed—"

"Harry."

"Uh, Harry. This is my wife Juli, and I'm George. We're on our honeymoon."

"Really? Never woulda guessed."

"Is it that obvious?"

"You kidding? You're the spitting image."

"As a matter of fact, we *were* kidding. We're really not on our honeymoon. We're not even married."

"You're pulling my chain."

"Well, yes and no. Why don't we go into the café and have a cup of coffee."

George and Juli led Harry into the café and sat him down to outline the plan they had in mind. They took turns talking, explaining briefly their idea to sneak onto shore in the dark, which, they told him, was to surprise a friend. By the time they finished, Harry's friendly, easy-going manner had changed slightly but perceptibly.

"I've been told you were coming," Harry responded. "I'm here to help." George and Juli stared at him, shocked at what he said.

"I report to Dave Price. I'm undercover for the F.B.I."

George and Julie stayed silent, not knowing what to say.

"You've heard of 'Our man in Havana?' Well, I'm their man in *Bermuda*. The F.B.I. has its tentacles everywhere."

Recovering her composure, Juli found her voice again. "You're in the *F.B.I.*?"

"Not exactly. I'm *really* a boat captain. But I like adventure, and the best part is they *pay* me to keep my eyes open."

"What do you know about us?"

"I know who you are and why you're here. Your background, your mission, everything."

"Are you okay with it? It could be dangerous," Juli warned.

"Count me in. I'm on board, mates."

"When they start shooting, you're not going to bail out and leave us?"

"We're a crew to the end. All for one and one for all."

"And you agree to keep this confidential and not tell anyone?"

"Aye, except maybe Dave Price. To the death, I swear."

During the next few hours Harry did his best to teach George and Juli how to don and use their scuba equipment. He worked with them for over an hour at the hotel swimming pool to show them how to drop down into the water and propel themselves beneath the surface.

"Why do we have to fall backwards upside down? Can't we just jump in?" Juli complained.

"Trust me. Do it my way and you'll be safe."

Harry also took pains to explain the operation of the aqua-lung. "You'll have plenty of air in the tank, but make it a habit to check the pressure gauge every so often, just to be sure."

When he was certain they were ready, Harry took them out on his boat for a practice dive in the daylight before their run at night. "Think of yourselves as frogs," he instructed, just before the two novices fell backwards off the side of the boat into the warm sea water. Sinking down into this strange ocean environment George and Juli let themselves float weightless at first, and then began to swim forward, paddling with their frog feet and guiding with their hands. It was an odd but wonderful sensation to move about in slow motion, seemingly defying the effect of gravity. Even odder was the feeling of being on the inside of a huge goldfish bowl as little fish swam effortlessly about, ignoring the presence of these large and lumbering land creatures.

The sunlight easily penetrated the clear blue waters and illuminated the ocean floor with its coral of red, orange and white and its sea plants bending this way and that with the current. Reflections of light and dark darted about in random patterns from the ripples and waves on the surface above.

Immersed suddenly in this strange new environment and surrounded by such varied and different life forms, George and Juli felt both uncomfortable and, at the same time, attracted and fascinated by this silent underwater world. Having escaped a sense of time, more than an hour slipped by before George realized they had better get back to their home world. He touched Juli on the shoulder and pointed upward, signaling his readiness to return to the boat and Juli, brought back to reality, nodded her assent. On queue, they both headed up with quick downward movements of their arms and hands.

When they broke through the surface, they looked around and saw the boat nearly a quarter mile away. "Over here!" George and Juli shouted, wildly waving their arms in the air.

Harry spotted them, rotated the rudder wheel on the boat and revved the engine, quickly covering the distance between them. "You sure had me worried, mates! I never lost a diver before but, man, you two were down one heck of a long time."

"Seemed like just minutes," Juli replied, apologetically, as she climbed the ladder in the rear of the boat. "Sorry!"

"Think you're ready for prime time?" Harry asked, revealing some concern in his voice.

Juli looked at George, who followed her up the ladder, and he gave her the thumbs-up sign. "We're ready!" she told Harry confidently.

Chapter 52

———◆◆◆———

As THE EVENING descended, Harry's boat bumped along at high speed, planing over wavelets on the calm sea while heading for Neptunus Rock at the end of the southern- and easternmost point of Bermuda island. Harry kept the southern coastline on his left as he sped eastward until he reached Howard's Bay at Castle Point. Slowing the boat somewhat, Harry carefully negotiated his way through Castle Cut, south of Castle Island, and then headed northeast, passing between South Cock Rock and North Cock Rock to reach Nonsuch Bay on the leeward side of Nonsuch Island.

By this time the faint jagged outline of the shoreline vegetation against the night sky had dissolved into darkness. Because of the overcast sky, Harry needed to rely solely on his GPS map for navigation. Traveling south from Nonsuch Bay, he rounded the southern point on Nonsuch Island and, switching off his running lights, he aimed his boat straight for Neptunus Rock at the end of the point where Financial Management, Ltd. had its compound. Cutting the engine back to a fast idle, Harry plowed slowly forward against the waves until he was within a few hundred yards of his destination.

There, in the blackness, Harry carefully lowered his anchor to avoid a splash. He let the boat drift in the current until it tugged lightly on the anchor line, causing the anchor to lock itself in place on the ocean floor. The boat secure, Harry turned his attention to his passengers.

Below deck, George and Juli suited up in their black wet suits, with rubber slippers and frog feet, and then helped each other don air tanks and aqua-lung equipment. When they were ready, they climbed the short ladder to the main deck and signaled Harry.

"Ready to go," Juli announced, not without nervousness in her voice.

"I'll be here waiting for you. Come on back, soon as you can."

"We'll just snoop around a bit. If they discover us, we'll be back in a hurry."

"If you're not back in two hours, I'm calling the police."

"Don't bother. The way we understand it, the police are on their side."

"Then be extra careful, ya hear?"

"We'll try."

"Just in case you find something interesting, here's a waterproof bag to put it in."

"You think of everything, Harry. Thanks." Juli handed the bag to George, who secured it to his waist with its two straps. Then, taking turns, they sat down on the gunwale of the boat with their backs to the water, gave Harry the high sign, and fell over backwards into the water.

Harry watched them disappear into the blackness of the sea and then checked his watch. It was 9:42 PM. Harry sat down on a cushioned bench and waited.

Juli and George made good time, swimming on the surface for the most part, although they were prepared to slip beneath the waves at a moment's notice to avoid being seen. As far as they could tell in the darkness, however, no one was patrolling the back of the building on the end of the point. It appeared Shelley Bernstein had called it right. Access from the sea was left unguarded.

Eventually, Juli and George got close enough to shore that they could touch bottom and stand upright with their heads just above water, peering at their destination. The ocean waves lapped quietly at their faces as they stood there for a moment and, seeing no immediate danger, walked slowly and carefully forward on the sandy sea-floor.

Within a few minutes they were climbing over the rocks that demarcated the shoreline.

Once secure on land, Juli and George dropped down on the grass and shed their frog feet and their aqua-lung equipment. Leaving this stuff in a neat pile in readiness for their return, they turned their attention to the building in front of them. It loomed large in the darkness without light from any of the rear-facing windows. Juli signaled to George to approach the building first, while she lay prone, and once he reached it, she crept forward and joined him.

Then, standing up and keeping their backs to the rear wall, they moved along as silently as they could, step by step, until they reached a rear door. George grabbed the door handle and carefully gave it a twist. To his amazement the handle turned, releasing the latch, and the door opened inward. George slipped into the building and Juli followed. George closed the door behind them, leaving them both in pitch-black darkness.

After standing silently for a couple of minutes, their sense of sight and sound awakened to full potential. They became aware of their surroundings, due to the faint light that entered from beneath an internal door, and they heard indistinct and muffled sounds of people talking in an adjacent room. Looking about, they realized they were in some kind of storage room or file room. Juli removed a penlight from her belt and switched it on.

There behind them, along the rear wall on both sides of the outer door through which they came, was a row of gray file cabinets. Juli directed her light toward the cabinets and illuminated file drawers, each of which bore a label in the middle. Scanning along the drawers as quickly as she could, she eventually found one with a label "Carrington – Copeland." Juli opened the drawer and aimed the penlight at the various upwardly protruding tabs, looking from front to back, until she and George came upon a thick file marked "Collingwood." George grabbed the file with his two hands, lifted it carefully out of the drawer, and held it tightly to his chest while Juli carefully slid the drawer shut. Then they both stealthily exited the building through the back door.

Once outside on the lawn George inserted the file in the bag that Harry had given them and the two set about donning their water gear. When they were ready, George strapped on the bag and he and Juli eased themselves over the edge of the rocks into the sea. Finally they swam back toward Harry's boat in the inky black water.

In the boat, Harry listened intently in the darkness for sounds of his two passengers. Pressing the button on the side of his illuminated digital watch, he could see it was 11:36, only six minutes before their self-imposed deadline.

"Damn," he muttered to himself. "What do I do now?"

Harry didn't have to answer that question because a minute later he heard a rustling sound in the water. Glancing sideways in the direction of the sound, so as to utilize the most light-sensitive portions of his eyes, he could detect movement, and eventually the forms of the two figures heading toward the boat.

"You're a sight for sore eyes!" he called to them under his breath, not wanting to be heard by anyone else. Then he scurried to the rear of the boat, grabbed a float at the end of a line and threw it out into the ocean as far as he could. Juli and George gratefully grabbed the rope and pulled themselves in. Panting heavily, they finally reached the ladder and climbed, exhausted, onto the deck. George untied and handed the bag to Harry and then, with Juli, collapsed, elated, on a bench.

"Thank God, you made it. Let's get out of here!" Harry cranked up the anchor, started the engine, switched on his running lights and sped away from Neptunus Rock.

Chapter 53

ALTHOUGH IT HAD been a strenuous day and Juli and George were tired when Harry finally delivered them back to the hotel, they were so excited they couldn't wait to pore over the contents of the Collingwood file.

They literally ran down the hall to their room and, dropping the key in the slot, burst through the door, their bag of papers under George's arm.

"What the fff....!" Stunned, Juli stopped abruptly and stared at the room.

George nearly bumped into her from behind, but what he saw made his eyes open wide: Their room had been ransacked and torn apart.

Clothes were everywhere. Drawers were pulled out and left on the floor. The bedcovers were missing and the mattress pulled off the bed. In the bathroom all of the toiletries and towels were strewn about.

"I guess while we were over there, they were over here," George ventured.

"Looks like they're on to us. Lucky there was nothing to find here."

"Now there is!"

"You're right. And they'll know it when they go back and look at the files."

"What do we do?" There was not just a little urgency in George's voice.

"Let's call Price, right *now!*"

The ringing signal growled a couple of times and a sleepy voice answered. "Huh, hello?"

"Agent Price? It's me. Juli Gables."

"Juli? Oh *Juli!* Uh, just a minute. Okay, I'm listening. What's happening?"

"They're after us."

"Who? Who is after you?

"The people at Financial Management!"

"Financial, *what?*

"Financial Management. You know, the subsidiary of Transport International!"

"The subsidiary—"

"In Bermuda!"

"Oh, Yeah. Yeah. Now I remember. So what's the problem?"

"They broke into our hotel room today, while we were out! We just got back and it's … it's *horrible!*"

"How do you know it's them?"

"Who else could it be? Everyone else thinks we're on our *honeymoon.*"

"Yeah, well maybe someone thinks you have money."

"*Price*"—Juli had never addressed him that way before and she now had an edge in her voice—"get *real!* You sent us here to do a job and we did it. Now we have to get out of here, *fast!*"

"You said you did *what?*"

"We went in there. We got the goods on them."

"Slow down. Slow down. You got what goods?"

"We got the Collingwood file from their office."

"You did? The Collingwood file? What's in it?"

"We don't know. We haven't looked at it yet."

"*You haven't looked at it?* Let me get this straight. You managed to go in and steal a file out of their office—and you haven't *looked* at it?"

"We have a slightly higher priority right now, *Price.* That's getting off this Island *alive.*"

"All right. All right. Let me think…. Okay, here's how we'll work it. At least I *think.* I'll have to make some calls. Bermuda isn't that far off the coast of North or South Carolina, whatever. I'll dispatch an F.B.I. helicopter directly from the mainland to pick you up. I'll send it over first thing tomorrow morning. I'll call to tell you the exact TOA. Where are you staying?"

"The Fairmont Southampton."

"Nice hotel. Been there. But they won't let us land on the golf course. Tell you what. I'll have the chopper go to a place called Dockside at the west end of the island. There's a big fort. They can land in the middle of it. Can you get there?"

"We have a scooter."

"A *scooter?* That's a hoot."

"It gets us around."

"I'll bet. It's a tiny island."

"Where do we spend the night?"

"Good question. Don't touch anything in the room. And whatever you do, don't tell the management what happened."

"Why not?"

"They'll clean up the mess and destroy evidence. We'll send our investigative team in there in the morning. Get fingerprints, hair samples, lint, DNA, whatever we can, to find out who was there. Maybe we can nail the bastards."

"So where do we sleep?"

"Go to the front desk. Tell them you're having a fight and you want to sleep in separate rooms. Then get another room and go to bed."

"A fight on our *honeymoon?*"

"Believe me, it happens all the time. Even to me, but that's another story."

"Love to hear it sometime—once we get back safe and sound, that is."

"Good luck. Talk to you in the morning. Oh, and one more thing—"

"What?"

"Put a *DO NOT DISTURB* sign on both your doors. Trust me, the hotel ladies understand this stuff."

Chapter 54

GEORGE REGISTERED FOR another room. The desk clerk, female, glanced at him disapprovingly but didn't say a word. Couldn't he keep his new wife happy on her honeymoon, for God's sake? She recorded a plastic key to a room across the hall and shoved it at him.

In the meantime, Juli remained in the old room and picked out the few belongings they really needed for the trip home. When George returned from the lobby, they moved these things to the room across the hall. Finally, after about the longest day in their lives, they collapsed together, fully clothed, on the king-size bed and went right to sleep.

Less than five hours later, the rays of the morning sun beamed in through the openings in the window curtains. Juli awoke first. 7:15 AM. Time to get moving.

Juli stood under the running water in the shower, rinsing off aches on muscles she never even knew were there, and then stepped out onto the bathroom rug, refreshed and wide awake.

George took his turn in the shower, and by 8:00, they were both packed and ready. The few belongings they took with them, including the unopened Collingwood file, were stowed in a single duffle. George looped the strap over his shoulder letting the duffle hang low on his back, and they both headed downstairs for a quick breakfast and checkout.

At the front desk, the same woman was there, just getting ready to leave her shift. "We're checking out," George said, handing her four keys, two from each room.

"Had a rough night, eh?"

"You don't want to know."

"Marriage is tough." The woman looked at Juli, sympathetically.

Juli smiled back. "Depends on the guy."

"Well, better luck next time. Come on back when you find Mr. Right."

"You've got it all wrong. But we don't have time for that now. Someday we'll come back and explain it to you."

"Hope you do. Your bill's all paid. Have a nice life." She gave them both a friendly nod goodbye.

Juli led the way out the front door, with George right behind. He strapped down the duffel to its carrying rack on the back of the scooter with two elastic bands. As he held the scooter steady while Juli swung her leg over the seat behind him, he noticed a white van with a strange-looking antenna on the roof pull up to the front entrance of the hotel. A bald man got out from the front passenger seat and went inside.

"Juli, that could be them," George alerted her.

"Geez, I'll bet you're right. Let's sneak out of here."

George started the engine and slowly drove the scooter forward behind the parked cars. They kept their heads down as best they could to avoid being seen. Eventually they came to the exit from the parking lot and turned out onto the access road to the hotel. The van hadn't moved.

"I don't think they saw us," George called out.

"Hope not. Let's go!"

"Where to? It's too early for the helicopter."

"We have to hide somewhere. Why hasn't Price called?"

"Maybe we don't have service down this low." George was coming to the end of the access road that descended from the hotel to near sea level.

Juli pulled out her phone and looked for the bars. There weren't any. "Oh, my God! That's the problem!"

"We need to go higher. The phone worked on the third floor of the hotel."

"Take a right here. That's the direction to the Dockside."

George took a right on the shoreline road. Juli looked behind but no one was following, at least not yet.

She looked up toward the right and saw a lighthouse at the top of a hill. "The lighthouse! Let's go up there." Juli pointed.

"How do we get there?"

"How should *I* know? We need to take a right somewhere."

Juli had no sooner said this than a road appeared on the right. There was a sign in the shape of an arrow that said *LIGHTHOUSE*.

"Turn here!"

George turned onto the side road, and the scooter groaned as it wound up the hill. The road twisted and turned but eventually leveled out. Near the top was a narrow driveway off to the left with another lighthouse sign. George followed the driveway all the way up until he reached the lighthouse parking lot. There were a number of other scooters there, so he drove up and stopped next to them. He let Juli off and then pulled the scooter back onto its kickstand.

Juli looked at her phone again and noticed two bars. "Reception's okay now. But let's climb up in the lighthouse. I'll bet it's even better up there."

She bought entrance tickets for George and herself and they headed up the stairs. About halfway up the stairs she looked at her phone again as they passed a small window. "It's three bars now. Let's keep going."

Juli reached the top landing first and looked out. "Wow! This view is *fantastic!*"

"You can see the whole island from here!" exclaimed George. "Look! There's the Dockside." George pointed to a port with the ancient fort in the distance.

"I'd better call Agent Price," Juli said, "Hello? Agent Price? It's Juli."

"Where have you been? I've been trying to reach you all morning. I left three messages."

"Out of range, I guess. We just realized it, so we're at the top of a lighthouse now."

"It worked yesterday."

"Yeah. We were on the top floor of the hotel."

"No matter. The helicopter's all arranged. It will be there at 10:30. He needs to stop at the airport to get fuel for the trip back. Can you go there?"

"I don't think so. The bad guys have a compound right next to the airport and I think they're after us already. Can't we get picked up at the fort, like you said? We're closer to that."

"Affirmative. We'll stick to the plan. Go to the fort and I'll have the helicopter drop in."

While Juli was talking, George looked for the van they had seen at the hotel. It was no longer parked at the hotel entrance—it was heading their way! As George looked down, the van turned right, where he and Juli had turned just fifteen minutes before, onto the winding side road.

George watched the van inch its way up the hill. They can't possibly be coming here, he thought. How would they know? The van approached the top of the hill and the entrance to the lighthouse driveway. Just keep going, George prayed to himself. But the van stopped briefly, as if undecided what to do, and then turned into the driveway.

"Juli! They're coming up here!"

Juli looked out and saw the van approaching up the driveway. "Omigod! We've got to go!"

Juli flew down the steps of the lighthouse with George clattering as fast she could behind her. Tourists who were climbing the stairs heard the commotion and pressed their backs to the outer wall to clear the way as the coupled hurtled downward. In a flash they were at the bottom and, first peeking out the doorway to make sure the coast was clear, they dashed for the parking lot.

"They must have homed in on your cell phone!" George shouted as they ran.

They reached their scooter just as the white van was pulling in. George freed the kickstand and started the motor, all in one motion, while Juli jumped on the back. In less than a second they were off, heading straight for the entrance of the lot with the van coming in their direction. George dodged the van, drove past it out of the parking lot, and sped down the driveway.

Chapter 55

GEORGE DROVE HEADLONG down the hill on the road without using his brakes even once, until he came to the end at the shoreline road. Even then, he braked only briefly at the stop sign to avoid traffic coming from the left, and when he saw the road was clear he turned right without stopping and headed west.

The van took some time to turn around and get out of the parking lot, and even then it couldn't travel down the winding road as fast as the scooter.

Once on the shoreline road, however, the van could accelerate to full speed, and it began to catch up.

The scooter was also traveling at its top speed, but this was only 45 miles per hour. Juli kept turning her head to look back, seeing nothing at first but then noticing the van in the far distance. Each time Juli looked back, the van appeared closer than before.

"Hurry!"

George swerved around a corner at full speed and almost lost control as his back tire slipped sideways slightly.

The van, which was traveling much faster, had a more difficult time negotiating the turn and ended up scraping the bushes on the left side of the road. It slowed down abruptly to avoid getting bogged down in the ditch, but then sped up as soon as the danger was over.

The scooter was able to widen the gap, but not for long. Juli looked back again and found herself staring at a gun that the man in the passenger seat of the van held out the window. It was pointed in her direction!

"Omigod! He's going to shoot!" she shouted to George. Just as she said that, she heard a bullet whizz past her head and, a second later, they heard the sound of the shot.

"Shit!" cried George. "What's that!"

Up ahead, George saw the road rising – like a ramp moving upward. He scrunched his eyes half closed in an attempt to see better, but the wind in his face and the vibration of the road made it difficult to make out what was happening.

"It's a drawbridge!" Juli screamed, holding tight to George's waist. "And it's going up!!"

The road at this point was not very wide. Signs on both sides warned that the road narrowed to the width of the small drawbridge over a channel that separated the west end of Bermuda from the main portion of the island. The west end was an island unto itself, connected only by this drawbridge.

George made a split-second decision to keep going at full speed and kept the throttle wide open. The scooter hit the ramp, just as it began to angle upward, and was catapulted into the air like a huge cannonball. Then down it came on the other side, landing square in the middle of the road, and it continued to travel forward as if nothing had happened. George sat frozen in his seat, holding the handlebars as firmly and straight as he could, but he was so shaken after they landed that he applied the brakes and stopped to catch his breath.

Juli, who had closed her eyes and held on tight, had greater faith in George's driving than he did himself. With the scooter momentarily motionless, she looked back and saw the drawbridge continuing to rise to a fully upright position, blocking the view of the van—and the path of bullets from the van.

"Hold it a minute! I have an idea," she said excitedly, and slipped off the back of the scooter. "You get off too."

"What, the…" George did as he was told, after placing the scooter on the kickstand.

Juli quickly unhitched the straps holding the duffel bag on the back of the scooter, and handed them to George. "Quickly, use these! Tie the duffel on my back!"

George caught the concept immediately. He grabbed the duffel and held it upright against Juli's back. Juli reached behind her and held the duffel in place while George wrapped the elastic straps around the bag and around her chest and connected the ends together.

"Too tight?" he asked, concerned.

"I'll manage. Now let's go!" Juli glanced over and saw a sailboat moving under motor power slowly but steadily through the channel in front of the drawbridge.

First George, then Juli climbed back on the scooter, with the duffel bag behind Juli extending up from the seat to the height of her head as protection against gunfire. George revved the engine, popped the clutch and off they went again, just as the drawbridge began to move downward behind them.

The white van started up even before the drawbridge had completed its travel. The weight of the vehicle forced the bridge down the rest of the way, stripping the mechanical drawbridge gearing as it did so. The van quickly accelerated.

Chapter 56

Up ahead George and Juli zoomed along the narrow road, turning this way and that without slowing down. The curves equalized the race somewhat because the van could not go much faster than the scooter. With the slight advantage it had, the van began to catch up, and the gun appeared again out the passenger side window aimed straight ahead.

A shot rang out, and this time Juli both heard a thud and felt the impact as the bullet penetrated the duffle bag.

"We're hit! He shot the duffle bag," Juli screamed. Then came several more shots that luckily passed them by.

By this time, George had reached a large parking area in front of the fort. He drove straight through an alcove, which served as a gate to the center of the fort, before applying the brakes. He and Juli dashed on foot into an entrance to a tiny shopping area and sought shelter inside. The few people who were there looked at them strangely, especially Juli with the duffel on her back, but kept out of the way.

The van pulled up and stopped outside the fort. Two men stepped out, both carrying guns, and raced toward the building. They heard the distant flutter of helicopter blades and, looking up, they identified a speck on the otherwise silent sky, approaching quickly from the east. The two men stopped and stood still for a moment, as if contemplating what to do next, and then dove into the building to continue their pursuit.

George and Juli moved quickly from one area to the next, to avoid being seen. They split up but kept within speaking distance of each other, all the time keeping their eyes open for the men with guns. They entered a museum with exhibits from early colonial Bermuda, including pictures and drawings of ships used in the slave trade. One of the drawings showed slaves lying on their backs, side-by-side tied hand-and-foot on the deck of the ship. Life was certainly more civilized today—or was it?

Juli glanced at her watch: 10:35. She signaled George to get his attention and then pointed to her watch. He nodded. If they could only hold out a bit longer they might be rescued.

Then, as if on queue, they heard the helicopter overhead, rattling the windows with its choppy wind. George and Juli ran to the exit door of the museum that faced the central courtyard. They watched the big machine descend, with tourists staring and scattering out of the way. Painted white on the side of the dark blue craft were some small numbers plus three large letters: *F.B.I.*

When the chopper settled down, blades still turning, a side door parted and an agent with an automatic rifle stood in the opening. Propping the gunstock on his belt and holding it with one hand, while bracing himself inside the chopper with the other, he looked around expectantly for his two passengers. Juli and George started running toward him from the museum doorway. In an instant, the agent recognized them and jumped out of the helicopter to render assistance. At the same instant, however, the two men from the van appeared in another doorway and started shooting. One of the men trained his fire on the agent in front of the helicopter while the other aimed at George and Juli.

George and Juli kept running, hand-in-hand, toward the waiting helicopter. The duffel bag on her back slowed Juli down somewhat, but George pulled her along. Somehow, in the hail of bullets, they made it to the helicopter door and climbed aboard. The agent had jumped in first to help by pulling them in.

Just as Juli was framed in the doorway, one of the bullets slammed into the duffel bag, giving her an extra boost into the cabin. The agent shut the door behind her while the helicopter roared and lifted off, stirring a cloud of dust. The two men from the van kept firing away, but their bullets just bounced off the armor shields on the sides and bottom of the craft.

Juli and George were on their way home!

Chapter 57

JULI AND GEORGE were ushered into Agent David Price's office in the Hoover Building that afternoon. Juli carried a large folder with the papers she and George had taken from the files of Financial Management, Ltd. in Bermuda.

Agent Price came out from behind his desk to greet them as his secretary led them into his office. He shook their hands warmly and, offering seats, he teased, "How was the honeymoon? I want to hear everything, blow by blow."

"Everything?" Juli replied with a friendly smirk. "It was a, you know, a *honeymoon*."

"Okay then, *almost* everything. Just don't leave out the best parts."

"We think you'll be satisfied when you see what we brought with us." Juli placed the folder on Price's desk and opened the cover. Inside was a stack of papers about two inches thick. Juli lifted the majority of papers from the stack and placed them upside down on the cover to the left, revealing an accounting sheet with some numbers on it. Oddly, the sheet had a hole right through the center.

"Most of this stuff has to do with Collingwood's aircraft, his patents and the lawsuit he brought," Juli explained. "We went through it on the helicopter ride to Charlotte and then on the airplane trip up here to Washington."

As she spoke, George reached carefully into his jeans pocket, took out a metal slug and gently laid it on Price's desk. "This bullet was embedded right in the middle of the file. These papers saved Juli's life!"

Agent Price looked amazed, first at the bullet hole and then the bullet. "These papers stopped the bullet?"

Juli nodded. "I hope they're still good evidence," Juli said hopefully.

"Even better. Shows the papers are genuine. They'll send someone to jail if we can match the bullet to a gun."

"And look at this!" Juli pointed to the accounting sheet. "It shows a number of wire transfers from this account at the Bank of Bermuda. They total $990,000."

"My, my. Are you thinking what I'm thinking?"

"Follow the money trail. That's what you told us to do and that's what we did."

"You did real good. *Real* good."

"Is there any way to find out where the money *went*? There is a Betty Falmouth, who was on the jury in Carl Collingwood's lawsuit against Transport International. After turning the jury against Mr. Collingwood, she moved into this gigantic new house, and—"

"Just a minute." Price raised his hand briefly, signaling silence, and typed a few commands into the computer on his desk. Within seconds, the number of the account that received the funds, as well as the names of the account holders, appeared on the screen.

Robert B. Falmouth

Elizabeth L. Falmouth

"You can do that?" Juli asked incredulously. "I'm impressed!"

"You'd be surprised what we can do. But just because we can do it, doesn't make it legal."

"What do you mean?"

"We have to have probable cause. Otherwise we can't investigate."

"What if you just accidentally discovered the information?"

"We couldn't use it in a court of law. Or any other evidence we found as a result of our discovery. It's called 'fruit of the poison tree.'"

"But if George and I, private citizens, were to bring you this evidence—"

"Exactly! That would give us probable cause to investigate."

"So what do you think?"

"I think Transport International, and Mr. Snead in particular, have some explaining to do. But we have to dig further."

"You don't think it's a slam dunk already?" George wanted to know.

"With these corporate types, you never know. Some don't have any moral compass. They think nothing of lying under oath, so it's never over till it's over. Even if you have them on video dead to rights, bribing some guy or whatever, they always seem to explain it away with a reason why what they were doing was perfectly legal. They're not much better than mobsters, but a heck of a lot smarter. They very seldom do time. And on the rare occasion that they do get caught, they serve only a year or two in one of the Federal prisons, where they play tennis."

"But they tried darn hard to get this file back," pointed out Juli. "They were *shooting* at us, for gosh sakes."

"Jury tampering is a serious offense. For them it's damage control. They'll take risks if they have to."

"Yeah, risks with *our* lives."

"You know what I mean. Normally they don't go around shooting. They work quietly behind closed doors."

"So send us out. We'll collect more evidence."

"Not very likely. You're not trained in law enforcement."

"We did a pretty good job so far."

"Anything else you do would be too dangerous, and also against the law, by the way. I don't care what you do in Bermuda, but I don't want you breaking-and-entering or anything else like that in this country."

"So let's get this straight: You're firing us! We bring you the goods on a silver platter and that's *it*?" Juli was indignant.

Price just smiled. "Well as a matter of fact, there *is* something you can do that would help."

"What's that?"

"More important than the evidence sometimes, is the power of the media."

"So?"

"Go back to your TV station and broadcast the news."

"Oh sure. We got *fired,* remember?"

"So? You're going to be heroes now, like Woodward and Bernstein. You'll never have to worry about a job again."

"Come to think of it, you may be right! For the past week we've been so focused on investigating that I almost forgot what we're about. We *are* the media, and we have a breaking story. So, George, let's you and I get to work!"

"Really?" George broke into a grin. "*Vous et moi?*"

———◆◆◆———

Chapter 58

ANDREW ("ANDY") ROSIN couldn't believe his luck. The boss of the New York office himself, the famed U.S. Attorney, Rene "Gotcha" Perez, had casually stopped in to Andy's office and had plopped a thick file on Andy's desk. The label in the upper right corner, in large capital letters, said it all:

COLLINGWOOD, CARL
COLLINGWOOD, BRUCE

It was almost a non-event when it happened, but now that Perez was gone, Andy just sat there and stared at the file. This was a prosecutor's dream. He would be right in the center of a media storm with a case that was a sure-fire win for the good guys.

He lifted the phone and dialed the number for the F.B.I.

"Hello? This is Andy Rosin at the U.S. Attorney's office. I'd like to speak with…" Andy squinted at the data on the outside of the file folder. "Uh, Price. Agent David Price. I believe he's in the Washington Office." Andy squinted again. Yes, Hoover Building."

"I'll connect you."

"Agent Price, speaking."

"Agent Price...David, I'm Andy Rosin with the U.S. Attorney's Office in New York. I've been assigned to prosecute the Collingwood case."

"Really? Ol' Gotcha didn't grab this one himself?"

"Guess he figured the case was too easy. Everyone knows the Collingwoods did it. It was on national TV. More people watched it than saw O.J. Simpson's slow-mo getaway with the white Blazer."

"Yeah, but do they know *why* they did it?"

"What difference does it make? Hijacking. Kidnapping. Aggravated assault. Resisting arrest. Reckless endangerment. How many counts we got? Maybe a hundred?"

"I agree. Sure looks bad on paper, but—"

"You're not waffling, are you? I understand you almost got yourself killed back then."

"I think you should cut them some slack."

"Whoa! Where's this coming from? Doesn't sound like the *slam-'em, bang-'em, take no prisoners* Price I've heard about."

"This one's different."

"How?"

"Collingwood got a real raw deal. He tried using the law but it didn't work. He thought he had no other choice."

"That's it?"

"Well, in a nutshell, yeah."

"No other choice than hijacking and kidnapping? How about taking your lumps and moving on? That's what most people do. And should do."

"It's not so easy to give up a lifelong dream. We're talking major mind adjustment here. In a way, I feel for the guy."

"You're going to testify, right?"

"Of course. I'll tell the truth too. He could have killed me on that train, but he didn't. As a matter of fact, he didn't really hurt anyone. Worst thing one can say is he inconvenienced a lot of people."

"I thought he tried to kill you."

"He was just defending himself."

"Resisting arrest."

"Defending himself. I wasn't trying to arrest him, I was trying to kill him."

"Geez. Don't say that in court. Looks bad for the good guys."

"Don't worry. I know what to say and what not to say. But if you and his defense attorney could make a deal, there'd be no trial."

"Not bloody likely. What else you got?"

"A whole lot of background on the victim who got himself kidnapped."

"Mike Snead? Okay, I'm listening."

"Piece of work. I got to know him real well on the train and we've been investigating him since then. I've got a lot to tell you."

"Relevance?"

"Let me put it this way. If there ever was a guy who deserved what he got, it's him."

"He was kidnapped, right?"

"A 'civil arrest' you might say."

"Kidnapped. So I ask you again: Relevance to the crime?"

"It's relevant to a plea bargain."

"No, it's not. Come on, Price. You should know better. Have you gone soft on us?"

"I just want you to know all the facts. We've gotta discuss it, and soon."

"When's your next trip to New York?"

"Is tomorrow soon enough?"

"You're on."

THE GABLES REPORT

Juli Gables *ONLINE!*

HOME * MISSION * ARTICLES * CONTACT* LINKS * PODCAST * BLOG

JULI   *GEORGE*

WELCOME TO OUR WEB SITE

YOU ARE THE

000,597,328th

VISITOR

www.juligables.com/home

MISSION STATEMENT

Our mission is simple: To shine a bright light on criminals and their criminal activity.

Our mission is to proactively investigate criminal activity, and to pass the information we uncover along to the police and to the public as rapidly as possible.

After all, the police could use a little help!

By the way, if *you* have information about possible criminal wrongdoing, contact *us*.

www.juligables/mission/

ARTICLES

Breaking story...

TI's Mike the Malevolent Denies Knowledge of Jury Tampering

Wherever he goes, Mike Snead, CEO of Transport International, Inc., familiarly known as "Tee Eye," is followed by reporters, seeking information on the allegation that a wholly owned subsidiary of TI in Bermuda transferred nearly one million dollars to a member of the jury in a civil action against the company and Snead personally, brought by a small firm, Hummingbird Aircraft, owned by Carl Collingwood. The subsidiary, Financial Management, Ltd., transferred $990, 000 to Elizabeth "Betty" Falmouth who subsequently purchased a million-dollar home in Chappaqua, NY.

Snead, popularly known as "Mike the Malevolent," denies any wrongdoing. He insists that the transfer of funds to Betty Falmouth was perfectly legal because it occurred *after* the jury announced their decision. The money was paid to Ms. Falmouth, he said, "as an expression of gratitude" for having swayed the jury to "vindicate my company in that specious lawsuit." A phone message left at Falmouth's home was not returned.

Carl Collingwood and his son, Bruce, are scheduled to stand trial next month in White Plains, NY, for commandeering a commuter train to deliver Snead into the hands of a Congressional Committee in Washington, D.C.

Visit our Web Site EVERY DAY to follow this story.

www.juligables.com/articles/collingwood

Other Stories to Watch!

There oughta be a law, department:

GE Board Approves Golden Parachutes for Top Officers
Corporate greed knows no bounds

Boeing CEO involved in Sex Scandal
Talk about robbing the cradle!

There is a law department:

Tyco CEO Charges Company for Wife's Birthday Bash
IRS *finally* investigates income tax evasion

www.juligables.com/articles/

Your comments are welcome!

How come you know this stuff before anyone else?   Randy29

Free the Collingwoods! BabarAndCeleste

That Bruce sure looks cute!   LolaGetz

Wish there were more investigative reporters like you. Taki-T

www.juligables.com/weblog

Chapter 59

◆━◆❈◆━◆

SHELLEY BERNSTEIN WAS in his office, studying a government report, when Mike Snead strode in to the executive suite. Both Shelley's office and a conference room were on one side of the reception area of the suite on the eighteenth floor; Mike's huge office was on the other. The reception area was beautifully appointed with a circular, cedar secretarial desk right in the middle, and two lounge chairs, a table and a couch forming a sitting area behind it. The sitting area was bounded by two big bay windows overlooking Central Park in Manhattan.

Shelley always left his office door ajar so he could see who came and went. When Mike arrived that Monday morning, Shelley was not in a good mood. He gave Mike a few minutes to settle in to his office and then pounced.

"Got a minute?" he asked, poking his head in Mike's open door.

"What *now*?" Mike said impatiently.

"We just received a report card on our wireless communicators. Look's bad." Shelley's voice, already gravelly, was even deeper with the word "bad."

"Whose report?"

"The U.S. Army. They've been using these walkie-talkies for a few years now, and they've had some complaints."

"Yeah? So?"

"So they did a study. And it doesn't look so good."

"Why am I not surprised? No one's ever satisfied."

"It's worse than that. They claim the radios are causing brain tumors."

"What! Gimme a *break*."

"No, *really*. They say the radiation they give off when they're used right near the head is causing a higher-than-average incidence of brain tumors, in young soldiers, no less."

"That's *bullshit*."

"Let's hope so. If this problem is real, then—"

"Why just *our* radios? What about the competition?"

"Ours have a higher wattage. That's our competitive advantage."

"Higher radiation means greater range."

"The competition knows that too, but they don't go that high. They say it's unsafe."

"Well, is it?"

"This report says so."

"Who wrote the report?"

"The guy in the Army who did the study, I guess. It's preliminary."

"Can we keep it confidential?"

"Depends on the guy."

"Let's get him on the phone."

"Shouldn't we talk about it first?"

"What's to talk about? We just have to do damage control."

"Maybe we should think about pulling the radios—"

"Oh? Well, let's take a look." Mike stroked a few keys on his computer and stared at the screen. "We sold a total of two point three five million of these things to the military, about five hundred and fifty thousand in the last year alone. At two-hundred-and-forty dollars a pop that's over five-hundred-and-fifty-million dollars. Figure a gross margin of fifty per cent, we netted two-hundred-and-twenty-five million in profit so far."

"Yes, but shouldn't we look into this? I mean if they are really causing brain tumors—"

"How can they prove the radio's the cause? Could be a million other things."

"That's what the tobacco companies said about cigarettes. No causal relation to lung cancer. And they lost."

"Not at first. Those damn companies won every lawsuit. They just pushed it too far. Took twenty years to bring them down. What's the product life of our radios? Five, maybe six, years? We'll have a new model to replace it before anyone gives a shit."

"What about the present model? We could do a recall and adjust the power to reduce the radiation."

"You have *any* idea how much that would cost?"

"The adjustment wouldn't cost much. Put them back on the assembly line and open them up. Maybe ten dollars a unit."

"Yeah, but the Army'll charge fifty just to ship it to us. I know those bastards. They'll jump at the chance to sock it to us."

"The whole recall would cost us one hundred dollars a unit, tops."

"We sold over two million. That's two hundred million bucks!"

"And what if those soldiers with brain tumors sue?"

"Let them try. You can defend a lot of lawsuits for two hundred million."

"So that's your strategy? *Stonewall*?"

"Damn straight. So let's get this Army guy on the phone. What's his name?"

Shelley looked at the report. "Schuffenecker. Dr. Emil Schuffenecker."

"Well, let me speak to Emil *Schnuff*—whatever. Set up a meeting and we'll see if we can keep this damn thing under wraps."

Shelley just looked at Mike, and shook his head.

"Well? What is it now?"

"With all due respect, Mr. Snead, you're going to *ruin* this company."

"Is that what you think?"

"Someday, one of these things is going to come back and bite us in the butt."

"I don't *think* so, Shelley. Stop worrying and let me take care of these little problems." Mike patted Shelley on the shoulder and led him out of the office. "That's why they pay me the big bucks."

Chapter 60

———◆———

SYLVA COLLINGWOOD NEVER really recovered from that day when Carl and Bruce kissed her goodbye in the early morning and left for the train station in Wassaic. Sylvia had been through rough times, especially when Carl had fought for his rights against the huge corporation that stole his invention, his livelihood and his dignity. However, even that had not prepared her for the unrelenting gloom which had descended and enveloped her when she realized that the two people whom she loved and cherished would not be coming home, perhaps ever. She was *bereft*

But now, it was different. Her men would finally be facing the government prosecutor at their criminal trial and Sylvia had a *purpose*: *To get them out of jail.*

Energized by hope and the realization that she could *do something* to help her men, she focused on finding an attorney who would champion their cause.

At first the task seemed easy. With the upcoming trial in the news almost every day, a number of lawyers contacted *her* to offer their services free of charge. Since the case was a sure loser anyway, no attorney could be faulted even if Carl and Bruce were convicted and sentenced to a long term in prison. The attorney who represented them would surely benefit from the exposure, no matter what the outcome of the case might be. And he or she would not have to work very hard.

Sylvia was tempted to retain one of these "free" attorneys, particularly because her own finances, and those of her parents who came to her support in this time of need, were strained to the limit. But she resisted all of these offers, after checking out each attorney who had solicited her business, with the conviction that she would retain only the best possible representation for her husband and son, and then worry about the cost.

She first tried Googling "Lawyers NYC" and got 1,440,000 hits. At the top of the Google list were a whole lot of search firms which, she surmised, charged money from lawyers to place ads on their referral lists. Since Google, in turn, charged these search firms to place their names at or near the top of Google's list, the whole system seemed to be just an advertising scheme, skewed toward those lawyers who wanted to pay the most for advertising.

She looked up the number for the Association of the Bar of the City of New York. The receptionist answered in a sing-song voice. "Bar Association. How may I direct your call?"

"I need advice on choosing a lawyer."

"Just a moment, please. I'll connect you."

So far so good, Sylvia thought. They even have a special person that handles this kind of thing.

"Referrals!" a bright female voice came on the line. "Tiffany speaking."

"Tiffany? My name is Sylvia. Sylvia Collingwood. My husband and my son have both been charged with a crime and I need—"

"Collingwood? You mean Carl and Bruce?"

"Well, yes, have you heard of them?"

"Mrs. Collingwood, *everyone in New York* has heard of them," Tiffany gushed. "I am *sooo* sympathetic. What that big corporation did to them. Everybody I know thinks that Carl and Bruce should go free."

"As a matter of fact, that's why I'm calling, they need a lawyer."

"I can give you names, Mrs. Collingwood. We have a list of our members here that do criminal defense."

"I need more than just names. I need to know who is who. What I really need is advice on choosing the right one."

"All I can do is give you the names and firm affiliations of our members."

"Can't you tell me who is the best?"

"All of our attorneys are fully qualified."

"But some are better than others, don't you think?"

"I'm very sorry, Mrs. Collingwood. Even if I knew, which I don't, I wouldn't be allowed to say."

"I understand. So you'll give me the names? How many are they?"

"Roughly 300, more or less."

"300 lawyers?! So how am I supposed to choose one?"

"You will have to do that research on your own."

"How do I do that?"

"Use the Internet. All of their law firms have web sites."

"I tried that. It just seemed like they were *advertising.*"

"I'm not sure I understand. But if you start with the members of our Association who do criminal work, you can't go wrong."

"All right. I'd like to get your list."

"Is email okay?"

Sylvia gave Tiffany her email address and was about to conclude, when Tiffany added one more thought.

"By the way, did you or your husband ever use a lawyer before?"

"Well, yes. Carl did, for his company, a long time ago."

"Why don't you ask *him?*"

"How would he know?"

"That's usually the way it's done. Lawyers know the lay of the land."

"Oh, well, then I'll do that. Thanks very much. You've been a big help."

"And Mrs. Collingwood?"

"Yes?"

"Everyone in New York is rooting for you. Everyone in the country probably is too."

Sylvia Collingwood hung up with a good feeling.

Chapter 61

◆◆◆

Sylvia's next call was to Jason Litchford, Carl's corporate attorney. After exchanging pleasantries with the receptionist in Jason's firm, she was put through.

"Sylvia, it is so nice of you to call. I've been following your husband's travails in the news. If there is anything I can do—"

"Yes, Jason, as a matter of fact, there is." Sylvia's voice revealed the stress and urgency of her quest. "I need to find an attorney for Carl and Bruce. I want to get the very best, you understand. They will only have one chance to defend themselves. If they lose, they may spend the rest of their lives in jail."

"Have you contacted Bill Lawson?" Bill was the attorney who had represented Hummingbird Aircraft in its civil action against Transport.

"No, not yet. I thought I'd call you first. You've been representing us from the very beginning when Carl started his company."

"Well, to tell the truth, nothing occurs to me, Sylvia. I'm not too well connected with the criminal bar."

"It was you who referred us to Bill, remember? He did a wonderful job, until that juror Betty." Sylvia choked on her words in mid-sentence and could not continue.

Jason quickly picked up the thread to spare her embarrassment. "I know. Bill did an amazing job and he should have won. I'll never forget the shock when the jury came back and found for the defendant."

"It was horrible, Jason. I can't tell you."

"Have you heard from Bill since then?"

"Not really. It's not for his lack of trying. When we lost the case, Carl, Bruce and I just couldn't handle it. We closed our doors and shut ourselves off. We didn't – couldn't – talk to anyone. "

"Maybe its time to give him a call. I'm sure he'd like to hear from you."

"I will, Jason. Thank you for all you've done."

"I've done nothing. I'm just sorry I don't know the right person to refer you to."

"That's all right. Maybe Bill does."

Sylvia hung up, took a breath, and dialed Bill's number. After all this time she still knew the number by heart.

"Uh, hello? This is Sylvia Collingwood calling. May I please speak with Bill Lawson?"

"Oh, yes! Just a moment, Mrs. Collingwood. I'll put you right through."

Bill's gravelly voice reverberated though the receiver. "Oh, my goodness! Sylvia how *are* you?"

"I'm okay. It's been a bit tough, you know."

"I can only imagine. I'm so sorry."

"Don't be. You did your best. It wasn't your fault."

"I still feel responsible. I didn't see it coming."

"Who could?"

"Those *bastards*!"

"I know."

"I understand there will be a trial."

"That's why I'm calling. They need representation."

"You don't have anyone?"

"No."

"You'll want the absolute best."

"I know. I just thought—"

"I don't do criminal defense."

"I'm not asking."

"You want a referral?"

"Yes, if you can help me."

"I'm not sure I know the right guy. I don't travel in those circles."

"What do you mean?"

"I mean, these guys are kind of special. They are nationally known."

"You can't recommend—"

"No. I mean I read the newspapers. Some of their names are household words. But I don't know them. I've never met them in court. I can't really vouch for their legal skills."

"So what should I do? Call them up?"

"You can try but I don't think they'll speak to you. You have got to have an awfully deep pocket."

"I'm determined."

"I know you are."

"I'm going to try."

"Well, then, I suggest you find out who represents the big corporate criminals. Like the guy who represents Mike Snead."

Chapter 62

———◆◆◆◆———

MIKE SNEAD SAT glumly at the conference table, facing Assistant District Attorney Andrew Rosin.

A bearded attorney, Burt Crowe, sat next to Snead and berated Rosin for wasting his client's time. "I will not have my client harassed like this. He's not answering any more questions."

"You're advising him to take the Fifth?"

"No, I'm informing *you* I'll go to a judge and get an order protecting my client from this chicken shit. Mike has been fully cooperative until now, but there has to be an end to this crap."

"Spare me the smoke screen. We've got enough for a grand jury already. You want to help your client, you'll play nice-nice."

"Go for it. I'll call your bluff."

"We have the complete money trail. We have Betty Falmouth. She'll spill."

"You don't have *mens rea*. You can't connect the dots."

"We will."

"This meeting is *over*." Burt Crowe stuffed papers in his briefcase, closed it and stood up. Rosin and Snead stood up, too, and eyeballed each other.

"Have a good day," Snead said, bowing slightly, and followed his counselor out of the room.

Outside, a glut of reporters rushed forward and shoved microphones in front of Snead and Crowe. Cameras flashed and two television cameras went live, their signal lights glowing red. Juli Gables was among the reporters, with her microphone tethered to George's videocam.

"We've got nothing to say," Crowe said cordially, with a smile on his face. "Why don't you boys and girls just go home and take care of business."

"This *is* our business. Were you under oath in there, Mr. Snead?" Juli called out.

"I'm sorry, kids," Crowe intervened. "My client has no comment on that today."

"Mr. Crowe, will there be a grand jury?" another reporter shouted.

"Ask Mr. Rosin. He hasn't asked for one for some reason. Maybe he knows my client is innocent. Now, if you'll excuse us, we have to go. Mr. Snead is in an amateur theater production and it's time to rehearse."

Instead of diffusing the reporter's enthusiasm, this news had just the opposite effect.

"Mr. Snead! Mr. Snead! Are you an actor?"

"I almost took up an acting career when I was younger. I loved the theater. Shakespeare especially. Now I just fill in for fun."

"What's the play?"

"*The Tempest*, at the Little Theater here in New York. I invite you all to come and see it. We open tomorrow night."

"What role do you play?"

"I'm *Prospero*. Now we really must go. I've got to get to the dress rehearsal."

Crowe and Snead moved off as the cameras panned, following them as they walked down the corridor in Federal Building. Sylvia watched the images on TV in her cramped home office. She saw her husband's nemesis smile at the cameras and engage the reporters like a Hollywood celebrity. She also recognized Juli as the girl who had done the most to expose Snead for the fraud that he was. Then in a last desperate attempt to find representation for her two men, she lifted the phone and placed a call.

"Channel 8 News. How may I direct your call?" Ariana said, automatically.

"Yes, I'd like to leave a message for Ms. Julianne Gables."

"I'm very sorry, she doesn't work here any more."

"Do you know how I may get in touch with her? "

"Who is calling?"

"I'm Sylvia Collingwood."

"Are you related to Carl Collingwood and Bruce Collingwood?"

"Yes, I'm Carl's wife and Bruce's mother."

"Omigod! Please hold the line. I'm sure that Juli would like to speak with you. If you wait just a minute I'll try to patch you in."

"Thank you!"

"It's the least I could do, Mrs. Collingwood. I'm so sorry about what happened. Hopefully, we can, thank goodness! Juli's answering her cell."

Juli's voice came on the line. "Hello?"

"Juli, it's me, Ariana. I have Mrs. Collingwood on the line. You know—

Carl Collingwood's wife?"

"Really? Mrs. Collingwood? She wants to speak to me?"

"Go ahead, Mrs. Collingwood."

"Ms. Gables, it is an honor to speak to you."

"The honor is mine, Mrs. Collingwood. You have been through so much. I've been meaning to contact you, but I thought it might be intrusive and—"

"If you could help me—"

"Anything. Just ask."

"I desperately need an attorney for my husband and my son for their their *criminal* trial." Tears of desperation and sadness came flooding forward. Sylvia wiped her eyes with the back of her hand and could say no more.

"Mrs. Collingwood, I don't know much about these things, but I promise you: I'll research it and put you in contact with the very best criminal lawyer in this country within twenty-four hours. You can rely on me."

Sylvia left her number with Juli, placed the receiver carefully on the hook, and then wearily lowered her head. With her hands in her face, she wept quietly.

Chapter 63

Juli looked at George. "I promised to get Mrs. Collingwood the best lawyer in the country," Juli blurted out, "and I have no idea how to go about it."

"Call Deep Voice?"

Juli brightened. "George, you're brilliant!" She dialed Shelley's number and put the cell phone to her ear. As usual Shelley didn't answer but Juli left a message for him to call. He rang back within seconds.

"Hello, Juli," came the familiar deep voice.

"I need another favor," Juli began meekly. She filled Shelley in.

"I do believe I can help you. There is one man who I consider to be the best at his craft, at the top of his game. The man *I* would hire if I were in trouble with the law. His name is Derek Taliz."

The name was vaguely familiar to Juli. She recalled that Taliz had defended a Senator from California in some kind of bribery scandal. She listened intently.

"The trouble is, he's outrageously expensive. He charges $1,000 an hour for himself. His associates get $500."

"She can't afford that."

"Who can? I'll contact him for you and see what we can do."

Within an hour, Sylvia Collingwood's phone rang.

"Mrs. Collingwood? I'm Derek Taliz. Juli Gables suggested I call."

"Do you know my situation?"

"Yes. Juli and the people at Transport International filled me in. I also spoke to Mike Snead's lawyer, Burt Crowe. We've crossed swords a few times in the past." Taliz waited for a response, but when none came, he continued. "If you wish, I can defend your husband and son."

"I wish you could, but I may not be able to afford—"

"My charges have been taken care of."

"What?"

"If I represent your family's interests, someone else will pay my fees."

"Who?"

"I'm not at liberty to say. As a matter of fact, the fee arrangement has to be held in strictest confidence."

"Oh. Why are they doing this, whoever they are?"

"Mrs. Collingwood, your family has been through enough hardship. The wrongs that have been done to you have to be made right."

Chapter 64

⸻ ◆❖◆ ⸻

MIKE SNEAD COULDN'T remember an opening night he had anticipated as much as this one. The audience was packed with friends, executives from his own company, executives from other major corporations, reporters who were following the Collingwood case, and even theater critics from the New York newspapers.

Mike had started this theater project some months before, when his attorney, Burt Crowe, suggested he do something to soften his public image. They had discussed different possibilities at length. Mike suggested starting a charitable foundation, like Bill Gates had done, but Burt thought such an activity, just at this time, would be viewed as a blatant and transparent attempt to curry favor with the public, which of course it was.

Eventually, Mike and Burt gave up trying to change "Mike the Malevolent" into something else, something he wasn't. As acting had been his outlet and his passion ever since those formative years in high school, Mike tried out for a part in *The Tempest* and impressed the play's director so much with his ability to "do Shakespeare" that he landed the lead. Mike surprised even himself that his talent was still there after all those intervening years.

Mike Snead was a natural for this part. It fit his own personality so precisely that the words rolled off his tongue with a conviction rarely seen in the theater. The audience vacuumed up every nuance.

In his last act soliloquy, Prospero having achieved redemption, he was at his absolute best.

Unless I be relieved by prayer,
Which pierces so, that it assaults
Mercy itself, and frees all faults.
As you from crimes would pardon'd be,
Let your indulgence set me free.

Snead exited the stage to thunderous applause. When he took his bows, the audience wouldn't stop shouting and clapping in their enthusiasm. In a word, his performance was a triumph. Mike the Malevolent had morphed into Mike the Marvelous.

Chapter 65

◆━◆━◆

SHELLEY WAS ON the phone when the intercom buzzed. He put his caller on hold and responded to the buzz. "This is Shelley – Oh yes. Please send him up."

Shelley wound up his call, then got out of his chair and walked over to Mike Snead's office. "Dr. Schuffenecker is here."

"What'd you say his first name was?"

"Emil."

"I like that name. Bring him in when he comes."

"Have you decided what you are going to discuss with him?"

"Yes, I have."

"Well?"

"Well, what?"

"What's our position?"

"I think you'll be pleasantly surprised."

"That's it?"

"You'll know in a moment. Here he is—" Snead nodded to Shelley to turn around.

There stood Dr. Emil Schuffenecker in the reception area. Shelley politely waved him in to Mike Snead's office. Snead came forward to greet Dr. Schuffenecker warmly with an outstretched hand.

"Dr. Schnuff – er – can I call you Emil?"

"Certainly, sir. Everyone does."

"Won't you have a seat?" Snead motioned toward a comfortable sitting area in his office by the window.

"Wow! The view is *great!*" Schuffenecker said, glancing out as he took his seat.

"I know. We're on top of the world." Snead acknowledged. "Can we offer you some coffee? Soda?"

"Coffee would be very nice."

"Cream and sugar?" Shelley asked, ready to *gofer* coffee.

"Both. I like it sweet."

"Shelley, I'll have a cup too. Make it sweet. Same as Emil," Snead added.

When the coffee was served, all three men sat comfortably and sipped.

"Now, Emil. Let's get down to business," Snead began. "I understand there may be a problem with our walkie-talkies."

"That's an understatement, Mr. Snead. If what I think is true, people may die from an overexposure to radiation."

"We read your report. It is alarming."

"What are you prepared to do?"

"First of all, Emil. Would you tell me who knows about this?"

"What do you mean?"

"Who did the study?"

"I did."

"And who has been copied on the report?"

"No one, yet. It's only a preliminary report. A draft. I sent it to your attention as a courtesy. I wanted to give you the opportunity to respond before it was circulated."

"Oh, well, thank you. We're a big outfit but, even so, this radio has represented a significant business for us. It's on the radar."

"I've seen the numbers—"

"It's a big profit center, and it will be a shame to kill it."

"You intend to stop production?"

"Of course," Snead replied firmly. Shelley did a double-take and stared at Snead, wide-eyed.

"How about the ones in the field?"

"We'll recall them and fix them."

Shelley couldn't believe his eyes and ears.

"Mr. Snead, I want to tell you that you have restored my faith in big business."

"How so?"

"It seems you intend to do correct the situation."

"Trust me, we'll make this right."

Shelley was squirming. He could hardly contain himself, but said nothing.

"Well, I never would have guessed it. I came here expecting a completely different reaction from you."

"I hope I didn't disappoint."

"Not at all. In fact, I have a surprise for you. I'm really not Emil Schuffenecker."

"*What?*"

"Yes, that guy is just a fiction. I'm Agent John Marshall from the F.B.I. and I came here to get evidence that you would try to bribe a government official. See—" Agent Marshall began to unbutton his shirt. "I'm wearing a *wire.*"

"Why, you *son-of-a-bitch!*"

"You look upset."

"I don't exactly *like* being spied upon."

"There's nothing to be concerned about. You did the *right thing!*"

"What if I didn't?"

"The government may be slow, but we eventually catch the crooks."

"It's comforting to know that you guys are out there. And while you're at it, could you look into my friend Shelley here? I think he's cheating on his taxes."

Shelley froze. Agent Marshall looked at him suspiciously.

"Ha, ha. I'm just pulling your chain! "

Shelley gave a huge sigh of relief. "You had me there, Mr. Snead. For a moment there I thought I was going to get *caught.*"

Marshall smiled at Shelley's joke and stood up. "Well, gentlemen. I've done my job, so I'll get going. I see this company is in good hands."

"We wouldn't have it any other way," Shelley said as he led the Agent out.

—◆‹◆›◆—

Chapter 66

DEREK TALIZ KNEW that changing the venue to find jurors who knew nothing about Collingwood was not in the realm of possibility, nor did he really want to change the venue. The Federal Courthouse in White Plains, in the center of wealthy, sophisticated Westchester County, was just fine with him. Jurors tended to be educated and even somewhat knowledgeable about the judicial system.

Derek was hoping for some upwardly mobile suburban housewives who could relate to the Collingwoods' plight – especially that of Sylvia Collingwood, who stayed at home and watched a big evil corporation dash her husband's dreams. That is, if he could get the entire sad Collingwood story admitted into evidence. The prosecutor, Andy Rosin, would do his best to keep it out.

Also, Derek knew the scales of justice were weighted in the prosecution's favor. Even without considering the clearly undisputed facts in this case, some of which were shown on television news for all to see, a jury had a tendency to believe the defendants in a criminal trial were guilty. Otherwise why would the State have wasted its valuable time and money in presenting the case?

In order to get a conviction, however, the prosecuting attorney would have to obtain a unanimous verdict from the jury. One holdout would result in a mistrial.

Conversely, in order to achieve an acquittal—one that would completely and finally relieve the defendants from jeopardy—Derek would need a unanimous jury too: unanimous, that is, for acquittal. This result, he knew, was unlikely. The best he could reasonably hope for was a mistrial that presented such difficulty for the prosecutor that he would hesitate to prosecute again. At least then Derek might stand a chance to make a deal for his clients.

Derek was sizing up and getting used to working with the judge during pretrial, and he liked what he saw. Judge Helen McMann was both even-tempered and even-handed, a good combination for the "good guys" side. However, there was one critical motion Rosin had filed, a Motion to Exclude Testimony of certain people on Derek's witness list, that Derek felt he *had* to win, and he lost. He was unable to convince Judge McMann that the testimony of the kidnapping victim himself, Mike Snead, would be sufficiently relevant to outweigh the negative influence on the jury of the backstory that motivated the crime.

The judge's language was not entirely dismissive. She wrote:

Normally the testimony of the victim of a crime is a necessary component of the prosecution's proof of the elements of the crime. In this case, however, the defendants *have asked to take the testimony of the victim to show justifiable and exculpatory reasons for the defendants' actions. However, without some offer of proof that Mr. Snead's testimony, as to facts which occurred* prior to *the crime, may establish legal justification, I find the marginal relevance of such testimony would be outweighed by its clearly prejudicial effect on the jury.*

Getting this testimony in was going to be an uphill battle.

The *voir dir* took an entire week. When interviewed, out of thirteen jurors, twelve panelists and one alternate, only two had never heard of the Collingwood case. The remaining jurors were able to convince both the prosecution and the defense that they would be unbiased, and would make their determination based only on the evidence presented in open court.

Derek got his wish, sort of, that some of the jurors would be suburban housewives. Four of the jurors were homemakers, while three women worked outside the home. Two of the working women were Hispanic and the other was Caucasian. One of the homemakers was African-American, the wife of a successful African-American businessman who had come from a welfare family. The others were men who held various positions in government and private industry. One of the men was the owner of a small company in Elmsford that developed computer software.

On the day of the trial, Sylvia took the commuter train from Wassaic – the same morning train her husband and son had hijacked— and got off at White Plains. She had declined Derek's offer to pick her up at the station and she walked the four long blocks to the Federal Courthouse. After passing through security in the lobby, she made her way to Judge McMann's courtroom on the fourth floor.

Arriving early she was assured of a seat in the spectator's gallery. Within minutes, however, the gallery filled up with reporters and other interested members of the public. Eventually security blocked the door to the courtroom and refused to let any other spectators in.

Andy and Derek passed through security and took their places at the counsel tables, Andy on the right and Derek on the left. Two uniformed officers led Carl and Bruce Collingwood in through a side door. They took their seats next to Derek at the defense counsel table.

"All rise," called out the bailiff, and Judge Helen McMann entered the courtroom from a door in the rear. She took her seat at the bench, surveyed the assembled audience and, apparently satisfied with the decorum, said, "Please be seated."

The bailiff announced the proceedings. "The People versus Carl Collingwood and Bruce Collingwood."

The trial was on.

Chapter 67

<hr/>

Judge McMann looked squarely at Andy. "Counselor, you may present your opening statement."

"Ladies and gentlemen of the jury," Andy addressed his audience with decorum. "The defendants, Carl Collingwood and his son, Bruce Collingwood, stand accused of hijacking a train at gunpoint, and also holding one of its passengers, Mr. Michael Snead, hostage on that train. The facts are not in dispute."

Andy went on to describe the hijacking and kidnapping in some detail and then concluded: "During this trial we will present live testimony, and we will show you videos taken contemporaneously with the hijacking, that will convince you, without a shadow of doubt, that these facts are true. You will *know* that the defendants deliberately planned, and carried out their plan, to commandeer the train that Mr. Snead would take that Monday morning. Instead of allowing Mr. Snead to travel to New York City, his desired destination, they delivered him, against his will, to Washington, D.C."

Andy bowed politely to the members of the jury, and returned to his seat.

Derek Taliz remained in his chair and surveyed the jury.

"Mr. Taliz," urged the judge, somewhat impatiently. "You may proceed."

Derek carefully raised his large frame from his seat and walked slowly toward the jury box, his head cocked, thinking as he walked.

Derek was dressed in dark blue slacks and a Harris tweed jacket. He wore a pink tie and had a matching pink handkerchief poking up from his left lapel. Derek's speckled gray-white beard seemed to match his jacket.

Derek stopped in front of the jury box and surveyed its members. He looked at them, each juror in turn, giving them due respect and acknowledging their importance, and then commenced his opening statement.

"Ladies and Gentlemen, it is your role, and your duty as jurors, to seek the *truth* of what happened on that Monday morning. By the *truth*, I mean not just the facts that, I'm sure, the prosecution will ably present, but also the *reasons* for these facts.

"The *truth* about this case includes *two things*: the *actions* of the defendants and the *thoughts* of the defendants on the day in question.

"In order for you to understand the defendants' thoughts, we are going to take you back to an earlier time to find out what motivated the defendants to take the actions we will be considering at this trial. You will learn that the defendants were, and are, law-abiding citizens. You will learn that one of the defendants had a dream, an invention, which he pursued with passion and determination – but that his dream was squashed like a bug—" Derek pressed his right thumb into the palm of left hand for effect. "Squashed and extinguished by one man, 'Mike the Malevolent' Snead, who was and is president and CEO of Transport International.

"You will learn that the defendants sued Transport International to recover the intellectual property rights that were unjustly taken from them. They used the justice system that the founders of our nation established just for this purpose, to right the wrongs done to them. But the justice system failed them. It failed them miserably.

"Through their actions, the defendants didn't mean to harm anyone. And in fact they *didn't* harm anyone. They may have inconvenienced a few people on their way to work. They surely inconvenienced an engineer by taking him to Washington, D.C., instead of New York City." Derek smiled briefly to show he meant that last line to be funny, and paused to allow the titters in the courtroom to die down. Then his countenance became serious.

"But there was one man that they intended – truly intended—to inconvenience—and that was Mr. Michael Snead. They took him to Washington to face a Congressional hearing on corporate corruption."

Derek paused again to let the word *corruption* sink in and then concluded his remarks.

"Ladies and gentlemen of the jury, I ask you—the defendants ask you – to withhold judgment in your mind until *all* of the evidence is presented. The prosecutor will present some of the facts; I will present the *complete truth*."

The courtroom was quiet as Derek returned to the defense table and took his seat.

Chapter 68

———◆◆◆———

"PLEASE CALL YOUR first witness." Judge McMann directed her request to Andy Rosin.

Andy slowly got to his feet and, without leaving his position, announced: "The prosecution calls Philip Davis to the witness stand."

Phil Davis, who was sitting in the middle of one of the benches in the gallery, excused himself as he stepped gingerly over and in front of people's feet to reach the aisle. He made his way confidently down the aisle to the bar separating the gallery from the heart of the courtroom. Finally, pushing open the railing at the bar and entering the *inner sanctum*, he just stood there, looking at Andy with a smile on his face.

"Would you please take your seat *here?*" suggested the Judge, pointing to the witness box while trying not to reveal her exasperation.

Phil climbed up behind the small desk in the elevated witness box, looked around the courtroom for effect, and sat down.

"Would the witness please stand," called the bailiff.

Phil stood up again and, finally, paid attention.

"Raise your right hand."

Ever so briefly, Phil had to ponder a moment to select his right hand from his left. He raised his right.

"Do you swear to tell the truth, the whole truth and nothing but the truth?"

"Yes, I do."

"You may be seated."

Andy stepped forward to address him. "Mr. Davis, could you please state your full name and address for the record?"

"Philip W. Davis. I live at…" Phil stopped. "Do I have to say where I live?"

"It's not really necessary, I don't think. It's just a formality."

"Then I'd rather not. There are a lot of kooks out there, you know what I mean?"

"I'm sure they can find you if they try hard enough. Are you a U.S. citizen?"

"Yes."

"That will do. Uncle Sam knows where you live. What is your occupation, Mr. Davis?"

"I'm a train dispatcher for Metro-North Railroad."

"Just generally, could you describe what a train dispatcher does?"

"My job basically is to allocate tracks for the trains that run in and out of Grand Central Station. I control the tracks and the trains that run on the tracks."

"Do you respond to emergencies?"

"All the time. Power outages, storms, fires, train collisions, medical emergencies; and even suicides on occasion. People jumping in front of trains, whatever."

"How long have you had this job?"

"About five years now."

"In all of that time, have you ever known a train to be commandeered by someone?"

"No, I haven't. Oh, excuse me. Yes, just once. A year ago last October."

"We'll get to that in a moment. Were you trained for this position you hold?"

"Yes. There is a lengthy training period and then a period of apprenticeship."

"During your training period, was there ever any mention of the possibility that a train might be hijacked?"

"Yes."

"There was? You mean you were trained in some way to respond to this type of emergency?"

"Yes."

"What were you supposed to do if a train was hijacked?"

"You're to do whatever the hijackers want, and then you call the cops."

A slight twitter of laughter could be heard in the courtroom.

"Now did there come a time that a train was hijacked during your watch?"

"Yes."

"Could you tell us about it?"

"Well I got a call from one of our engineers. His name's Jack. He was calling in from the first morning train from Wassaic. Said there was some kind of a problem."

"Did he say what the problem was?"

"Yes. Code 99."

"Code 99? What's that?"

"That's our highest level of alert. Someone is holding a gun on railroad personnel or, God forbid, a passenger."

"You mean you even have a special code for this emergency?"

"That's right. Though nobody used it on my watch before and I almost forgot what it meant."

"What was your reaction when you heard it?"

"I thought it was a joke."

"A joke?"

"Yeah, you know, like I was being punked."

"Okay, so what happened next?"

"The engineer – Jack – gave the phone to one of the hijackers and he told me he had a gun. He said he'd shoot Jack unless I did what he said."

"Did you realize then it wasn't a joke?"

"Not right away. I thought it might be a training exercise, especially when the hijacker told me what he wanted."

"What was that?"

"It was a crazy request. He said he wanted the train switched through to Washington, D.C."

"What did you do?"

"I gave the hijacker some static. I told him I couldn't do that."

"Wasn't that exactly contrary to your training? Weren't you to 'do whatever the hijacker wants and call the cops?'"

"I know, I know. I just didn't figure."

"But then you realized the engineer's life was in danger."

"Yes. At least I *thought* so."

"So what did you do then?"

"I followed the rule. I did what the hijacker wanted me to, and I called the cops."

Having set the stage, Andy thanked the witness and looked up at the judge. She didn't appear to have any questions herself so he turned around, gave a little bow to the defense and announced, "I have no further questions."

Derek rose slowly from his chair, then stepped out from behind the defense table and walked pensively toward the witness.

"Mr. Davis," he began. "What were your hours of duty on the day when all of this transpired?"

"I was on the morning shift from six AM till noon."

"Did you indeed switch the train through to Washington, D.C.?"

"No. I just handle the Metro-North trains. Once the train was switched onto an Amtrak line, it was out of my jurisdiction."

"Do you know if the train ever made it to Washington?"

"Objection!" shouted Andy. "Hearsay."

Derek backtracked without being told. "Did you ever receive any reports of harm – physical harm – to anyone on the train?"

"No, I didn't."

"What happened to all the passengers on the train?"

"Objection!"

"Sustained," replied the judge.

"I'll rephrase the question: Did you order the passengers off the train at any time prior to its destination?"

"Yes."

"Where?"

"I ordered the train to stop at the Southeast station and to discharge its passengers."

"What did the passengers do then?"

"Objection."

"I'll allow it." Judge McMann was trying to be fair to both sides.

"They took the next train into the City."

"So they weren't inconvenienced very much?"

"Objection. How would he know their state of mind? "

"Sustained. Mr. Taliz, ask proper questions, if you please. I know you can do it."

"When did the next train at Southeast leave for the City?"

"About five minutes later."

"No further questions, your Honor."

"Redirect, Mr. Rosin?" Judge McMann looked at him quizzically.

"No, your Honor."

"Then, Mr. Davis, you may step down," the judge offered politely. "We are sorry to take you away from your interesting work for a day."

"May I add something, your Honor?"

"I am not sure. That depends on what you have to say."

"I just want to say that—"

"Objection!" Andy cut him off.

"But he is your own witness, Mr. Rosin."

"This is highly unorthodox, your Honor. There is no telling whether Mr. Davis will say something prejudicial or just plan contrary to the rules of evidence."

"Mr. Taliz? What do you say?"

"I'll roll the dice."

"You have no idea what Mr. Davis will say?"

"No idea."

"Then let's allow it and see what happens." Judge McMann said definitively. "Mr. Davis, you may continue."

"I just wanted to say that there was one person left on the train whose commute was interrupted."

"And who was that?"

"Mr. Michael Snead, your Honor."

Chapter 69

"I WOULD LIKE to call John Springer," Andy announced and, as if by magic, a thin, wiry man with a leathery face appeared at the gate of the bar. Andy held the gate open and motioned for him to take his place on the witness stand.

Jack faced the room somewhat self-consciously, waiting for someone to tell him what to do next.

"Raise your right hand…" The bailiff went through the ritual and told Jack to be seated.

"Mr. Springer, what is your full name and occupation?"

"My name's John C. Springer. I work for Metro-North as a train engineer," Jack answered respectfully.

"Mr. Springer—"

"Call me *Jack*. Everyone does. Most people don't even know my last name."

"Not John?"

"No, Sir. Just *Jack*."

"All right, Jack. What does a train engineer do?"

"The official title is 'Senior Train Operator.' I drive a train."

"How long have you worked for Metro-North?"

"Going on twenty-five years now."

"As a train engineer?"

"Nope. I worked my way up. Started in the yard as a junior mechanic, fixing locomotives."

"How long have you been an engineer?"

"About eighteen years, give or take."

"In these eighteen years, have you ever been threatened by any passenger… strike that. Have you ever been placed in fear of your life by someone other than a Metro-North employee?"

"Someone…like my wife?"

Until now so quiet one could hear a pin drop, the gallery nearly exploded in laughter.

"No, I mean on the job."

"Well, let me think… sure, lots of times."

"Really? You were in fear of your life?"

"Depends on what you mean by 'fear'. You mean like someone driving across the tracks in front of the train? Happens all the time."

"No, I mean at gunpoint."

"Well, that, yeah, only once. Last year."

"Can you tell us about that?"

"Sure. Guy comes up behind me while I'm on the morning run from Wassaic to the City. I didn't notice him 'cuz I was paying attention to the signals and such. Anyway, he scared the bejesus out of me. At first I thought I was a goner. But then he explained that he didn't want to hurt me. Just take the train to Washington, he says."

"What did you do then?"

"I took the train to Washington. The Diesel engine at least. No, it was a different engine, come to think of it. We switched engines in Metropark, in Jersey."

"Why did you do that?"

"Because of the fighting with the F.B.I. agent. It broke the front window on the first engine."

"I see. You didn't feel threatened by the fighting?"

"Not really. The F.B.I. guy scared me more than the guy with the gun. I could see he was pissed. I could have caught a stray bullet."

"Let's go back to the beginning. What happened when you first realized there was man with a gun?"

"He asked me to call the dispatcher."

"Who was this man? Did he tell you his name?"

"Not at first. Later I learned his name was Bruce somebody."

"Do you recognize him in this courtroom?"

"Yes. He's right over there." Jack pointed at the dejected-looking young man sitting at the defense-counsel table.

"Let the record show that Mr. Springer pointed to the defendant Bruce Collingwood. Now, Jack, did you do what you were told? Call the dispatcher?"

"Yes, of course."

"Who did you speak to?"

"Phil."

"Do you know his last name?"

"No. To me he's just *Phil.*"

"All right. What did you tell Phil?"

"I told him I needed to stop the train at Southeast and let all the passengers off. Said there was a serious problem with the engine."

"Did Phil let you do that?"

"Yup. That's what we did."

"Then what happened?"

"Then this Bruce told me we were going to Washington."

"Did he say why?"

"No, but later I found out we were carrying this high-level exec to Washington to testify. He didn't get off the train with the other passengers."

"Why not?"

"Objection!" Derek, who appeared to be bored with the testimony, didn't even rise from his seat. "Did he use mental telepathy?"

"Sustained."

Andy began anew. "Did there come a time when this high-level executive entered the locomotive?"

"Yeah, he did."

"Did anyone else enter the locomotive with him?"

"Yeah, another guy held a gun on him while Bruce tied him up."

"This other guy, do you see him in this courtroom?"

"Yeah, he's sitting right there." Jacked pointed to Carl.

"Let the record reflect that Mr. Springer identified the defendant Carl Collingwood."

"That will be all for now, Jack. Your witness, Mr. Taliz." Andy returned to his seat with a smug look on his face.

Derek stood and approached the witness with a kindly smile. "I'll bet," he began, "that was a very harrowing experience for you."

"Yeah, it was quite a day. Harrowing is maybe not the right word."

"Oh? How else would you characterize it?"

"Kind of, uh...*exciting.* Sure beat the boring routine run to the City."

"You just testified that you weren't scared, except when you first became aware of the defendant Bruce Collingwood. Is that correct?"

"Yes, Sir."

"Why is that?"

"I dunno. Because of what Bruce said. And because I could tell he wasn't a bad guy."

"Can you elaborate?"

"Well, over the years you get to be a pretty good judge of character. I could just tell that Bruce was okay. That other guy was too. I think he said he was Bruce's father."

"Let me try to understand this. These two men, who are now sitting there at the defendant's table, held you up at gunpoint and made you drive a locomotive 300 miles out of your way and you say they are 'good guys?'"

"Objection! The witness didn't say they were 'good guys'. Just 'okay!'" Andy was taking a chance on this and he knew it.

"Were they 'good guys?'"

"Yes, I would say so. It's the other guy – that big shot they were taking to Washington – who was a snot."

Andy sat glumly in his seat.

"This other guy, the 'big shot'. Do you know his name?"

"Yeah. Mike Snead."

"He was a snot, you say?"

"Yeah, he was."

"How so?"

"He was...well, *angry.* You could tell he was used to getting his own way."

"No further questions."

For a moment there was silence in the courtroom as Andy sat

there, thinking of what to do next. He wanted to blunt the effect of the witness's testimony, but he certainly didn't want to make the situation worse. He decided to give it a try, even though he didn't know what the witness was likely to say. This was a basic mistake that a seasoned trial attorney learns from experience to avoid.

Andy rose and said. "I'd like to ask a few follow-up questions, Jack."

Judge McMann nodded to Andy with an amused look on her face.

"Sure." Jack sat back in his chair, appearing almost relaxed.

"You testified that Mr. Snead was angry. Is that right?"

"Yeah, he was."

"You also testified that he was held at gunpoint, tied up and taken to Washington against his will, when all he wanted to do was go to New York City on the commuter train. Isn't that right?"

"Yup. That's true."

"Then don't you think he had a *right* to be angry?"

"Sure I guess so. But—"

"That's all, Jack. Thank you, you may step down."

"But—" Jack just sat there wanting to finish the sentence.

"You answered the question. It was a 'yes or no' and you answered 'yes'. You may step down now."

"But there's more—"

"Your Honor, the question has been asked and answered. It is time to move on," Andy urged Judge McMann.

"Let him finish," she responded.

Everyone in the courtroom looked at the witness, expectantly. He didn't disappoint.

"From what I hear," Jack said, "the guy had it coming."

Chapter 70

——————◆◆◆——————

ANDY ROSIN FACED a dilemma: Who should he call next to testify about the basic facts of the crimes charged against the defendants? He needed to prove that Mike Snead was kidnapped and held hostage against his will and that the defendants resisted the efforts of the police to end the hijacking and to free the hostages. Besides the two defendants and Jack, the engineer, there were four other people on the locomotive: Mike Snead, David Price, Julianne Gables and her cameraman, George.

Andy had viewed the video footage George took while on board the locomotive several times. While it clearly confirmed that a crime was being committed, it could also be taken as exculpatory. More than anything, the video would garner sympathy from the jury for the defendant Carl's alleged mistreatment by Mike Snead and his company, Transport International. If at all possible, Andy had to keep this information from reaching the jury.

If he allowed even the tiniest *hint* of this backstory to sneak through, Andy was in danger of losing his right to object on the grounds that the defendants' *reasons* for the hijacking and kidnapping were wholly irrelevant to their guilt or innocence. In fact, if Mike Snead's prior actions became an issue at all, they would open the door for the defense to elicit full testimony on the subject.

In view of the last comment Jack made about Mike – that he "had it coming" - Andy decided that Mike would go next on the witness stand to nip this "character thing" in the bud. He wanted the jury to take with them to the jury room the idea that Mike was an unfortunate victim of the defendants' crimes.

Therefore, at nine the next morning, just after Judge McMann called the court to order, Andy dramatically announced that Mike would now testify. Although the jury had been cautioned not to read the newspapers or watch the news on television, they would surely realize that this witness promised to be the highpoint of the trial. The media had indeed been full of anticipation and speculation about Mike's appearance in the courtroom. How would the mighty chief executive of Transport International comport himself? Would he seek vengeance for the ordeal he had endured at the hands of the defendants? The humiliation he had suffered? Would he pretend to be unbowed and take the high road?

"The prosecution calls Michael Snead, the Chief Executive Officer of Transport International."

All eyes turned toward the back of the courtroom. The gallery was packed with members of the fourth estate and the few trial fans who had arrived very early and managed to snatch an available seat.

Not one of the persons in the gallery stood up to come forward.

Andy stood there a moment, staring hopelessly for some sign of his famous witness who had promised to be on hand for the opening session. He reached in his pocket for his cell phone, but just then the double door in the rear of the courtroom swung open and Mike Snead made his entrance.

He wore a pinstriped charcoal black suit and a white shirt with French cuffs and gold cufflinks. A navy blue regimental tie and matching pocket kerchief contributed to and accented his sophisticated appearance. Clearly this was a man, dressed for success, who confidently filled the role of world-class executive.

Andy breathed a silent sigh of relief and invited Mike to come forward. Unlike the previous two witnesses, Mike knew where to go.

When he took the witness stand, the bailiff swore him in and then nodded to Andy. Andy took the cue and began.

"Mr. Snead, please state your name and residence address for the record."

"Michael H. Snead. 29 Willow Lane, Millbrook, New York."

"What is your present occupation?"

"I am President and Chief Executive Officer of Transport International, Inc." Mike's answers were short and snappy, but not without warmth. He smiled slightly as he provided the information.

"How long have you held this position?"

"For about twelve years now."

Gag me with a spoon! thought Derek, sitting at the defense table between Carl and Bruce. He's just too sanctimonious. I'll have to prick his balloon.

"In your position as CEO of Transport International, where do you usually work?" Andy continued.

"I have an office in New York City. It's the World Headquarters of TI."

"And where is that? What is the address?"

"300 Park Avenue. It's walking distance from Grand Central."

"Do you commute each day from Millbrook to New York City?"

"Oh, no. I come in to the city on Monday mornings and stay until Friday. I have an apartment there. Then on Friday evenings I commute back out to my farm in Millbrook."

"Is that pretty regular? Do you take the train almost every Monday morning?"

"Most of the time, unless I'm traveling on business or I'm on vacation."

"Do you recall a particular Monday morning when the train didn't take you to the City?"

"Certainly."

"Would you please tell us about it, Mr. Snead?"

"I'd be happy to. It was quite a train ride. The excitement started soon after we left my station. A man with a duffel bag walked by and sat down in the empty seat next to me. I was working on my laptop and didn't think anything of it at first but then, within ten minutes or so, there was an announcement that everyone should get off at the next station. Just as I was about to stand up and leave the train, this man, Carl Collingwood, pulled out a gun and told me to stay. After all the other passengers on the car got off, he forced me at gunpoint to go to the restroom and we stayed there until the train started moving again."

"Why do you think he did that?"

"Objection." Derek stood up this time to address the judge.

"Sustained. Go on, Mr. Rosin."

"Could you point out the man you said held you at gunpoint? Is he in this courtroom?"

"Yes, of course. He is sitting right over there."

"Let the record reflect that Mr. Snead pointed to Carl Collingwood, one of the defendants. What happened next, Mr. Snead?"

"Do you really want me to tell the whole story? It is rather long and involved."

"Why don't you continue. I'll interrupt you if I think we should shorten the testimony."

"All right then. Well, I knew right away, when I recognized Carl, that he was up to no good."

"Just a minute, Mr. Snead. You say you *recognized* Carl?" Andy suddenly froze and turned pale.

There comes a time when a baseball pitcher throws a ball and he knows, just *knows*, even before it leaves his fingers, that the ball is destined to go right over the middle of the plate at waist height, and that the batter is going to swing and hit that ball out of the park. And there is nothing he can do to stop that ball and snatch it back. This is how Andy felt at that moment.

"He sued me once, and lost."

Uncharacteristically, Andy was almost at a loss for words. "I have no further questions of this witness, your Honor," he managed to say in a quavering voice and returned to his seat.

Derek sat for a moment, dumbfounded, without moving. Andy had handed him his defense on a silver platter. Eventually he stood up and came forward toward the witness. He began softly and carefully.

"Mr. Snead, I know you are a very busy man, and I promise not to take too much of your valuable time—unlike my clients over there who so rudely interrupted your work for a whole day."

Mike smiled at the joke, as did some members of the jury. "No problem." Mike replied amiably.

"Now, Mr. Snead. At any time during the day in question, were you physically injured or hurt?"

"No, not at all. Except for the duct tape they used to tie me up. That hurt a little."

"That was certainly unfortunate. Would you have tried to escape if they hadn't tied you up?"

"Objection!" Andy had gotten his voice back.

"Overruled. I'll allow it," replied the judge.

"Of course."

"Why do you think that you were held at gunpoint? Strike that! Where did you end up going on the train?"

"To Washington, D.C."

"What happened when you got there?"

"They let me go."

"Let you go? They untied you?"

"Oh, they had untied me long before. We were in the locomotive. When it finally stopped in Washington, I just got off."

"And what happened to the defendants? If you know."

"They were arrested."

"Did you see the police arrest them?"

"Yes. The F.B.I."

"The F.B.I.? "

"Yes, they committed Federal crimes."

"Your Honor, I move to strike that answer." Andy's confidence had returned, at least for the moment.

"Motion granted," Judge McMann agreed. "Jury, you are instructed to disregard that answer. It is *your* job to determine if any crimes have been committed."

"How did you know that the F.B.I. arrested the defendants?"

"Well, one of the agents, Special Agent Price, I believe, was in the locomotive with us. The others had the letters *F.B.I.* on their shirts."

"You had an F.B.I. agent on board?"

"Yes, that's right."

"Then is it safe to say that you were not concerned about your safety?"

"Well, no. But that's not—"

Derek cut him off. "Even at the beginning, when defendant Carl Collingwood held you at gunpoint."

"No, not really. I knew he wouldn't shoot me, unless I tried to grab the gun or something."

"Mr. Snead, in your position as President and CEO of Transport International, what is your salary?"Andy jumped to his feet. "Objection! Relevance?"

"Where are you going with this, Mr. Taliz?" asked the judge.

"Strike that, please. Mr. Snead, I believe you stated that the defendant Carl Collingwood 'sued you once and lost.' Is that correct?"

Andy Rosin sank slowly into his seat. He knew what, inevitably, was coming.

"Yes."

"What did he sue you for?"

"He claimed that I stole the intellectual property rights to his invention."

"Let me get this straight. He claimed you stole his invention, right?"

"His intellectual property rights."

"You mean his patents?"

"Yes."

"That sounds pretty bizarre to me. I thought one needed a written assignment to get ownership of a patent. Is that true?"

"Objection. Mr. Snead is not a patent lawyer."

"I just want his understanding, your Honor."

"I'll allow it."

"Yes, I believe that's true."

"Did the defendant assign his patents to you in writing?"

"Yes, he did."

"Why did he do that?"

"My company was prepared to loan him money and we needed collateral. He gave us a contingent assignment that said my company would get the patents if he defaulted on the loan."

"Did he default?"

"Yes, he missed a payment."

"A monthly payment?"

"Yes."

"How much was the payment?"

"Five thousand dollars."

"Did he eventually make the five-thousand-dollar payment?"

"Yes, he tried to pay late, but we told him the loan was in default and he owed us the entire amount of the loan with interest."

"You didn't accept the late payment?"

"No, it was late."

"How late?"

"I believe it was three days late."

"Let me get this straight, Mr. Snead. You say that the defendant Carl Collingwood missed a five-thousand-dollar payment by three days and you insisted that he repay the entire loan with interest or you would retain ownership to his patents?"

"Well, yes. That's right."

"Did Mr. Collingwood ever repay the loan?"

"Yes, we counter-sued and got our money back."

"But you kept the patents?"

"Yes."

"You received your money back *and* kept the patents?"

"Yes. That's what the lawsuit was about."

"And you won?"

"Yes, we did."

"Now, Mr. Snead, I am going to ask you just one more question, and I expect a truthful answer."

"Of course."

"You realize that you are under oath?"

"Yes, I do."

"And that if you answer falsely, you can be prosecuted for perjury?"

"Yes."

"Do you also understand that you may exercise your Fifth Amendment right not to answer any question under oath that may tend to incriminate you?"

"Yes, I do."

"Well, then, here is the question: Mr. Snead did you, or anyone in your employ or under your control, offer payment to any one of the jurors in that lawsuit?"

Andy Rosin sprang to his feet. *"Objection!"*

"Counselors, please approach the bench!" the judge demanded.

The two attorneys came forward and looked up at the judge. "Your Honor," Andy began emphatically, "that question is completely out of order. The very *asking* of such a question is prejudicial. I move for a mistrial."

"I'll take that under advisement, counselor. In the meantime, let's consider what to do with your objection. Mr. Taliz?"

"Your Honor, I am privy to some very damning evidence of malfeasance on the part of Mr. Snead. I would like to get his statement on the record."

"Evidence? What evidence?" interrupted Andy.

"Ask your own witnesses, Mr. Rosin. I'm sure it's no secret."

"What witnesses?"

"They're on your witness list. Take your pick. Julianne Gables, David Price, Shelley Bernstein. They're all aware of this, I'm sure." Derek's voice had an uncharacteristic edge to it.

"All right. All right," agreed the judge. "I'll allow it. As I see it there are three possibilities: one Mr. Snead will confirm he bribed a juror. Highly unlikely, but certainly a possibility. Two, Mr. Snead will invoke the Fifth Amendment. Also unlikely, I think.

And three, Mr. Snead will deny any wrongdoing. The most likely response to the question. Mr. Rosin, what is wrong with that?"

"*If* that's the answer, I have no objection."

"Then let him answer," said the judge, decisively.

Andy returned to his seat and Derek returned to his place in front of the witness.

"Could you read the question back, please?" Derek asked of the court reporter.

The young lady reached forward and picked up the paper tape from the basket of her steno machine. She looked through it, stopped at the right section, and repeated the question verbatim: "Well then, here is the question: Mr. Snead did you, or anyone in your employ or under your control, offer payment to any one of the jurors in that lawsuit?"

"The answer is emphatically *no*."

"Thank you, Mr. Snead. That is all I have."

"I have no redirect, your Honor," said Andy, conclusively. "Mr. Snead, you may step down."

Mike Snead stood up, flashed a broad smile at the jury, and strode out of the courtroom.

Chapter 71

———◆◆◆———

JULI AND GEORGE arose at four AM each day of the trial to make sure they would secure a place in the courtroom gallery. The first train from Grand Central to White Plains left at 5:40 in the morning and they wanted to be on it.

After they had returned to New York from their "honeymoon" in Bermuda, George, who still lived with his mother in her brownstone apartment in Brooklyn, had invited Juli to come to dinner. With great curiosity about George's home life, Juli eagerly accepted.

She had taken the A train down the Upper West Side to Bowling Green and then switched to a subway that traveled beneath the East River to a station in Park Slope just two blocks away from the address George had given her.

As she walked up the street, looking at house numbers, George spotted her in the distance and came running, arms open wide, to embrace her and welcome her into his world. They hugged and kissed as enthusiastically, as if they had been apart for months, not just two days.

George took Juli by the hand and led her tenderly back to his building and up the steps of the stoop to his front door. It was there that Juli had met "Mama."

After some heated debate, arguing the pros and cons, it was a group decision by all three of them that George would move into Juli's apartment in Manhattan, and not *vice versa*. Much as Mama would have wished for and enjoyed the additional company, she knew it was time that her one and only son find his own way in the world. She urged him to move out and, giving in also to Juli's coaxing, he reluctantly agreed to do so.

Mama had done her best to stifle and hide her tears on the day he packed his things, but she was unable to keep her feelings in check, and finally succumbed at the moment of his departure. As he was about to leave by taxicab, bags on board, for the trip to the City, she enveloped him in her trademark bear hug for such a long time that the cab driver honked impatiently. Then George gently eased away from the warmth of his mother's arms and climbed into the passenger seat of the cab. The driver quickly sped away, leaving Mama alone on the Brooklyn sidewalk.

Living and working together as investigative reporters, Juli and George had forged a deep respect and love for each other. Soon after George moved in, Juli took him home to meet her own mother in upper Harlem. Eventually the two mothers also met. After considerable time traveling between their two homes by subway to visit each other, adjusted to their odd but endearing idiosyncrasies.

Meanwhile, Juli's web site attracted increasing attention by the media, as well as the public, for its timely and newsworthy content. It soon received so many hits per day that advertisers took notice and started contacting Juli to place some tasteful and seemingly inconspicuous banner ads on the site. Juli and George worked hard to follow leads and expose previously-hidden corrupt practices throughout industry and government, many of which would never have come to light without their efforts. As they posted their up-to-the-minute news reports on the web site, they often found that some anonymous blogger would enhance a story by adding further facts and comments that only an insider would know.

Over time, Juli and George developed a fan base of information junkies who clicked on the web site each day, and often several times a day, to catch the breaking news on the latest exposé.

As Gables Fables gained popularity, more and more of the persons exposed to the media glare became furious and attempted to close the web site down; however, Juli and George were protected by the law that favors freedom of the press. When they learned that some executive or politician became upset by their reports, it only made them dig deeper with greater diligence to unearth the truth.

On this second day of the trial, Juli and George sat together and watched the proceedings from the gallery, both of them taking careful notes. Recording devices were not allowed in the courtroom, so these notes were all they could take away with them. The "no recording" rule actually worked to their benefit because other members of the media had to rely on note-taking too, and Juli and George had merged their efforts, forming an unbeatable tag team. At the conclusion of Mike Snead's testimony, George promptly left with their notes to write the report and post it on the web site.

Just after he left, Andy addressed the jury and announced, "I would now like to call Julianne Gables as a witness."

Juli knew she was on the witness list, but she wasn't at all sure she would be asked to testify. What did Andy Rosin have in mind? Now that her name had been called, she suddenly became nervous. She stumbled over the feet of the other spectators who filled the long gallery bench as she made her way out.

Andy motioned for her to take the witness stand.

"Raise your right hand," the bailiff began. She raised her left hand by mistake, then pulled it down, embarrassed. There was laughter in the court, which relaxed the tense mood. Juli winced and raised her right. The bailiff swore her in.

"Would you state your name and address for the record please?" Andy began.

"My name is Julianne Cheryl Gables. I live at 345 West 123rd Street in New York City."

"What is your occupation?"

"I'm a news reporter."

"Where are you employed?"

"I'm self-employed. I work at home."

"Have you been in the gallery, watching this trial, since it started?"

"Yes, I wouldn't miss it for the world." The gallery tittered with approval.

"Have you written news reports about this trial?"

"Yes."

"Have you had occasion to write a report on the lawsuit that Carl Collingwood filed against Michael Snead and his company, Transport International?"

"Yes."

"Were you present at that trial?"

"No, I wasn't."

"Let me understand this: You say you wrote a report about that trial but you weren't present at the trial?"

"Yes, that's correct."

"Then where did you obtain the information that you wrote about?"

"I'm an investigative reporter. I have my sources."

"I'm not asking you to reveal your sources, Ms. Gables. I just want to know: Have you ever committed a crime in order to obtain information about a news story?"

"A crime?"

"Yes, like breaking-and-entering."

"Objection!" Derek roared, feigning anger at the audacity of the prosecutor to ask such a question.

"On what grounds, Mr. Taliz?" queried the judge, cocking her head. "Sounds like a fair question to me."

"First of all, the witness is not an expert on criminal law and, second, she is being asked, under oath, to incriminate herself!"

"She can invoke her Fifth Amendment right, if she wishes. Go ahead, Mr. Rosin."

"Did you ever commit the crime of trespass to obtain information for your story about the lawsuit brought by the defendant Carl Collingwood against Mr. Snead and his company?"

"I guess I have to invoke the Fifth Amendment, as the judge said."

"Do you realize that the Fifth Amendment only applies to crimes committed in the United States?"

"Uh, no."

"Did you commit the crime of trespass in Bermuda, to obtain information for your story, Ms. Gables?"

"I'm invoking the Fifth Amendment."

"You can't do that. Your Fifth Amendment right doesn't apply to crimes committed outside the United States."

"It doesn't?" Juli looked hopelessly over at Derek, who responded by silently raising his hands and looking skyward. There was nothing he could do to help her.

"Answer the question," Andy growled, almost fiercely now.

"Yes, I did."

"Where was that?"

"At the offices of Financial Management, Ltd. A subsidiary of Transport International."

"Now, Ms. Gables. Did anyone tell you to do that?"

"Yes."

"Who was that?"

"I refuse to say."

"Refuse to say? *Refuse* to say?"

"I won't reveal a source."

"I'm not asking for a source. Did you ever speak to an F.B.I. agent about breaking into the offices of Financial Management?"

"Yes, I did."

"Who was that?"

"Agent David Price."

"What did you tell Agent Price?"

"Objection! Hearsay."

"Your Honor, I'm asking the witness what she herself said to Agent Price!"

"Sustained. That's hearsay, Mr. Rosin. Law school, Evidence 101"

Andy turned back to the witness and took another tack. "What did Agent Price say to you?"

"Objection! Assumes a fact not in evidence."

"Sustained."

"Did Agent Price ever speak to you about breaking into the offices of Financial Management?"

"Yes."

"What did he say?"

"He said that if he or one of his agents had obtained information that way, it would not be admissible in court."

"But the information *you* obtained in this way would be admissible evidence?"

"Objection! The witness is not a legal expert."

"Your Honor, I'm just asking what Agent Price said."

"Overruled. Go on."

"Did Mr. Price say that?"

"That was the sense of it, yes."

"That's all the questions I have. Your witness, Mr. Taliz."

Derek was on his feet in an instant and charged forward to take center stage. "Ms. Gables," he began, "you testified that you obtained some information about Mr. Collingwood's lawsuit by breaking and entering the offices of Financial Management, Ltd. Is that correct?"

"Yes."

"What information did you obtain?"

"Objection. Fruit of the poison tree!"

"Are you a private citizen, Ms. Gables?"

"Yes, I guess so."

"You are not an agent of government, are you?"

"No, I am not."

"Then you may answer the question."

"Objection! Same grounds."

"Your Honor!" Derek protested. "The fruit is free for the picking by a private citizen. The rule protects against unwarranted investigation by the police."

"He's right, Mr. Rosin. I'll allow it."

Derek turned his attention back to Juli. "You may answer the question."

"What was the question?"

"What information did you obtain from Financial Management, after breaking and entering?"

"We – that's my partner, George, and I – we obtained an accounting sheet that showed that nearly one million dollars had been transferred to an account in the U.S."

The jurors listening to this testimony leaned slightly forward to catch every word.

"Would you recognize that accounting sheet if I showed it to you?"

"I certainly would."

"You would?"

"Yes, I would."

"How could you tell it was the same sheet?"

"Because people in Bermuda shot at me and there is a bullet hole in it."

The jurors' eyes widened further. They could hardly believe what they were hearing.

"Your Honor, I would like to mark for identification the defendants' Exhibit D-1, an accounting sheet with a bullet hole, right in the middle."

Derek handed the document to the court reporter, who first finished typing the transcript of what he had just said and then removed a self-adhering sticker marked "Defendants' Exhibit D-1" from a backing sheet and placed it at the bottom right corner of the exhibit.

Derek took back the exhibit, now officially marked, from the court reporter and walked it over to the prosecutor's table. He let Andy examine it while he grabbed a couple of copies from his own defense table. He then had Andy relinquish the original in return for a copy, and handed the original to Juli.

"Is this the accounting sheet that you took from Financial Management?"

"Yes, it is."

"How can you tell?"

"It has the bullet hole."

"I won't ask how come this hole ended up in the document but not in you," Derek remarked, off-handedly.

"Objection," Andy protested. "Your Honor, that is uncalled for."

"You know better, Mr. Taliz. Ladies and gentlemen of the jury, disregard that remark."

"My apologies, your Honor. Juli, can you tell us what is on the document?"

"The document shows that funds were transferred from the Financial Management account in Bermuda to an account here in the United States. It is identified here only by an account number."

"Does the document give the date of the transfer?"

"Yes, it does."

"Does that date have any significance?

"Yes, it is two days after the jury found in favor of Transport International in the lawsuit brought by Carl Collingwood."

"And who owned the account in the United States that received the money?"

"Objection!" Andy shouted, nearly at the top of his lungs "How would the witness know that?"

"Foundation, Mr. Taliz?" asked the judge.

"Did you have occasion to find out who owned the account that received the funds?"

"Yes."

"How did you find out?"

"I saw it on a computer screen."

"Whose computer screen?"

"Agent Price of the F.B.I."

"All right," said the judge, satisfied. "I'll allow it."

"Who owned that account?"

"The owners were listed as Robert Falmouth and Elizabeth Falmouth. Betty Falmouth was one of the jurors in the Collingwood case."

"Are you implying that money was paid to Mrs. Falmouth in exchange for lending her support to Mr. Snead and his company as a juror in that case?"

"Objection!"

Before either the judge or Derek Taliz could say anything, Juli interjected her answer: "It's pretty obvious, isn't it?"

Chapter 72

❖◆❖◆❖

"THE PROSECUTION CALLS as its next witness, F.B.I. Agent David Price."

Price stood up from his seat in the gallery, buttoned the center button of his sport jacket, and came forward to take the witness stand. He had been through this routine many times before.

"Raise your right hand," said the bailiff, and Price did so. "Do you swear to tell the truth, the whole truth and nothing but the truth?"

"Yes, sir. I do."

"You may be seated."

Andy came forward and approached the witness. "Agent Price, could you state your name and address for the record?"

"Special Agent David Price. 546 East Capitol Street, Washington, D.C."

"You are an F.B.I. agent, are you not?"

"Yes, I am."

"Did you have occasion to investigate an incident last October involving a commuter train?"

"Yes, I did."

"Could you tell us about it?"

Andy Rosin took Agent Price slowly and carefully through the events of the day. For his part, Price set forth, without embellishment, the basic circumstances of his direct involvement in the hijacking, from the moment he had received the call to action in New York City to the time he stepped out of the locomotive onto the platform at Union Station in Washington.

The colloquy with Andy took most of the remainder of the day, with a break for lunch, but this was just fine with Andy. He wanted to save the best for last, and he wanted the best to be heard the next morning, when the jury was fresh and would listen intently and understand the import of Price's testimony.

Finally, when all the salient facts had been elicited, Andy asked, "Would you recognize Carl and Bruce Collingwood again if you saw them?"

"Of course."

"Are they here in this courtroom?"

"Yes."

Almost reluctantly, Price pointed out the two defendants, the father and son who sat glumly at the defense table.

"Your Honor, it's four-thirty and I still have quite a few questions for Agent Price. This might be a good time to break for the day."

"Agreed. That's fine with me. The court will recess until nine-thirty tomorrow morning." Judge McMann banged her gavel, stood quickly and retired to chambers while everyone else scrambled to stand up also, as court etiquette required.

At nine-thirty the next morning, all were in their seats when Judge McMann entered through the rear door in the courtroom.

"All rise!" intoned the bailiff. Everyone stood until Judge McMann took her seat at the bench and gaveled the day's proceedings to order. Then everyone sat down again.

The judge waited for the hubbub in the courtroom to die down and then commenced. "Mr. Rosin, you may continue with the examination of your witness."

"Thank you, your Honor," Andy replied, respectfully, and invited Agent Price to take the witness stand again.

"Agent Price, I just want to remind you that you are still under oath."

"I understand."

"Yesterday you testified as to the events that occurred on the train and on the locomotive – or I should say locomotives – until you finally arrived in Washington, D.C. Today I am going to question you about facts that occurred *after* you got off the locomotive and the defendants were arrested."

"Objection." Derek shot to his feet. "Of what relevance is this?"

"Mr. Rosin?" Judge McMann raised an eyebrow.

"I am laying a foundation, your Honor. It will become clear in a moment."

"All right. Be brief."

"Where did you go that day when you left Union Station?"

"I took the Metro to the Hoover Building and went to my office."

"What did you do there?"

"I looked at the mail, checked my email, made a few calls, that sort of thing."

"Did you have any visitors?"

"No, not that day."

"Did there come a time that Julianne Gables visited you in your office?"

"Yes, the very next day. She and her cameraman, George, came up to the office."

"Did Ms. Gables say why she wanted to visit you?"

"I can't recall. I just know she visited. With George."

"Why did you agree to see them?"

"Why wouldn't I? We had spent practically the whole day together the previous day under very unusual circumstances."

"All right. What did you speak about when she visited you?"

"We talked about the possibility that Michael Snead had been involved in bribing a jury."

"What jury was that?"

"The jury in the Collingwood lawsuit against his company, Transport International."

"What did Ms. Gables, Juli, tell you?"

"Objection. Hearsay."

"Overruled."

"She said she had evidence of such jury tampering."

"Did she show you any such evidence?"

"No."

"Did she have any such evidence in her possession?"

"No."

"Did she say she could obtain such evidence?"

"Yes."

"When and where?"

"She said she needed to go to Bermuda for that."

"What did you tell her?"

"Be my guest. I can't stop you."

"Did you say anything else?"

"Not really."

"You didn't ask her, and her cameraman, to go on government business?"

"No."

"They went on their own accord?"

"Yes."

"You didn't ask them to go?"

"No."

Derek stood up again with feigned impatience. "Your Honor. I really must reassert my objection. Mr. Rosin has exhausted this witness's recollection. There is no relevance whatsoever to this testimony."

"I tend to agree," replied the judge. "Mr. Rosin, is there a point?"

"I believe so, your Honor. I am trying to show that Ms. Gables and her cameraman were agents of the U.S. government."

"That's preposterous!" Derek shouted. "Anyway, you asked that very question and Agent Price denied it."

"If you please, your Honor. Permit me to ask one more question."

"All right," said Judge McMann, exasperated. "Just one, and then let's move on."

Andy stood there for a moment, trying to formulate a question that would salvage a situation he knew was important. Finally he said, "Did Juli and George go to Bermuda at their own expense?"

"Well, not exactly."

"What do you mean, *not exactly*?"

"The government paid for—"

"The *government* paid?"

"Yes."

"Just a minute. Maybe I'm missing something. Reporter could you read a portion of the transcript back, please?"

The reporter picked up her tape and looked at Andy "Where do I start?"

"Where it first talks about a trip to Bermuda."

The reporter read verbatim: "Question: 'When and where?' Answer 'She said she needed to go to Bermuda for that.' Question: 'What did you tell her?' Answer: 'Be my guest. I can't stop you.' Question: 'Did you say anything else?' Answer: 'Not really.' Question: 'You didn't ask her and her cameraman to go on government business?' Answer: 'No.'"

"Agent Price, I want to remind you again you are under oath. First you clearly testified that Ms. Gables did not go on government business, and then you said that the government paid for her trip? Is that not inconsistent?"

"No."

"It is not?"

"I testified that she could go as my guest, if she wanted to. And she wanted to go. I couldn't stop her."

"You didn't order her to go, is that right?"

"She is a private citizen. She can do as she pleases and do what she wants."

"But she decided to go to Bermuda."

"Yes."

"All expenses paid by the U.S. Government."

"Well, yes."

"Who wouldn't want to go under these circumstances?!"

The whole courtroom broke out in laughter. Andy was suddenly on a roll.

"Why did you agree to pay her expenses?"

"She convinced me that she could bring back some evidence of jury tampering."

"Did she, in fact, obtain such evidence? She and George?"

"Yes, they did."

"What evidence was that?"

"Defendants' Exhibit No 1. The accounting sheet with the bullet hole in it."

"Your Honor, I move to strike all the testimony relating to jury tampering and all the evidence obtained by Juli and George during their trip to Bermuda."

"The grounds?" Derek demanded.

"Both Juli and George were agents of the U.S. government who, by Juli's own admission, obtained the evidence in Bermuda by breaking-and-entering without a search warrant. All evidence is therefore tainted and inadmissible."

Judge McMann reacted, her voice tinged with anger. "I want to see both prosecution and defense counsel in my chambers, immediately!"

The two attorneys followed her out through the rear door of the courtroom while the rest of the people in the courtroom stood up at attention.

When they entered her chambers, she motioned for them to sit on opposite sides of the long table that protruded forward from the front of her desk. She then went around behind the desk and stood there, glowering furiously.

"What in devil's name is going *on?*" she began.

"I'm not sure, your Honor," Andy began. "You could see that Price was holding out on me. He almost perjured himself out there."

"Your Honor, if I may," Derek interrupted, "it seems that no one wants these men to go to jail, not even the F.B.I. agent that pursued them. Clearly he didn't want the reasons for my clients', uh, indiscretions, excluded from evidence."

The judge was still livid and she showed it. "Well, as far as I'm concerned he's gone over the edge this time. First he pays these people to commit a crime in Bermuda and then he practically lies about it under oath. I'm not sure he shouldn't be brought up on charges himself."

"My motion, your Honor." Andy said hopefully, now that he thought the judge might be siding with him. "With the government acting this way, they are part-and-parcel of the unwarranted search. The evidence of money transfer has to be excluded."

"All right, let's reconvene. I'll grant your motion, Mr. Rosin."

The attorneys took their leave and returned to the courtroom the same way they came. A short time later Judge McMann also left her chambers and reentered the courtroom. All eyes were on her as she announced her decision.

"I will grant the motion of Mr. Rosin to exclude all evidence relating to the *reasons,* however valid and exculpatory they may be, for the defendants' actions that gave rise to the charges against them.

"Ladies and gentlemen of the jury, I now instruct you to *disregard* all testimony you heard in this courtroom *except* that which directly relates to the activities of the defendants on the commuter train on that Monday in October.

"Mr. Taliz, you may now cross-examine this witness."

Derek stood and announced: "I have no questions, your honor." Now there was nothing Agent Price could say that would favor the defense.

Chapter 73

———◆•◆◆◆———

"The prosecution rests, your honor," said Andy and sat down, satisfied that he had made his case.

"Very well. Mr. Taliz, you may call your first witness."

"The defense has no witnesses, your honor. However, I move to dismiss. The prosecution has not presented a *prima facie* case to support the charges against these defendants." Derek knew his motion, which he made at the end of every criminal trial to preserve his right to appeal, stood no chance at all of being granted.

"Motion denied," said the judge irritably. "Then we'll move right on to the closing statements. Are you ready, Mr. Rosin?"

"Yes, your Honor."

"You may proceed."

Andy walked forward from his table and, for the first time since making his opening statement, addressed the jury directly. He looked at them for a moment, as if to get acquainted again, and then launched into what seemed more like a fireside chat than a speech.

"Ladies and gentlemen of the jury, first I want to acknowledge your valuable service to your community – for leaving your homes and your jobs and coming here to sit through two days of testimony in this case. In behalf of the community and on behalf of our judicial system, I thank you.

"Very shortly we will ask you to meet together in the jury room, to deliberate and to make a decision as to the defendants' guilt or innocence. I know that you will take this task seriously and that you will come to the correct, and just, decision.

"My job now is to summarize the evidence for you, so that you can make that decision, based solely on the facts as they were presented. I believe you will agree that the facts are not in dispute."

Andy took the jury carefully through a tour of the testimony, witness by witness. Using the elements of each charge against the defendants as a basis, he pointed out those facts, elicited in the testimony, that were required to prove that crimes were committed. It was an easy run because, unlike most cases he had prosecuted, the facts were clearly supported by the evidence.

When he finished his summary, Andy paused for a moment and then took a step closer to the jury box, as if to speak with each juror privately.

"In closing," he said, "I would like you to imagine you were on that commuter train that fateful day last October. Imagine you were a passenger on the train that left Wassaic early in the morning, before the sun came up. As a commuter you probably had a monthly pass you carried with you, or if you traveled infrequently you may have had a ten-trip ticket. You showed your pass or your ticket to the conductor as he passed by and then settled down to read your newspaper, work on your laptop, or even sleep as the train made the routine trip to New York City. But on this day the train didn't go there. Just as you got comfortable, you were ordered to get off and take another train, which was so full you probably couldn't get a seat. You had to stand all the way. Why? Because the defendants wanted to take your train to Washington!

"Now I ask you to imagine again that you were the engineer on that train. You were doing your job, as you had done many times before, safely bringing that train with all its precious passengers to Grand Central Station in New York City. And then suddenly you realize that there behind you in the locomotive stands a man holding a gun to your head. He looks like he may kill you at any instant if you do not do what he says. You are in fear of your life.

"At the end of the day you are still alive, but you have been ordered to take that locomotive to Washington, three-hundred miles out of your way. Why? Because the defendants wanted to go there.

"And last, but not least, imagine, if you can, that you are Michael Snead, the CEO of a major corporation. You board the train as you have done each Monday many times in the past to commute to New York City. You have a full day's work ahead. You are already thinking about the day's agenda and what needs to be done. And then suddenly the man sitting next to you takes out a gun and orders you to stay on the train while all the other passengers get off. You comply because you are in fear of your life. Later on you are tied up, hand and foot, and taken three-hundred miles out of your way to Washington. Why? Because the defendants wanted to take you there.

"There ought to be a law against this, you say. We can't let anyone do such a thing. We can't let them put other people in harm's way; we can't let them threaten people and tie them up; we can't let them interfere with the legitimate operation of a railroad; and we can't let them inconvenience so many innocent people who are just trying to get to work on a Monday morning. Well, as I am sure you know, there *is* a law, in fact *many* laws against such wrongful actions, both Federal laws and state laws.

"You can be sure the defendants knew the laws existed, too, and yet they went ahead and carried out their plan, in spite of these laws.

"Before you are asked to deliberate, Judge McMann will explain these laws to you in excruciating detail. It then will be your final task to consider the facts of this case and determine whether these defendants before you have violated these laws.

"When you finally sit down to deliberate together, you will find that the facts will speak for themselves. The only rational decision you can possibly make is that these two defendants violated the laws of this state and this country and are guilty of the charges against them.

"I thank you for your attention." Andy gave a respectful bow to the jury and walked back to his seat.

The judge called to the defense. "Mr. Taliz?"

Derek stood and came forward to address the jury.

"Hello again." He said, smiling almost to himself while scratching his head. "After a summation like that from Mr. Rosin, you are probably wondering what I am going to say.

There is quite a bit to say, really, if only I were permitted to do so.

"You heard Judge McMann's ruling that you are to disregard all evidence of malfeasance by Mr. Snead—"

"Just a minute!" shouted Andy. "You can't go into that. Your Honor, object!"

"What have I said?" responded Derek. "I just called attention to her Honor's ruling."

"Continue," said the judge, her voice revealing extreme annoyance.

"Mr. Rosin has asked you to imagine that you were on that commuter train on the day in question. Fair enough. I would like you to imagine you were on that train too. Only this time I would like you to imagine you are the defendant, Carl Collingwood, or his son, Bruce. Take your pick.

"What went through your mind as you boarded the train, knowing that you were going to try to take it out of its way, to Washington, D.C. Why would you do such a thing? You would be putting your own life in danger and, if you did manage to survive the trip, you would surely be arrested when you got there.

"The defendants *must* have been extremely desperate to carry out such a plan, a plan that was doomed to failure from the start. They went ahead with it anyway, not motivated by malice or revenge, for they were very careful not to hurt anyone, but simply to call attention to their plight.

"The judicial system had failed them and they had nowhere else to turn to rectify the wrong that was done to them."

"Objection!" Andy howled at the top of his lungs.

"Sustained!" Judge McMann exploded in anger. "Mr. Taliz, you are *not* to touch on any facts not in evidence. The court reporter shall strike that last statement from the record and, ladies and gentlemen of the jury, I instruct you to disregard it.

"Mr. Taliz, your comments are completely out of order and *you know it*. If you make one more such reference to the defendants' issues with the past, I will hold you in contempt of court."

"Yes, your Honor," Derek said contritely. Then he turned his attention back to the jury and said to them conspiratorially, "As you can see, my hands are tied." Derek winked to emphasize that it was <u>them</u>, the judge and the ADA, versus <u>us</u>, the defendants, the jury and him.

"That is all that I can say. The defendants' future is in your hands. After listening to all the testimony here – oops, excuse me – after listening to the testimony you were allowed to hear, I trust you will do the right thing. You will return with a verdict in favor of the defendants, a verdict of *not guilty*."

Derek sat down. He had said the words, but he was a beaten man. No reasonable jury could acquit the defendants, based on the overwhelming evidence of their guilt. He had done his best, but his best was not good enough.

Derek hardly listened as the judge charged the jury. He had reviewed Andy Rosin's proposed charges and, with some minor alterations, had approved them. There was nothing further he could do.

After reading the charges, Judge McMann asked the jury to commence their deliberations. It was late in the day, but they could start by electing a foreman and proceeding with a preliminary poll. They had at least an hour before the court closed and it might be helpful for them to know where each jury member stood before they retired for the evening. This would pave the way for their deliberations the next morning.

Chapter 74

<hr />

Forty-five minutes later the jury informed the judge that they had reached an agreement. Judge McMann was surprised, but with such overwhelming evidence, it was probably to be expected that the decision would come quickly. She immediately asked the bailiff to notify both parties, as well as the media.

Andy and Derek returned to the courtroom and the defendants were brought in, Judge McMann had the bailiff notify the jurors that the court was in session. One by one, they filed out of the jury room, taking their seats in the jury box in the oak-paneled courtroom. Intentionally expressionless, they sat there like statues, looking straight ahead and avoiding the eyes of both the prosecution and the defense.

"Has the jury reached a verdict?" asked Judge McMann.

"Yes, we have, your Honor," said the jury foreman.

"For both defendants?"

"Yes, your Honor."

"On all counts?"

"Yes, your Honor."

"Please share your verdict with this court."

The bailiff took a folded slip of paper from the jury foreman and handed it up to the judge. Judge McMann opened it, peeked at the writing, and then quickly folded it again as she sucked in air and stifled an expression. She handed the paper back to the bailiff, who returned it to the foreman.

"What is your verdict?"

"We, the jury, find the defendant Bruce Collingwood *not guilty* on all counts." There was a rustling in the courtroom, which quickly turned into a hubbub. Judge McMann banged her gavel.

"Continue!"

"We, the jury, find the defendant Carl Collingwood *not guilty* on all counts."

The courtroom exploded with noise. People stood and cheered. Reporters rushed out of the room to contact their media. Sylvia Collingwood let out a joyous scream and rushed forward through the barrier gate to hug her husband and son.

Derek sat numbly in his seat for a moment, astounded at the success of his defense of Carl and Bruce.

Andy Rosin, too, could not conceive of this outcome. The jury had completely ignored the facts in this airtight case and had freed the defendants. Under the American system of jurisprudence they were allowed to do this – to find justice, notwithstanding the demands of the law – but such an action would require a unanimous decision by every juror.

Andy stood and addressed the judge. "Your Honor," he began but the room was too noisy so that no one heard. Through his actions, however, the judge realized that Andy was trying desperately to say something. She banged her gavel and shouted, "Silence!" The room went instantly quiet while someone said "Shhh!" Andy continued.

"Your Honor, I would like to request that the jury be polled."

"A reasonable request under the circumstances. Bailiff, if you please." Judge McMann nodded to her bailiff.

One by one, the bailiff called the names of the jurors and, one by one each juror repeated, "Bruce Collingwood, not guilty on all counts and Carl Collingwood not guilty on all counts."

HOME AGAIN

Chapter 75

"WELL, THAT WRAPS *that* case," Juli said to George, as she posted the final report of the trial on their web site. "Too bad we couldn't nail Mike Snead but, hey, as they say, 'All's well that ends well.'"

"After all the trouble we went to, trying to get the goods on him," George countered.

"Trouble? You call that trouble? I thought it was a honeymoon."

"I'm not complaining, you understand. It was just about the best three days of my life, except maybe for the last hour or so when we were getting shot at."

"Do you want to go again?"

"Now that you mention it, I've been thinking about that a lot lately. But there is something I'd like to do first."

"Oh? What's that?"

"Well, you know before people go on a honeymoon, they usually get married."

"And? What's your point?" Juli teased.

For the first time ever, George was hesitant to speak his mind. "Would -- would you marry me?"

"You're my good luck charm, George. You're the best thing that's ever happened to me."

"*Moi?*"

"*Oui, vous.*"

"So you'll marry me?"

"I thought you'd never ask." Juli took George in her arms and planted a big wet kiss on his lips. "Yes, yes, a thousand times yes."

When George came up for air, he looked at her lovingly. "And this time *we'll* pay for our honeymoon trip to Bermuda."

Sylvia Collingwood couldn't believe their good fortune. Her family was home again and their troubles with the law were over for good. She couldn't stop smiling.

"I don't think I'll ever let you two ride on a train again," she joked as she spread her arms wide and wrapped both her men in a big bear hug. It was not the first time she had hugged them since the trial, and it wouldn't be the last.

"Well, there was this airplane we were working on," her husband retorted. He winked at Bruce.

"Yeah, Mom, who needs trains anyway."

"But there's just one problem." Sylvia let go of Carl and Bruce and made a face.

"What's that?" they asked together.

"You didn't finish that darn plane!"

Just then the phone rang. "I'll bet that's another one of those reporters. They kept calling when you were away, and now it's starting again. Do you want to speak to them?"

"Sure! We're glad to speak with anybody after being locked up all this time, aren't we, Bruce?" Bruce nodded in happy agreement.

"Well, now that I've got my husband back, we've got some catching up to do." Sylvia grabbed his arm and pulled him in the direction of the stairs. "Bruce, you answer the phone."

Bruce went for the ringing phone as Carl and Sylvia disappeared upstairs.

"Hello, is this the Collingwood residence?" The voice was gravelly and deep.

"Yes, who is this?"

"My name is Shelley Bernstein. I work for Transport International."

"Oh, yes, Mr. Bernstein. You're Mr. Snead's assistant. My father has told me a lot about you."

"Is your father there?"

"Well, yes and no. He's, uh celebrating at the moment."

"I can imagine. Bruce...your name is Bruce, isn't it?"

"Yes, I'm Bruce."

"Mr. Snead would like to speak with you. Do you have a moment?"

"Sure."

"All right, I'll put him on."

There was silence on the line for a second and then Michael Snead came on.

"Hello, Bruce? This is Mike Snead."

"Hello, Mr. Snead."

"I'll get right to the point. I'm sure you have a lot of catching up to do. But frankly, Bruce, I'm calling to apologize to you and to your father, Carl."

"Oh!"

"Yes. It was an awful thing I put you through and I want to make it up to you. I'm having my attorneys assign all of your father's patents back to him. I sincerely hope you both continue with the project. We have looked at it, you know, and think it's worthy of pursuing. We'd ask you to work on it with Transport International, but I'm sure that you and your father won't want anything to do with us any more."

"I guess you're right about that. But, thank you, that's awfully generous."

"You shouldn't have any trouble getting financing now, with all the publicity you got from that girl Juli Gables."

"Maybe so."

"Good luck to you both."

Bruce ran upstairs shouting, "Mom! Dad! Wait till you hear this!!"

❀

"Well, that's done," Mike said. "I feel much better now."

"I knew you would. It seems you have a conscience after all," Shelley replied.

"It's funny, I never knew I did."

"What did you tell him?"

"I told him we'll give the patents back. I apologized too, would you believe."

"Is that all?"

"Well, yeah. What else was there to say?"

"What about the twelve million dollars you're spending?"

"Oh, that! How'd you find out about that?"

"I have my ways. I know everything there is to know about this company."

"Oh, yeah? Good thing you're loyal. You know where all the bodies are buried."

"So? You going to tell them?"

"Tell them what?"

"That you're funding the development of their aircraft."

"What makes you think that?"

"It says so right here on the ledger. The money is being transferred today."

"True, that's what the ledger says the money's *for*. But look who it's being transferred to."

Shelley shifted through the ledger sheets and looked closely at the fine print.

"Oh, I see."

"This will never happen again, I assure you."

"You're cured?"

"Cured. A new leaf. Starting over. Whatever."

"Mike, I like that. I think I'll stick around and watch."

Meanwhile, the twelve jurors met secretly and waited for a visitor from Bermuda. They had complied with Snead's request to acquit the Collingwoods and they would each receive a million dollars in cash. That would go a long way toward purchasing a house and putting the kids through college.

THE AIRCRAFT

By Karl Milde

Chapter 1

HI, MY NAME is Julianne Gables. "Juli" for short. If you've read about the hijacking of the commuter train to New York City, you know all about my husband, George White, and me. We got married just a year ago, and honeymooned in Bermuda. Oh, that honeymoon: that incredible, two-week romantic fantasy of sun and sin. It was what every young girl dreams about, only it was *real*!

When we came back home to New York and set to work again, our news-breaking web site, www.thegablesreport.com, just kind of *took off*. We've been getting thousands of hits a day and every day there's more.

We post up-to-the-minute news on the site before it's reported on TV or in the newspapers. We leave the murders and break-ins to the local media and focus on political and corporate corruption. We also do sex scandals when they touch a presumably responsible public figure, but I'm getting ahead of myself. Let me start from the beginning and tell you what happened to the man named Carl Collingwood. Tighten your seatbelt, dear reader, and hear me out…

George and I left early in the morning and drove way out to the Suffolk County Airport in Westhampton, Long Island. When we arrived at the airport gate, we stopped and asked directions to our final destination, the Hummingbird Aircraft Company. The security guard handed us a sheet with a map of the airport and, with his finger, pointed out a route that led to the back of the facility. We finally pulled up in front of a huge metal hanger with the word "HUMMINGBIRD" painted in large white letters on the side. There, on the tarmac, in front of the open hanger door, stood the thing Carl Collingwood, the CEO of Hummingbird, called a "Personal Aircraft," or just "PAC" for short (pronounced "*pack*," not the letters "P" "A" and "C.").

The aircraft looked like an immense frozen bird, motionless with its wings outstretched in the take-off position, ready to fly away. It was *showtime*! Carl and his son, Bruce Collingwood, had asked us to come this morning to watch the very first test flight.

All summer long Carl and Bruce had worked with their team to build this prototype: an airplane with wings that could fly fuel-efficiently, using about the same amount of gas per mile as a car, and yet could take off and land *vertically*. It was based on some novel principal that Bruce had explained to me once but I never understood. Something about blowing wind over the top of the wings to produce lift, even when the aircraft was stationary.

George and I got out of our car and walked into the cavernous building. Carl and Bruce were over in the far corner on the right, holding coffee cups and chatting with their guys. There were five of them in all – members of his team, I mean - each with a different skill-set that was needed to build an aircraft. No one was indispensable.

As we walked up, we saw Carl and Bruce locked in a heated exchange while the team looked on with amused smirks on their faces. His handy-cam always at the ready, George held back and started quietly to record the scene.

"You've got to be kidding, Dad. You're twice my age! Pardon my saying so but your reflexes are a bit *s-l-o-w.*" Bruce dragged out the last word for effect. "The PAC's going to act more like a bucking bronco than an aircraft."

"But I know all the different twists and turns it can make. I've done the math. It won't make any moves I can't keep up with."

"Why don't we let our people decide?" Bruce turned to his teammates for assistance.

"Yeah, right," Carl said sarcastically. "If they choose you, I'll be pissed at them, and if they choose me, you'll be pissed at everyone, including me."

"Okay, here's Juli! Maybe she can settle it."

Both Bruce and Carl broke into wide smiles and took turns giving me bear hugs. "Welcome stranger!" Carl held my face between both his hands and looked at me squarely in the eyes. "How've you been, dear Juli? Survived that Bermuda honeymoon? Where the heck's the lucky man?"

I nodded in George's direction, and the entire crew walked over to greet him too. George stopped recording and shook their hands warmly. As he did so he glanced in my direction with those dreamy brown yes, and winked. I just love it when he does that. "Our honeymoon was... uh..*okay*." He replied, pursing his lips to show he was trying to be cute.

"Just *okay*?" Bruce took the bait. "Tell us, man. We want *details*."

"Just kidding. How about *tres* okay?"

"Now we *really* want details."

"Sorry guys, but its time to get your asses back in gear," Carl remarked. "The military brass will be here in a minute to watch this test flight. If it goes well, the Army'll pay us a whole lot of money for our plans to the PAC, and the aircraft will go into certification for production – big time."

We had asked for, and Carl and Bruce had granted us, an exclusive on this story. We were the only reporters allowed anywhere near the hanger today. Whether the test was a soaring success or a fatal flop, we were entitled to the first broadcast. After that, ours would be the only video footage available so we could license it at a tidy profit. Considering the publicity we got at the Collingwood trial, I figure there'd be a heavy demand for our pics.

"How're you going to run the test?" George asked, always thinking about his next shot.

"The aircraft will be on a tether," Bruce explained, "so it can't go too high. We'll just take it up, keep it there for a few minutes, and bring it down."

"That's it?" I asked, somewhat disappointed. "You brought us out here for *that*?"

"It's a big moment," Carl said proudly. "It'll be the first time a fixed-wing aircraft could do this, rising up from the ground, due just to the air flowing over the top of the wings."

"I still don't get it," I said. "What's the big deal?"

"The fixed-wing aircraft, as we know it, has been developed and refined for over a hundred years. It is incredibly efficient at producing lift, once you get it moving through the air. But this is the first time an aircraft of this type is going to go straight up and hover. No downward pointed jets; no spinning chopper blades, which are the helicopter's wings by the way. No complex mechanism to control those spinning blades. Less noise too!"

"Like flying a *magic carpet*?"

"Remember that expression for your story! It's *just* like that. Some day we'll all be able to take off from our own backyards. This is the beginning. You'll see."

There came a sound from behind them and all heads turned to see a black SUV pull up and stop just outside the hanger. Three men in uniform got out. I could tell by the stripes on his sleeve that the driver was a sergeant. The other two wore those military hats with gold graffiti on their visors proclaiming their elevated status. They all headed our way.

Carl just stood there, staring at them blankly, without moving. The arrival of the military had triggered something, and he froze. Maybe it was the enormity of this moment – to have arrived at this final test, which, if successful, would result in fulfilling his lifelong dream – or maybe it was fear: fear of authority, fear of the military, fear of the future, whatever. I didn't have a clue..

Sensing his father's difficulty, Bruce quickly stepped forward to greet the visitors. "Hi, I'm Bruce Collingwood." He held out his hand. "Thanks for coming."

"I'm General Bellamy, and this is Major Hendricks and Master Sergeant David Schulz."

They shook hands all around and Bruce introduced his father, still practically catatonic for some reason, and the other members of his team. Finally they got around to greeting George and me.

"So *you're* the ones who broke the story about that commuter train." The General seemed actually pleased to see us. "Good going. We never would have heard about this aircraft if it hadn't been for you."

The military was sucking up to *us*!

"Yes, Sir," I responded. "We had never heard of the aircraft either, that is until we got to know Carl and Bruce here."

"We'll, we're here to see what it can do. So let's get on with it."

"We still haven't decided who will fly it, Dad or me." Bruce continued, while Carl still seemed to be tongue-tied. I just couldn't believe it! "We'll have to flip a coin or something."

"Is that a problem?" the General asked. "It's *your* invention," he said, turning to Carl. "*You* fly it."

With that decided and without a word, Carl reached for his flight jacket and carefully put it on. George kept the camera rolling as Carl walked out to the aircraft. Bruce followed and helped him climb into the cockpit and close the door.

At Bruce's signal, Carl opened the side window and yelled "Clear prop!" I figure he had finally found his voice. The front propeller cranked a couple of turns and awakened the engine, which sputtered briefly before settling into a smooth roar. Then, strangely, a *second* engine, buried somewhere in the center of the fuselage, started up with a high-pitched whine. The combined sound was a bit much for my sensitive ears, but hey, I'm a reporter, right? I'm able to cover anything, no matter how loud it may be.

The wheels of the craft were blocked, keeping it from moving forward or back. Bruce moved in and grabbed little ropes that were attached to each chock, and pulled the chocks away, at first from the front wheel and then from the main landing gear under each wing. He backed off a safe distance, carrying the chocks, and watched the aircraft vibrate as its propeller appeared to churn the air.

The aircraft shuddered slightly as its engine noise increased further, and then moved forward a bit as it slowly lifted itself, seemingly by its own bootstraps, off the ground. The landing gear extended downward at first, leaving the wheels on the tarmac beneath, and then held firm and picked the wheels up off the surface. The craft was airborne!

The tiny group of people, who stood by with their eyes glued to the levitating aircraft, spontaneously broke into wild applause. "Hurray!!"

The aircraft continued to rise, first by a foot, then five feet, and eventually held steady at about fifteen feet off the ground, rotating horizontally a little as it hovered. We all stood there in awe, especially since it was impossible to see how the aircraft could fly at all. Except for a tiny shroud above each wing, the aircraft looked for all-the-world like a conventional airplane, but it was not flying forward. It was just sort of...defying gravity.

The aircraft remained motionless for a few seconds and then, without warning, there was a huge explosion and it ignited into flames right before our eyes. The fire burst forth and engulfed the aircraft, for all the world like the dirigible Hindenburg.

Printed in the United States
by Baker & Taylor Publisher Services